For Michel Roux Jr,
who suggested death by caramel

ORCHARD BOOKS
First published in Great Britain in 2015 by The Watts Publishing Group

1 3 5 7 9 10 8 6 4 2

Text © Christopher William Hill, 2015
Schwartzgarten map illustration by Artful Doodlers © Orchard Books, 2015
The Informant illustrations © Chris Naylor, 2015

The moral rights of the author and illustrator have been asserted.

A CIP catalogue record for this book
is available from the British Library.

ISBN 9781408314586

Printed and bound in Great Britain by CIP Group (UK) Ltd, Croydon, CR0 4YY

The paper and board used in this book are from well-managed forests and other responsible sources.

Orchard Books
An imprint of
Hachette Children's Group
Part of The Watts Publishing Group Limited
Carmelite House
50 Victoria Embankment
London EC4Y 0DZ

An Hachette UK Company
www.hachette.co.uk

www.hachettechildrens.co.uk

TALES FROM SCHWARTZGARTEN

MARIUS AND THE BAND OF BLOOD

Christopher William Hill

ORCHARD

The City of Schwartzgarten

CEMETERY

Bone Orchard Street

OLD TOWN

N
W E
S

1. Poisoner's Row
2. Abandoned Hotel –
   Headquarters of the Band of
   Blood
3. The Bureau of Forgotten Things
4. Borgburg Avenue
5. Mr Lomm's School
6. Donmerplatz
7. Mr Kobec's shop
8. Department of Police
9. Grand Duke Augustus Bridge
10. Governor's Palace
11. Beckmann Street
12. Schwartzgarten Bookshop
13. Bildstein and Bildstein
14. Schwartzgarten Museum
15. Edvardplatz
16. M. Kalvitas's Chocolate Shop
17. Duttlinger's Shop
18. Secret entrance to the lair of
    Franz the Forger

PUMPKIN BOY

In the Duchy of Offelmarkstein, where children were as plentiful as cherries on the tree, a Cobbler and his Wife were without a child.

'One day we will have the little child, yes?' said the Cobbler's Wife. 'With the dark hair and the pale face, and the sad eyes, and the red lips like smears of blood.'

'And the child will love me more,' said the Cobbler.

'No, the child will love me more,' said the Cobbler's Wife.

And they fought and they fought and hair was torn and blood was let, but no child was born to them.

Time passed as it did in those days, and still the Cobbler and his Wife fought.

'The child will love me more,' said the Cobbler's Wife.

'No, the child will love me more,' said the Cobbler.

But still no child was born to them.

Now, there was a legend that on the eve of the Festival of the Unfortunate Dead, when the moon was ripe, a wax figure placed amongst the pumpkins would bring a childless couple a babe by daybreak. But two things were needed to give the figure life – hair from a mother's head and blood from a father's arm. It just so happened that on the night in question the Cobbler had torn a hank of hair from his Wife's head, and the Cobbler's Wife had bitten her husband's arm until the blood ran red, enough to fill a cup.

So at dead of night the Cobbler and his Wife took a pumpkin from the pumpkin patch. They cut off the stalk and they scooped out the seeds. They melted down candles in a pot and sprinkled in the tufts of hair and the cup of blood, which they stirred into the bubbling wax. Together, the Cobbler and his Wife made a figure from the wax – a figure of a small boy. Carefully, the Cobbler's Wife placed the figure in the hollowed-out pumpkin and the Cobbler returned the pumpkin to the patch.

The Cobbler and his Wife were foolish people. They neither knew nor cared that only blood and hair that is given with love will turn a wax figure into flesh. So they sat beside the fire, without a care for the terror to come, and waited for daybreak.

And as they waited, a pale, waxen-skinned figure rose up from the pumpkin patch. He dragged his long, sinewy limbs along the dirt track and headed for the town.

'You must be our son,' said the Cobbler's Wife with a trembling voice, as she opened the door to the creature. 'You love me more,' she whispered as she clothed the Pumpkin Boy. 'Eat your father; he will not care for you as I will.'

'You love me more,' whispered the Cobbler as he fed the Pumpkin Boy. 'Eat your mother; she will not care for you as I will.'

But the Pumpkin Boy, who cared no more for one than the other, opened wide his fearsome jaws and devoured them both.

Taken from Woolf's Tales:
Stories Old and Peculiar

CHAPTER ONE

BLATTEN WAS a small town, clinging desperately and apologetically to the foothills of the Brammerhaus Alps. It was home to a dozen firms of weavers who, between them, manufactured the celebrated Brammerhaus tweed, for which Blatten was justly famous.

In the middle of the town, beside a spindly aspen tree, stood a large wooden house belonging to the Myerdorf family. Large though the house was, the only member of the family to occupy its four walls was Marius Myerdorf, who sat alone at the dining table, enjoying a breakfast of cream cheese on rye bread, with sliced dill pickle and caperberries. He was a boy of ten, with dark, sorrowful eyes, short raven-black hair and skin pig-pink from the buffeting mountain winds.

There was a tentative knock at the dining-room door and Marius's tutor hurried into the room, clutching a letter tightly in his hand. He was a small man, barely taller and hardly ten years older than his student.

'I'm afraid I have some terrible news,' he gasped.

Marius dipped his pickle in the mound of cream cheese. 'Are my parents dead, Mr Brunert?' he asked.

This was not an unusual question for the boy to pose. Marius often felt quite certain that his parents had been the victims of unfortunate accidents. And in the past he had always been wrong. But even a stopped clock tells the correct time twice a day, and on this occasion Marius was perfectly justified in fearing the worst.

'Yes,' replied Mr Brunert quietly. 'Your parents are dead.'

Marius looked up from his breakfast plate. 'You mean, really dead?'

The tutor nodded gravely.

'How?' asked Marius.

'It was a cable-car accident,' explained Mr Brunert. 'They had been skiing in the mountains, many hundreds of kilometres away from here.'

'They like skiing,' said Marius. He corrected himself. '*Liked* skiing.' He stared hard at Mr Brunert and spoke in a whisper. 'Was it quick?'

Sadly, the Tutor shook his head.

'The cable car dropped many hundreds of metres into a

ravine, but it seems it was cushioned by a fresh fall of snow. Your parents may well have survived the drop, were it not for the presence of—' He halted, mid-sentence, uncertain how best to continue.

Fortunately, Marius broke the uncomfortable silence. 'The presence of wolves?'

'It would seem so,' replied Mr Brunert.

'Mother said that Father's fear of wolves was irrational,' said Marius thoughtfully. 'I suppose she was wrong, wasn't she?'

'I suppose she was,' said the tutor.

Marius had imagined so many times that an unfortunate accident had claimed the lives of his parents that it was difficult for him to absorb the fact that they were now indeed dead in their graves. Or, rather, dead inside the bellies of a pack of ravening wolves.

———•——

The following morning the snow was falling heavily and Mr Brunert arranged by telephone to meet with Mr Offenhaus, bank manager to the Myerdorf family.

Mr Brunert had formed a peculiar aversion to the snow.

He shuddered at the prospect of stepping out through the front door and wrapped his striped woollen muffler tightly around his neck.

'We must be brave,' he said. 'Goodness knows how much money your parents have left you. I haven't been paid these last three months.'

Marius stared sadly at Mr Brunert; he was closer to a brother than a tutor, and the fact that the untimely and selfish death of his parents had further added to the man's woes troubled him greatly.

Forcing the door open against the howling wind, Mr Brunert guided Marius outside and together they set off for the banking house.

Mr Offenhaus was an old man, as fat as a bear and with hair as white as a mountain weasel. He snuffled as he moved slowly around his office, crunching hard on a peppermint throat lozenge which perfumed the musty air. The pigeonholes on the wall behind him were stuffed full of aged vellum deeds and yellowing envelopes, and he rifled through the papers carefully, searching.

'Ah!' said Mr Offenhaus at last, and his arthritic fingers alighted claw-like on the files in question. 'Myerdorf.' He tugged out the necessary papers and laid them on his desk before easing himself slowly into his leather armchair.

Marius and Mr Brunert sat patiently, listening to the wind as it howled mournfully through the town before hammering against the window of the office and rattling the latch. At long last, Mr Offenhaus looked up from the papers and his gaze settled on Marius's pale and tragic face.

'Dead, you say? Both of your parents?'

Marius nodded. 'Wolves,' he said quietly.

Mr Offenhaus shook his head sympathetically. 'Fond of them, were you? Your mother and father?'

'I don't think they were very fond of me,' replied Marius.

'Serves them right then,' said Mr Offenhaus, and his face ruptured into a broad grin. 'Wolves were too good for them, if you ask me.'

'Thank you,' said Marius politely. 'You're very kind.'

Mr Brunert attempted a gentle cough, which spluttered out of him like the beginnings of something tubercular. Mr Offenhaus shifted his gaze from boy to tutor and proffered his box of peppermint lozenges.

'How much money did the Myerdorfs leave?' ventured

Mr Brunert, sucking gratefully on a peppermint.

Mr Offenhaus frowned. 'But there is no money. Not a sorry curseling.'

'No money?' gasped Mr Brunert, choking quietly on his peppermint.

Mr Offenhaus shook his head. 'Unfortunately, Marius, your parents left you with a number of unpaid debts. The house must be sold, of course.'

'Then where will I live?' asked Marius.

'You have relatives, do you not?' replied the bank manager.

'I don't know,' said Marius. 'And even if I do, I don't want to live with them. Not if they're as bad as my parents. Can't Mr Brunert look after me forever and for always?'

Mr Brunert turned and stared sadly out of the window. He had barely enough money to support himself, let alone a boy with a fondness for cocoa and cream cheese. When he finally spoke his voice trembled and the words caught in his throat as painfully as the peppermint lozenge.

'Have no fear, Marius,' he said. 'I will make sure that you will be taken in and cared for and not removed to the Schwartzgarten Reformatory for Maladjusted Children.'

Every night for a week, Mr Brunert worked to compile a family tree for the Myerdorf family, sending telegrams first thing each morning in the hope of unearthing a kindly relative who would shower Marius with the love that his parents had always denied him. But it proved unaccountably difficult to trace surviving members of the Myerdorf family.

'Have you found anybody that actually wants me?' asked Marius gloomily one evening, as Mr Brunert sat working by the light of a flickering candle.

'Come, Marius,' said his tutor. 'It's not that your relatives don't wish to take you in. It's simply the fact that most of them are very unfortunately and inconveniently dead.'

It was hard for Marius not to take his family's high mortality rate personally. It seemed that they had selfishly chosen to die rather than offer him shelter.

But just when the boy was preparing to abandon all hope, a telegram arrived, delivered one evening as Marius and Mr Brunert were preparing to sit down to a simple supper of cocoa and spiced mountain cheese.

'It would seem you have a great-great-uncle in Schwartzgarten,' said Mr Brunert, reading from the telegram. 'M. Kalvitas. Did your parents ever speak of the man?'

Marius shook his head.

'How strange,' said Mr Brunert.

'My parents were very strange people,' replied Marius.

***

A week later a tiny white envelope arrived. It was addressed to 'Marius Myerdorf' in an inky scrawl. The envelope contained a one-way rail ticket to Schwartzgarten and a little money for Marius's expenses. There was nothing else. No card to greet the boy. No word of commiseration at the death of his parents. Nothing.

'I'm sure he's a very busy man,' said Mr Brunert, sensing Marius's disappointment. 'I have little doubt that he wished to despatch the railway ticket as quickly as possible and that there was not sufficient time for your aged relative to write an accompanying message.'

'How aged is he?' asked Marius.

'According to your family tree...' Mr Brunert stopped.

'Yes?' said Marius impatiently.

'It would seem that the benevolent gentleman is at

least eighty-eight years of age.'

'That's ancient,' said the boy with a frown. 'Do they keep him in a museum?'

'He may very well live for another couple of years... maybe even another five,' said the tutor with an optimistic note in his voice that belied his true feelings on the matter.

'He'll probably be dead before I even arrive there,' said Marius. 'He would have been wise to send a return railway ticket instead.'

He picked up the ticket and turned it idly in his hands. Written on the back was a message so small it was barely visible to the naked eye. Marius strained his eyes and read:

Bring no inferior chocolate with you...

And beneath these words, written in blood-red ink, the message continued:

...on pain of death!

CHAPTER TWO

———◆◆◆———

THE NEXT morning Marius prepared to set out from the Myerdorf house for the last time. Apart from a suitcase with a change of clothes and his pyjamas and dressing gown, he took with him only a pocket watch of polished steel (a gift from Mr Brunert) and a framed photograph of his mother and father from his bedside table, a sorry reminder of his unfortunate parents. He picked up a book from his desk – an Inspector Durnstein mystery – and dropped it into his overcoat pocket.

Marius and Mr Brunert trudged through the snow on their way to the railway station, the tutor pulling Marius's suitcase along behind him on an old wooden sledge.

'I am afraid to say your great-great-uncle did not send enough money to pay the extra needed for a seat on the train,' said the tutor with a despairing shake of his head. 'I had hoped that you would travel to Schwartzgarten in a first-class compartment all to yourself. But, as it is, you will have to make your journey by luggage wagon.'

'Please don't feel too badly,' said Marius. 'And anyway, it's often safest to travel at the back of the train in case there's a terrible crash...'

'Excellent,' said Mr Brunert. 'I find it is always best to dwell on positive thoughts—'

'...unless I'm crushed to death under falling luggage,' continued Marius. 'Which would probably be less likely to happen if I were travelling in a first class compartment and more likely in a luggage wagon.'

Mr Brunert, who could think of nothing useful to say, whistled a cheerful tune to pass the time.

As they made their way slowly along the streets of Blatten, the tutor handed his student an enormous wedge of nougat, generously studded with caramelised nuts and jewelled slivers of candied cherry.

'Sustenance for the long journey ahead,' explained Mr Brunert, with a smile. 'There was at least the money for that.'

'What is Schwartzgarten like?' asked Marius, as he carefully slipped the nougat into his pocket.

'From what I have heard it is a charming place,' said Mr Brunert, biting his lip and failing to meet Marius's gaze. 'I am certain you will find the Great City most diverting.' He held out the envelope that had been sent by the boy's aged uncle. 'Your relative lives in the most northerly corner of Edvardplatz. I have written his address on the back of the envelope. Guard this well, Marius.'

As they arrived at the small railway halt that passed for a station in Blatten, the steam train was already pulling alongside the platform with a screeching of brakes.

'You have your ticket safely secreted about your person?' asked Mr Brunert.

'Yes,' replied Marius, his voice catching in his throat.

'Very good,' said Mr Brunert. 'I do hope you'll write.'

'I will,' replied Marius, as his tutor helped him up into the luggage wagon and passed up his suitcase.

'I have put some stamped envelopes and writing paper in your suitcase. Send any letters care of Mr Offenhaus at the bank,' said Mr Brunert. 'Soon your parents' house will be sold to pay their debts and I shall be left without a roof over my head. I cannot tell for certain where I will be living next.'

The whistle sounded with a shriek and the train moved slowly from the station.

'Good luck in Schwartzgarten,' called Mr Brunert,

running along the platform. 'Make me proud and keep up with your studies!'

'Goodbye!' cried Marius, waving his hand so hard that his wrist ached. 'Don't forget me!' He waved until Mr Brunert was nothing more than a blurred speck against the white of the mountains.

'So you're off to Schwartzgarten, are you?' asked the Guard, sliding the heavy wagon door closed. 'To the Great City?'

'I am,' said Marius mournfully, presenting the Guard with his ticket, which was clipped and returned to him.

'Make yourself comfortable wherever you can,' said the Guard. He was a young man with a round face and a ready grin.

Marius settled himself on a mail sack between two large steamer trunks. 'I'm no better than a piece of luggage myself,' he thought, his teeth chattering from the cold.

'Beef broth, that's what you need,' said the Guard, lifting a kettle from a small stove in a corner of the wagon and filling a tin cup. 'That'll take the chill out of your bones.'

As the train snaked its way along the tracks, Marius sipped from the warming cup of peppery broth, following the journey on a pocket railway map which had been loaned to him by the Guard.

After two hours the train rattled to a standstill at the small village station of Ziggermund and the Guard climbed down from the wagon, heaving one of the steamer trunks towards the station building with its tall chimneys and snow-scattered roof.

The sky was bright blue but the air was icy. Marius watched from the window as a silver airship climbed over a distant snow-capped mountain, casting a rippling grey shadow across the brilliant white peaks.

'Do you like airships?' asked a voice.

Marius turned to see two women standing at the open doorway of the wagon. One was thin and the other was fat.

'All alone?' asked the thin woman, who wore a silver fox fur around her shoulders.

Marius nodded his head.

'Do you like chocolates?' asked the fat woman, clutching a small velvet-covered box in her hands.

Again, Marius nodded.

The fat woman lifted the lid of the box and leant inside

the wagon, proffering the box to Marius. Her red painted nails were chipped and ragged and she wore glittering diamond rings on every finger. In her hair was an amber clasp shaped as a smiling pumpkin lantern.

Marius selected a chocolate wrapped in orange foil.

'A cloudberry crème,' said the fat woman approvingly as Marius unwrapped the foil. 'An excellent choice.'

Marius bit through a crisp outer layer of milk chocolate which gave way to a centre of whipped cloudberry cream that was both sweet and sour. 'Delicious,' he murmured.

'Travelling like a parcel in the luggage wagon,' said the thin woman with a smile. 'Returning home to your parents, are you, my poor cherub?' she asked.

'My parents are dead,' said Marius.

'How sad,' said the fat woman. 'Would it upset you if I asked...' She hesitated. 'If I asked what they died of?'

'They died of wolves,' said Marius, staring out of the window deep in thought as the airship disappeared behind the mountain peaks.

'A poor little orphan boy,' said the thin woman quietly. 'With not a soul in the world to take care of him.'

'That's not quite true,' said Marius, turning back to

face the two women. 'I have an uncle. A great-great-uncle. A very old man. I'm going to live with him in Schwartzgarten.'

At this the fat woman frowned. 'Schwartzgarten is a wicked place,' she said. 'A wicked, evil place.'

'Is it really?' asked Marius, feeling suddenly more intrigued by the thought of the Great City.

The thin woman nodded her head in agreement. 'Terrible things have happened there,' she said. 'Terrible, terrible things.'

'What sort of things?' asked Marius quickly, his heart leaping in his throat. 'Please tell me.'

But the thin woman shook her head, as though the memory of these terrible things had temporarily robbed her of the power of speech.

It had often been Mr Brunert's sad duty to remind Marius that it was impolite to stare at strangers who struck the boy as peculiar. And though the memory of his tutor's words pricked his conscience, he could not help but gawp at the thin woman. Her face was caked with pale make-up, her lips were crimson and her eyelashes were spider-leg thick with mascara. In the lapel of her coat she wore a pumpkin brooch, its spiralling tendrils formed from tiny green emeralds. It seemed strange to Marius that both women should choose to ornament themselves with pumpkins; he wondered if they were sisters.

'A curseling for the orphans?' said the fat woman with a smile, holding out a collection tin and rattling it hard.

'For the orphans who don't have a soul to look after them,' explained the thin woman. 'Not the lucky orphans like you.'

Marius searched in his pockets for a coin and found a curseling that had become stuck to the wedge of nougat. He peeled off the coin and dropped it into the tin. As the Guard returned, the women smiled and stepped away from the door of the luggage wagon.

———

It was another three hours before the train reached the outskirts of Schwartzgarten. It passed through a vast forest of towering fir trees at the southernmost tip of the great city, before plunging into the sprawling Industrial District, where spindly factory chimneys befogged the sky with thick, grey smoke.

With a squeal of brakes the train drew slowly into Schwartzgarten's Imperial Railway Station.

'This is it,' said the Guard, pulling back the wagon door. 'The last stop. The Great City itself.'

Marius climbed to his feet, gathering his luggage together. 'Thank you,' he said, returning the pocket railway map. 'And for the beef broth.'

'You take care of yourself,' said the Guard, shaking Marius warmly by the hand. 'It's a strange city with strange people living in it. Keep your wits about you and your money safe.'

'That's all right,' said Marius as he stepped down from the wagon, dragging his luggage behind him. 'I don't have much money. Just a few curselings and some nougat.'

'I've known men have their throats cut for less,' said the Guard.

'Don't worry,' said Marius. 'I'm fast at running.'

Schwartzgarten's Imperial Railway Station was a bewildering place to a boy from the mountains and Marius walked slowly from the luggage wagon as if in a dream. Everything around him was grey; the station platform, the steam which burst from the funnels of the waiting trains, the faces of the citizens of the Great City as they bustled across the station concourse.

An elderly and bearded man sat at a table outside a small café, sipping from a glass of beetroot schnapps and sucking on a long briar pipe. Marius stared hard at the man, hoping that he would rise from his seat and introduce himself as Great-great-uncle Kalvitas. But the man only growled and waved the boy away.

Though he searched and searched, it soon became clear to Marius that no one was waiting at the station to meet him. No longer was he simply a piece of luggage; he was now an unwanted piece of luggage. He bought a raisin swirl from the café and waited.

Idly picking raisins from the pastry and throwing them to a raven that was foraging for scraps beneath the café tables, Marius noticed the two women from the train as they wheeled a large stack of wooden cake boxes across the concourse. He raised his hand to wave, but the women seemed oblivious to him and, for some reason which Marius could not quite comprehend, he felt relieved at this. He watched as the boxes were loaded into a waiting taxicab. The women climbed inside and the cab pulled away.

Marius glanced up at the great clock that hung high above the station concourse; he had been waiting for half an hour. Where was Great-great-uncle Kalvitas? Perhaps a motor car accident had occurred, he thought. Or perhaps the old man had dropped dead as he prepared to leave the house for the railway station. One thing was certain; he would never know the truth of the matter if he remained where he was.

Marius did not have enough money to pay for a taxicab, so instead he purchased a travel guide from a book kiosk and resolved to find his own way to the house of his great-great-uncle, following the address that Mr Brunert had written on the back of the envelope.

Printed in black on the red cloth covers of the book were the words:

MULLER, BRUN & GELLERHUND'S

SCHWARTZGARTEN:
AN ILLUSTRATED GUIDE
TO THE CITY AND ITS ENVIRONS

Marius turned to the back cover of the guidebook:

The history of Schwartzgarten has been coloured by warfare, murder, and intrigue – it is a bloodthirsty tale in the telling, and one from which the authors of this informative guide do not turn their faces.

The book includes additional notes on outlying towns and villages, especially those made famous during Good Prince Eugene's heroic battles to free Schwartzgarten from the despotic rule of Emeté Talbor.

Marius smiled to himself. He opened the book, turned to the first page and began to read:

"The traveller whose tankard is drained in a single gulp will be lost to the wolves by nightfall."
Traditional Schwartzgarten Proverb

Turning the page quickly to escape the thought of murderous wolves, Marius's attention was arrested by an encouraging greeting:

WE RAISE OUR HATS AND WELCOME YOU TO SCHWARTZGARTEN

Unless visitors are fortunate enough to travel by scheduled Airship Service, most will arrive in Schwartzgarten by way of the Imperial Railway Station in the south of the Great City. The railway was erected on the instructions of Good Prince Eugene, who was himself a great patron of the railways and an enthusiast for all things mechanical. Worthy of note are the statues of the Twin Travellers at the entrance to the station, their eyes shrouded by the hoods they wear – a reminder that all travellers stumble blindly in the darkness and none can ever be assured of their final destination.

The Emperor Xavier Hotel is but a short journey by taxicab from the railway station and offers superior accommodation for visitors of quality. Poorer travellers can seek room and supper in the historic Old Chop House (once a haunt of Emeté Talbor's despised Vigils) or, in the Old Town, at any number of boarding houses (though cockroaches are plentiful and bedbugs more plentiful still).

Wherever the visitor chooses to stay, Schwartzgarten is a glittering jewel of the North and should be explored at leisure. Places of special interest include Edvardplatz at the very heart of the city with its notable clock tower, the excellent Zoological Gardens, the Governor's Palace with its celebrated Traitors' Gallery, and the vast sprawl of the Schwartzgarten Municipal Cemetery.

The sky over Schwartzgarten was as black as a smudge of charcoal as Marius set off on his journey, with the aid of a folding map that had been affixed inside the cover of the guidebook. He walked from the Imperial Railway Station, passing the tall hooded statues of the Twin Travellers he had just read about. Everywhere there was noise and smoke and bustle. Taxicabs sounded their horns as they carried passengers into the Great City and trams rattled noisily along their tracks. Wherever Marius looked there were people; office workers, businessmen, elegantly dressed women on shopping expeditions, police constables, ragged street vendors, newspaper sellers, delivery boys.

More faces flashed past in a minute than Marius had seen in all his life tucked away in Blatten.

His luggage was heavy, so whenever he stopped to rest his arms he would seize the chance to read another page from the guidebook.

The most perilous approach to Schwartzgarten is along the treacherous mountain road, leading from Lake Taneva. Countless unwary motorists have plummeted many hundreds of metres to their deaths...

As Marius stumbled on along the frozen pavement he passed beside the River Schwartz, which wound its way darkly through the heart of the city. Stopping for a moment's rest he sat on his case and again opened the book.

The River Schwartz was deepened on the orders of Emeté Talbor, to flush from the city corpses that had become ensnared upon the rocks below his palace (now the residence of the Governor of Schwartzgarten).

Marius leant over the railings and peered curiously into the surging waters, but to his disappointment there were no corpses to be seen.

Fairs and Festivals were often held at wintertime on the frozen river, until a tragic incident when the heat from a burning brazier cracked the ice. Many citizens were swept down river and off through the dark forests outside the city, where the unfortunate survivors were killed and eaten by wolves and bears. It was a melancholy episode in the already melancholy history of the City of Schwartzgarten.

'Wolves again,' sighed Marius wistfully, lifting up his luggage and continuing on his way.

He followed the map to Edvardplatz, at the very heart of the New Town, dragging his luggage slowly across the cobbles to the northernmost corner of the square.

But the only building to be found was a shop and not a house at all, standing beside an antiquarian bookseller's. Marius stared up in bewilderment. It was a tall and narrow building with a striped canvas awning. Below the awning was a sign:

M. Kalvitas – Chocolatier

A second sign hung suspended above the door, painted in gilded lettering:

By appointment to his late Majesty, Crown Prince Eugene

Marius leafed quickly through the pages of the guidebook until his eyes alighted on a chapter dedicated to the shops of Schwartzgarten.

Chocolate shops are so plentiful in the streets around Edvardplatz that the area is known fondly as the Cocoa Quarter. The leading Chocolate Makers in the City are members of The Guild of Twelve, and can be identified by a gilded cocoa pod hanging beside their shop doors.

Sure enough, there, beside the door of the shop, was the

golden cocoa pod of The Guild of Twelve.

'Whatever sort of man he is, he must be good at making chocolate,' thought Marius hungrily. 'Maybe things won't be so bad in Schwartzgarten after all.'

He glanced further down the page until his eyes came to rest on a now familiar name.

M. KALVITAS, the oldest surviving chocolate shop in Schwartzgarten, is still home to M. Kalvitas, the oldest surviving Chocolate Maker in the Great City.

Marius closed the book. Blinds had been drawn at the windows, so he squinted through the glass panes of the door. The shop was in darkness and there was nobody to be seen.

Marius knocked gently but, though he waited for some minutes, no one came to admit him. With a deep sigh he reached out for the door handle and to his surprise found that it turned easily in his hand. A bell jangled loudly as he stepped inside; startled by the noise, he could feel his heart quickening.

Though it was not a wide shop, its deficiency in width was more than compensated for in height. It was a miraculous palace of confectionery, even in the failing light. Marius could make out the tall shelves, closely packed with chocolate boxes of velvet and satin tied with silk bows, and tins of Kalvitas's Excellent Cocoa Powder stacked in pyramids.

'Hello?' said Marius quietly. 'Is anybody here?' But, as before, there was no answer. 'Great-great-uncle Kalvitas?' he whispered. 'Are you dead?' He walked behind the counter and pushed open a door into a dark and narrow passageway, lined on either side with chocolate boxes and wooden crates marked Pfefferberg's Nougat Marshmallows.

At the end of the passageway was another door and this Marius opened, stepping into a small kitchen with a table and an ancient iron stove.

Still there was no sign of life.

Lying open on the table was a newspaper. An article had been circled in red. Marius placed his luggage on the floor and picked up the newspaper.

ANOTHER MEMBER OF THE GUILD OF TWELVE SLAIN

In the early hours of Tuesday morning the body of Chocolate Maker Helmut Fugard was discovered in his shop in the Cocoa Quarter of Schwartzgarten...

As Marius read on, a figure lurched out at him from the shadows, tugging the newspaper from the boy's hands. It was an old man, his skin as brown and lined as ancient leather and his hair as white as an alpine peak.

'Who are you?' demanded the man, his eyes hooded and watchful as he leant forward to squint at Marius through the gloom. 'Why have you come?'

Marius opened his mouth to speak but not a sound came out.

'Are you here to spy on me?' continued the man, jabbing his finger accusingly in Marius's direction. 'Who sent you? One of the Guild of Twelve, I suppose. Montelimar, eh? Becklebick?'

Still Marius could not answer the man. It felt as though his tongue had been cast from lead.

'Well? Speak, boy!'

'Are you K-K-K-Kalvitas?' stammered Marius.

The old man slowly lowered his finger. 'Yes,' he said. 'Of course I am Kalvitas.'

'Then I think I might be your great-great-nephew,' said Marius. He held out the envelope and the old man snatched it from his fingers, holding it close to his eyes and mumbling under his breath.

'This seems in order,' said Kalvitas, his voice quieter than before as he returned the envelope to Marius. It was fast growing dark and the old man lit a taper from the stove, which he used to light two gas lamps on the walls of the kitchen. 'So, you are my great-great-nephew, eh?'

Marius nodded. 'I've travelled by train from Blatten to get here.'

'And you're hungry now, I suppose?' said Kalvitas, pulling out a chair at the table and motioning for Marius to sit down.

Marius sat.

'What do you eat, boy?' asked the old man, picking up a pan and shuffling towards the stove.

'I...I don't know,' said Marius. His head had emptied of all thought, and try as he might he could not think of a single thing that he liked to eat.

'Then you'll have liver and onions and be grateful for it,' said Kalvitas, grasping a large brown onion and peeling away the skin.

Marius opened the guidebook on his lap and glanced down at the pages.

What should the visitor expect when sitting down to dinner in the Great City of Schwartzgarten? What culinary delights await?

He was certain that liver and onions was not a culinary delight, even in Schwartzgarten. Marius closed the book as Kalvitas prepared onion gravy and cut thick slices of bright red liver that he fried in a pan.

When at last the meat was cooked, the old man ladled the food onto the boy's plate and Marius took a spoonful, blowing hard to cool a steaming and gelatinous lump of liver.

'Where was it you said you come from?' asked Kalvitas, cutting the crust from a loaf of rye bread and buttering it thickly.

'From Blatten,' said Marius, sipping the thick, grey gravy from his spoon and swallowing hard. 'In the mountains.'

'Ah,' said the old man.

And not another word passed between them until the meagre meal had been eaten.

As Kalvitas stood at the sink, washing the pots and pans, Marius took out the bar of nougat that Mr Brunert had given him for his train journey, hoping it might take away the lingering metallic taste of liver. The cellophane wrapping crackled and Kalvitas swung round suddenly. 'What is that?' he demanded. 'Nougat?' He sprang forward, snatching the offending confectionery from Marius's hands. 'Inferior,' growled the old man, 'inferior in every way.' He tossed the nougat onto the fire and Marius watched despairingly as it bubbled and spat in the flames. 'Thought you could hide it from me, eh? There'll be no secrets here.'

'No, sir,' said Marius quietly, his eyes fixed on his knees so he would not have to gaze up into the face of his fearsome relative.

'What did I write to you?' chided Kalvitas. 'Bring no nougat. Didn't I expressly forbid it?'

'You wrote "bring no inferior chocolate",' said Marius defiantly. 'You didn't write anything about nougat.'

'Nougat, chocolate. It all adds up to the same thing,' said Kalvitas. 'Did I write "on pain of death"?'

Marius looked up and nodded slowly.

'Well,' said Kalvitas, with a dark twinkle in his eye, 'I suppose I'll let you live for now.' He struck a match and lit a stumpy candle. 'It's getting late and Chocolate Makers rise early. I suppose you'll be wanting to go to bed, boy?'

It was the very last thing Marius wished to do. He wanted nothing more than to pick up his suitcase and run from the shop, across the cobbles of Edvardplatz to freedom. 'I would run to the mountains and home to Blatten, if my legs could carry me there,' he thought. But as this idea fermented in his brain, Kalvitas extinguished the gas lamps, picked up the candle and walked quickly from the kitchen.

'Your room is this way,' murmured the old man.

Marius gathered his luggage and followed close behind, fearful that the dark would swallow him whole if he remained on his own in the kitchen.

Kalvitas led the boy up a steep and narrow wooden staircase, passing a cast-iron raven that stood sentry at the foot of the stairs.

Every step upwards seemed to carry them further back in time; framed portraits lined the walls, so blackened by the passing years that it was hard to make out more than an eye, a nose or a leering smile. There were daggers and battered helmets hanging from brass hooks and stuffed animals in cases, their glass eyes briefly sparkling with life in the flickering light of Kalvitas's candle.

Marius's arms ached as he hauled his luggage up the stairs, the suitcase bumping loudly against the wooden steps.

'So much noise,' grumbled Kalvitas, without turning to help the boy. 'It's enough to wake the dead.'

Halfway up the second flight of stairs a budgerigar chattered in an ancient brass cage, stirred from sleep by the leaping flame of the candle. Kalvitas pushed a piece of dried cuttlefish between the bars.

'It's good for her beak,' he muttered.

'What is she called?' asked Marius timidly.

'Call her what you like,' grunted Kalvitas and carried on up the stairs. 'She's a bird.'

It was a strange building, and the further they climbed the odder it became. There were so many peculiar objects hanging from the walls that it was impossible for Marius to take everything in without tripping on a stair and dropping his luggage.

'Relics from the wars,' said the old man mysteriously, tapping a long fingernail against a bronze medallion that hung from the wall in a tiny glass case.

Marius stopped to stare at the medallion but Kalvitas continued up the stairs, carrying the candle with him, and the boy had no choice but to follow.

When it seemed they could climb no further without stepping out onto clouds, the old man halted.

'In here,' said Kalvitas, opening a door and ushering Marius into a small, dark room. 'Don't steal anything. I'll know if you do.' And without another word he closed the door and was gone.

Marius lowered his luggage carefully to the floor, fearing that any loud noise might bring Kalvitas hurrying back. The blood slowly returned to his fingers and he flexed his hands gratefully.

The pale moon cast little light into the room, though it seemed to Marius that there was not much to be seen, except a narrow bed and a large and ancient chest of drawers, on which stood an old wooden box and an age-spotted mirror. He walked to the window and gazed down across the cobbled expanse of Edvardplatz, watching as a young police constable walked quickly across the square and disappeared inside a busy café. Marius closed the shutters and turned from the window. Blatten seemed so far away it might as well have been the moon and the thought stung him as though he had been stuck with a pin. In the gloom he could make out a candlestick and candle on a nightstand beside the bed. Striking a match from a pot on the chest of drawers, Marius lit the candle.

The bed had been made, but long ago. It was too cold to undress, so Marius took off his shoes and placed his pocket watch carefully on the nightstand. Taking the Inspector Durnstein book from his overcoat pocket, he shook a thick layer of dust from the quilt and climbed beneath the covers.

He opened the book and turned to a page carefully marked with an old postcard of Blatten and began to read.

...Inspector Durnstein gazed down at the dead body sprawled on the floor before him.

'No weapon, no witness, no motive for murder,' said the Inspector, his forehead creased as he thought the matter through. He turned to Constable Mandel who stood patiently at his side. 'But I'll tell you this much, Mandel. It's murder nonetheless...'

Marius's eyelids were heavy and the words were blurring before him. He closed the book and blew out the candle. From a corner of Edvardplatz he could hear the great

Schwartzgarten Clock strike the hour of eight. It seemed that a hundred clocks in the rooms above the chocolate shop were chiming in reply, causing the budgerigar to shriek in alarm from her cage.

He lay back in bed with his fingers in his ears. He closed his eyes and imagined that he was lying in his familiar bed in Blatten. But it was no good; the damp and musty smell of the room was more than enough to destroy the dream and it was not possible to block up his earholes and his nostrils at the same time. With a sigh that stirred a heap of dust on the nightstand Marius pulled his fingers from his ears and began to drift off to sleep.

And as he did so he was jolted awake by a curious noise that sent his pulse racing – it was as though a large and heavy object was being dragged slowly across the floor above him...

CHAPTER THREE

M ARIUS SLEPT a fitful and uncomfortable night in his new bed, shivering from the cold, his throat scratchy from breathing in dust from the ancient bedcovers. He awoke to the sound of frenzied squawking from the budgerigar on the stairs below and climbed out of bed, fumbling in his case for his dressing gown. Opening the ancient shutters, he gazed out of the window, down onto Edvardplatz. Schwartzgarten was stirring into life. Blinds were being raised in the windows of shops that lined the square and a waiter was setting out tables and chairs in front of the small café.

Marius picked up his pocket watch from the nightstand. It was gone eight, but he had not heard a sound from Kalvitas. What if the old man was dead? What if he had died in his sleep? What if Marius was alone in the world once more? He opened the bedroom door and crept out onto the landing.

He had expected the building to seem more ordinary in the daylight, but this proved not to be the case. If anything, it was even more peculiar than it had looked before. The wallpaper was a faded beige colour, with a swirling pattern of green fern leaves – but only a little of the paper could be glimpsed between the many portraits, framed photographs and tarnished brass battle relics that hung from the walls.

Across the landing a door was ajar and Marius spied Kalvitas standing at a shaving mirror. He watched as the old man took a razor from a steaming bowl of water and held the blade to his scraggy throat. His shirtsleeves were rolled back to the elbows, revealing smooth arms as white as marble, dotted here and there with dark-brown liver spots.

Catching sight of Marius's reflection in the mirror, Kalvitas turned and his face darkened. He quickly rolled down his sleeves and fastened them at the cuffs. 'Did you shave today?' he asked.

'No,' replied Marius.

'And why not?' demanded the old man.

'Because I'm ten,' answered Marius.

Kalvitas shook his head disapprovingly and lifted the blade of the razor to his cheek. 'I've been shaving since the age of six,' he muttered. 'Boys today don't know they've been born.' When he had finished with his ablutions, he turned to look at Marius properly. 'Those clothes won't do for the city,' he said. 'Those are mountain clothes. What else did you bring to wear?'

'Just one other set, exactly the same,' said Marius. 'My parents never thought that I needed more than one change of clothes.'

'Then we'll have to find you something.' Kalvitas opened his wardrobe and heaped shirts and pullovers and socks into Marius's outstretched arms. 'Keep whatever fits.'

Heavy-hearted, Marius returned to his room to try on the clothes. He re-emerged a few minutes later, half-hidden beneath an enormous pullover.

'You'll do,' said Kalvitas, turning back the sleeves to reveal Marius's hands.

'The socks are too big as well,' said Marius.

'You'll need these then,' said Kalvitas, rooting around in the bottom of his wardrobe and handing Marius two strips of black elastic. 'Sock suspenders.'

'What do I do with them?' asked Marius.

'Suspend your socks with them,' came the flat reply.

Marius followed Kalvitas down the many flights of stairs to the kitchen, where the old man whisked up a pan of chocolate on the stove, emptying the contents into two copper cups.

'Now drink it up,' said Kalvitas gruffly, pushing a cup across the table.

Marius sipped slowly. The chocolate tasted as thick and as strong as molten tar.

'I make it extra-strong to wake me up in the morning,' muttered Kalvitas, taking a deep slurp of the chocolate. 'It's better than coffee to get an old man's bones working.'

After breakfast, Kalvitas led Marius from the kitchen and out into the shop. The heavy blinds had been lifted from the windows and bright autumn sunlight poured in.

Marius gasped as he cast his eyes around the room. The glass of the shop counter was dazzling in the light, and he shielded his eyes with his hands. Wherever he looked there was chocolate, and the strong, sweet smell of cocoa filled his lungs. There were baskets of white chocolate figs stuffed with marzipan, prunes dipped in milk chocolate, white chocolate cornets and dark chocolate wolves. In front of the counter a large box overflowed with Pfefferberg's Nougat Marshmallows.

Two women appeared through a door, tying aprons around their waists. One was young and red-cheeked, the other plump and grey-haired.

'Good morning, Miss Esterhart. Good morning, Mrs Kurtz,' said Kalvitas. 'This is my great-great-nephew, Marius...' He frowned. 'Marius...'

'Marius Myerdorf,' said Marius, completing the old man's thought.

'Yes, yes,' said Kalvitas irritably. 'Marius Myerdorf. He has come from the mountains.'

Mrs Kurtz and Miss Esterhart smiled and bowed and Marius bowed back.

As the women opened boxes of chocolates to be displayed on the counter, Marius wandered idly around the shop. From a wall hung a sword in its silver scabbard.

'That's from your great-great-uncle's youth,' whispered Miss Esterhart. 'A hero, he was. Helped to free the city from—'

'That is enough,' said Kalvitas sourly. 'I don't want you filling the boy's head with thoughts.'

Miss Esterhart mumbled an apology under her breath and opened up a box of marzipan fruits.

In the very centre of the room was a glass cabinet housing a clockwork cocoa pod. Inserting a curseling in a slot in the side of the cabinet, Marius watched in amazement as the cocoa pod opened like a blooming flower to reveal a perfect miniature of Kalvitas's shop, carved from a block of dark chocolate.

'No time to stand and stare,' tutted the old man. 'There is chocolate to be made.' He beckoned Marius through a doorway. 'This is the mould room.'

It was a tall, narrow chamber, and seemed to Marius like the inside of a castle turret. A wooden ladder led up into the rafters where chocolate moulds of copper and tin hung from the high wooden beams, rattling together as a whisper of breeze filtered in through an air vent set high in the wall. Marius could dimly make out the tin mould of an airship and an ancient wooden mould of a pike locked in mortal combat with a writhing salmon.

'We don't have all day,' muttered the old man, leading

Marius through to a pristine chocolate kitchen. 'I need you to start tempering the chocolate for me.'

Marius gave his great-great-uncle a look of bewilderment.

Kalvitas frowned. 'You do know how to temper chocolate, I presume?'

Marius shook his head.

'Didn't your tutor teach you anything, boy?'

'He taught me very well,' said Marius hotly. He could not bear to hear the man speaking ill of Mr Brunert. 'He taught me maths and geography and algebra.'

'What use is that to a growing child?' said Kalvitas, his face darkening. 'A boy your age who doesn't know how to make chocolate? No wonder things are upside down. You're living in a dream world.'

To Marius it felt more like a nightmare than a dream. Only the day before he had been sitting down to breakfast in the Myerdorf house with the kindly Mr Brunert. But now everything had changed and nothing seemed right.

'You're no good to me here,' continued the old man, pouring cream into a copper pan and turning on the gas flame. 'Leave me to work and we'll talk later.'

'Where will I go?' asked Marius.

'What do I care?' snorted Kalvitas.

Dazed and unhappy, Marius climbed the stairs to his room and returned with his overcoat and guidebook. Taking an umbrella from a stand beside the shop door he set out nervously to explore the city, though the freezing rain was falling heavily.

The book was the nearest thing to a friend that he had and he turned the pages carefully, anxious not to expose it for too long to the fast-falling raindrops.

> ...*for the earnest traveller who seeks a fuller knowledge of the dark ways and customs of our Great City, might we humbly recommend the Schwartzgarten Museum as the place to begin your journey? It is a veritable treasure trove of ghoulish mementoes and bloodthirsty relics cataloguing over a thousand years of tragedy, warfare and intrigue. If your heart has quickened at the very thought of such a place, then you are the visitor we seek and we bid you welcome.*

Certain that the guidebook would not mislead him,

Marius made his way across the city to the Schwartzgarten Museum. He paid for his ticket and stepped into the grand entrance, shaking the rain from his umbrella and placing it in the elephant-foot stand beside the door.

It was a diverting way to spend a day. The museum's Wax Gallery was a particular source of fascination to Marius. Most thrilling of all was a wax figure of Otto the Poisoner, holding a bottle of acid and standing beside the very bathtub in which he had dissolved eight members of his family.

'I wish Otto the Poisoner had visited Great-great-uncle Kalvitas in *his* bathtub,' murmured Marius, then put the thought out of his head.

———

When he had at last exhausted the gruesome delights of the Schwartzgarten Museum, Marius returned home to Edvardplatz as slowly as he could possibly manage without coming to a complete standstill. On his way, he passed the door of another chocolate shop on the corner of Alexis Street. The outer walls of the building were decorated with carved cherubs, burnished with gold leaf, and high above the door was an elaborate clock face, set into a sculpted mountain peak. Beside the mountain stood a group of children; brightly painted figures with rigid grins and piercing eyes. A sign over the shop door read:

Akerhus and Hoffgartner –
Chocolate Makers of Distinction

There was no gilded cocoa pod hanging beside the door, and Marius was quickly thumbing through his guidebook to see if he could find mention of the shop when the Schwartzgarten Clock began to strike from across the rooftops. He lifted the watch from his overcoat pocket; it was four o'clock. A whirring noise from above captured his attention and he gazed up to see that the painted children had sprung to life, their mechanical arms moving backwards and forwards in time to a haunting tune played from deep inside the carved mountain. Now the figures began to move their legs, which carried them with jerking steps towards a large gorge that had slowly opened up in the mountainside. The music grew louder as one after the other the painted children disappeared inside the gorge. Such was the effect on Marius's imagination that he could almost hear the screams of the disappearing children.

The music stopped, the gorge closed and all was silent again.

'A magnificent feat of mechanical engineering, don't you think?' said a voice.

A thin man with a pinched face had appeared beside Marius, wearing a long white apron. In his hands he held a silver tray piled high with milk chocolates, each topped with a single, crystallised cloudberry.

'I've never seen a clock quite like it,' said Marius.

'And you never will again,' said the man. 'It is unique. You know *Woolf's Tales*, of course?'

'I don't think I do,' said Marius, who had spent more time with Mr Brunert reading books on mathematics and algebra than works of fiction.

'Wonderful stories,' continued the man. 'There is a tale of the greedy children of a far-off town who were told that a cave hidden deep in a mountain was full of chocolate, theirs for the taking. And in their eagerness to find that magical place they were lost to their parents forever.'

The door in the carved mountain swung open and the figures of the children reversed out along their tracks. They juddered to a halt and stood motionless as before.

'The clock strikes every hour,' continued the man. 'It is a wonderful spectacle and draws visitors from far and wide.' He held out the silver tray to Marius. 'Try one,' he said. 'They are quite delicious.'

Marius took a chocolate.

'Greetings!' came a voice. Marius turned as a second man, much larger than the first, appeared from inside the shop. 'Perhaps you would care to take a guided tour of our humble premises? My name is Mr Akerhus. My colleague, with whom I see you are already acquainted, is Mr Hoffgartner.'

Hoffgartner bowed and held the door open for Marius.

Marius felt sure that his great-great-uncle would disapprove and it was this thought that guided him inside.

The shop was larger than Kalvitas's, but the ceiling was lower, with dark, wooden beams. It felt to Marius as though he had entered into the cave beneath the mountain. Dark though the shop was, gold glittered everywhere – on burnished chocolate gargoyles, and the faces of gilt cherubs with dark chocolate demons perched upon their shoulders.

The sweet aroma of strawberries and cloudberries filled the air and Marius breathed deeply.

'You might like one of these,' said Akerhus, holding out a chocolate, wrapped in a twist of cellophane. 'A strawberry fondant, for which we are famous throughout the Northern Region.'

'Please take it with our compliments, Marius,' said Hoffgartner.

Marius started. 'How did you know my name?' he asked.

'Are you not the great-great-nephew of Kalvitas the Chocolate Maker?' said Akerhus with a twinkling smile. 'News travels fast in Schwartzgarten.'

———

When Marius at last reached Edvardplatz he stood outside Kalvitas's shop to consume the strawberry fondant in secret.

Slipping silently through the kitchen door he was

horrified to find his great-great-uncle waiting for him.

'Where have you been?' demanded the old man.

'I...I visited the Schwartzgarten Museum,' said Marius. 'I took my guidebook. I've been exploring.'

'Empty your pockets,' said Kalvitas.

'But Great-great-uncle—' stammered the boy.

'I said, empty your pockets.'

Marius turned out his pockets onto the table, staring in dismay at the cellophane wrapper of the strawberry fondant.

'You've been to Akerhus and Hoffgartner,' said Kalvitas, pouncing and holding up the wrapper.

'No,' whispered Marius. 'I...I haven't...I...'

'Don't lie to me, boy,' growled Kalvitas. 'What did I tell you before? No...inferior...chocolate!'

Marius's face burned though the room was cold. He wanted desperately to defend himself but, as was often the case, no words came out. With tears stinging his eyes he turned and ran up to his bedroom. Closing the door he took paper and a stamped envelope from his case, sat down on the end of his bed and began to compose a letter to his former tutor.

The Chocolate Shop
of M. Kalvitas,
Edvardplatz
Schwartzgarten

My dear friend Mr Brunert,

Could you please look at my family tree again
and see if there is someone else who will take pity
on an orphan? Someone who is not so old and
perhaps kinder?
I hope you are happy and not too poor.

Your very loyal student,
Marius Myerdorf

He folded the letter and slid it inside the envelope, licking the gummed strip and sealing it firmly, as if all his hopes for the future were contained inside. He wrote the address on the envelope, then crept back down the stairs, where Kalvitas was busying himself at the kitchen stove.

'Where are you going now, boy?'

'For another walk,' said Marius concealing the envelope behind his back and slipping it into the sleeve of his pullover. 'I won't be gone for long.'

'It won't bother me if you're gone forever,' muttered Kalvitas.

Marius set off across Edvardplatz, the envelope in his hand. A bearded man in a greasy top hat had set up a barrel organ at the southern corner of the square. Marius dropped a curseling into the collection box and the man removed his hat and bowed his head, all the time slowly and smoothly turning the handle of the mechanical organ. The mournful warbling of the music gave Marius an uneasy feeling in the pit of his stomach.

He reached the postbox, which stood in a corner of the square close to the great clock tower. 'Help me, please, Mr Brunert,' Marius whispered under his breath as he dropped the letter in the box and made his way slowly back across the cobbles to Kalvitas's shop.

CHAPTER FOUR

THE DAYS passed slowly in the chocolate shop. Kalvitas could not hide his irritation that Marius was not versed in the art of chocolate making, but showed no inclination to teach the boy himself. So Marius was left to his own devices, exploring the great city with the help of his trusty guidebook, all the time waiting for Mr Brunert's return letter. But when nearly a week had slipped by and Marius had still not heard back from his tutor, his mind naturally strayed towards the terrible tragedies that must surely have befallen the man. Perhaps there was to be no hope of rescue after all.

One evening, returning from the Schwartzgarten Zoological Gardens, Marius found Kalvitas sitting disconsolately in the kitchen, an untouched plate of onion crackers and blue cheese on the table in front of him.

'Aren't you hungry, Great-great-uncle?' asked Marius tentatively.

'I don't want to eat,' muttered Kalvitas.

'But you have to eat,' said Marius, sitting down at the

table. 'If you don't eat you'll die.'

'What do you care?' grunted the old man. 'I'd be better off dead and in my grave.'

'I think I might become a Chocolate Maker one day,' said Marius casually, hoping that the news might be enough to cheer the old man.

But Kalvitas only shook his head miserably. 'Chocolate-making is no way to live a life,' he grumbled. 'All the time struggling to make ends meet. I get cheated on the weight of cocoa beans, and the price of almonds is going up all the time. There's not enough money in chocolate to keep a rat alive. Life's getting harder every day. Even my customers are deserting me.' He held up a copy of *The Schwartzgarten Daily Examiner* and tapped his finger against a full-page advertisement:

AKERHUS AND HOFFGARTNER ARE PROUD TO
ANNOUNCE THE OPENING OF THEIR FIRST CHOCOLATE
FACTORY – SUPPLYING THE GREAT CITY OF
SCHWARTZGARTEN AND BEYOND WITH THE FINEST
STRAWBERRY FONDANTS AND CLOUDBERRY CRÈMES.

'Their chocolates are too sweet,' grumbled Kalvitas.

'But the world is changing and I'm too old to belong.'

'You have me with you now,' said Marius.

'You say that as though it's a good thing,' said Kalvitas, staring sullenly back at the boy. 'You think I wanted you to come? Well, I didn't. I've never wanted anybody else here. I am a solitary creature and that's the way I like it. I wish your wretched tutor had never written to me in the first place.'

This was too much for Marius and he felt his face burn with anger. 'Maybe you didn't want me,' he shouted, jumping up from the table. 'But I didn't want you either. I wanted to stay in Blatten. I could have lived my life happily there without ever coming to Schwartzgarten.'

'Go back there then,' snapped Kalvitas, climbing up from the table. 'No one's chaining you here, are they, boy?'

'All right,' said Marius, his voice quavering. 'I'll go.'

'Good,' said Kalvitas, as he stalked from the kitchen, slamming the door behind him.

———◆———

Little more than half an hour later Marius crossed the Princess Euphenia Bridge into the Old Town. It was difficult to decide whether he had run away from home or not; he had no bags with him, just his guidebook, the Inspector Durnstein mystery and a pocket flashlight, in case he had need to hide in shadows.

He was in a dark mood and thought it would be appropriate on such a day to visit the Schwartzgarten Municipal Cemetery, the better to enjoy his feelings of creeping gloom. He flicked open his guidebook:

...the Municipal Cemetery occupies a quarter of the Great City.

For more than two hundred years Schwartzgarten was blighted by civil unrest, bloody sieges, battles and political assassinations. This, of course, resulted in a vast quantity of bodies, all in need of burial. It was the suggestion of Princess Euphenia that a substantial plot of land, to the North of the Old Town, should be set aside for a new cemetery.

Marius studied the map closely, working out his route to the cemetery, and found himself following a half-starved and flea-bitten cat as it prowled along the pavement in front of him; within a few blocks it became his constant companion. But turning a corner, he found that the cat had vanished.

'Where are you, cat?' he called.

'Don't wake my mother!' hissed a voice from above, and Marius looked up in alarm. A man had appeared at a window, leaning out over pots of sickly red geraniums that struggled to bloom on a shadowy ledge.

'I didn't mean to wake anybody,' said Marius apologetically. 'I'm walking as quietly as I can.'

'Stealthily, if you ask me,' said the man, suddenly suspicious and narrowing his eyes. 'Up to no good, are you? There's a thief on every street corner...if you believe what you read in the newspapers.'

'I don't read the newspapers,' said Marius. 'I'm not from—'

'We live in fear of our very lives!' interrupted the man, shouting now. 'I should telephone to the Inspector of Police and report you. That's what I should do. And if I had a telephone I would!'

An old woman appeared at an upstairs window, a moth-eaten black shawl wrapped tightly around her shoulders. 'What's all this shouting about? We weren't expecting visitors, were we, Hans?'

'He's not a visitor,' said the man. 'He's a murderer. Come to do you in, Mother, most likely. And who can blame him?'

'But I'm not a murderer,' protested Marius. 'I'm lost. I'm not from this city.'

'Don't contradict,' snapped the old woman. 'Murderers had manners in my day.'

'Get going, stranger,' barked the man, arming himself with one of the potted geraniums. 'We don't want your sort around here!'

'The murdering sort,' added the woman for good measure. 'That's what he means.'

'Shut up, Mother,' said the man.

Marius had never been mistaken for a murderer before, and somehow this gave him confidence as he pressed deeper into the Old Town. Ominous black clouds hung low above Schwartzgarten, seeming to press down against the rooftops. But Marius was a curious boy and the grimmer the streets became, the further he wanted to explore. Abandoning his plan to visit the cemetery, he turned to the next page of the guidebook.

The streets of Death's Doorstep, one of the darkest areas of the Old Town, are not to be explored by the unwary traveller come nightfall. Ruffians and pickpockets inhabit its streets and are all too grateful for any rich visitor who may unwittingly cross their paths...

Marius lowered the book. He had the unmistakable sensation that he was being watched. As he walked on, he heard hard-soled boots fall into step behind him. Whenever his pace slowed, so the footsteps slowed. He turned, flashlight in hand, the beam glinting from oily puddles. But there was no one there. He hurried off the street into a dark alleyway but stopped abruptly; it was a dead end. Marius turned and a sturdy figure stepped out in front of him, blocking his path. The figure was accompanied by a small brown pug dog, growling and straining at the end of a long piece of rope.

Marius was trapped. He looked around desperately for a way to escape – but there was none. His mouth was dry and his pulse was galloping.

The dog was clawing at the cobbles, a deep growl rattling at the back of its throat.

'Easy, Boris,' whispered the boy, for sturdy-looking though the figure was, Marius could now see that the stranger was only a little older than he was. Not that this gave him much comfort. As Mr Brunert had often commented, a wily child can be twice as dangerous as a dull-witted man.

Suddenly the growl exploded into a volley of ear-splitting barks. The boy gave the rope a sharp tug and the dog yelped.

Marius took a tentative step backwards.

'And where do you think you're going?' asked the boy.

'I'm new to the city,' stammered Marius. 'I took a wrong turn and lost my way. I'm going home now.'

'No you're not,' growled the boy and clicked his fingers. Two figures materialised from the shadows, their hands clamping down on Marius's shoulders. 'You're coming with us.'

CHAPTER FIVE

———◆×◆×◆———

MARIUS STRUGGLED, but it was no good; his captors were too strong for him.

'Come on,' said the boy with the dog. 'Quickly. Before anyone sees him.'

Marius was hurried out of the alley, along a narrow side street and through a low door that was slammed shut behind him as soon as he entered. He blinked in the darkness and turned his head to see that he was flanked by two boys. The taller boy with the dog stood before him.

'Who are you?' demanded Marius. 'Are you going to murder me?'

One of the boys at his shoulders gave a sudden laugh. 'He thinks we're going to murder him, Yurgen!'

Candlelight was flickering up ahead, revealing a floor of polished black granite, rippled with streaks of red. An unlit chandelier hung lopsidedly from a high ceiling, quivering alarmingly with every gust of breeze that passed through the building. Glimpsed dimly in the gloom, a grand staircase wound upwards, its copper balustrade dull and tarnished. Everywhere candles flickered in empty tin cans. A mournful gramophone record played from somewhere deep inside the dark and cavernous building.

A bedraggled throng of children appeared one by one from the shadows, silently approaching and crowding around Marius.

A bespectacled boy, one of his lenses cracked, pushed his way forward, a fringe of black hair hanging low over his eyes. 'Who is he?'

'My name is Marius. Who are you?'

'I am Cosmo,' said the boy.

'We found him wandering on his own through Death's Doorstep,' said Yurgen.

Marius observed his captor with interest. The boy was at least two years older than he was, with a long face and a flop of light-brown hair, parted in the centre. Attached at his belt was an odd collection of keys, bottle openers, and other assorted implements. A small grappling hook hung down as low as his knees.

'Don't you know how dangerous it is to walk on your own at night?' said Cosmo. 'You could have been snatched off the street and then where would you be? Not here, that's for certain.'

Marius could not understand why anybody would want to snatch him but he thought it safest not to ask awkward questions.

The cat from the street made its appearance again, purring quietly as it rubbed its back against Marius's legs. The boy reached down to stroke the creature.

'That's Bag-of-Bones,' said a tall girl with wavy brown hair and a freckled face. She bent down, lifting the cat from the ground and cradling it in her arms. 'He's my cat.'

'He's not your cat, Lil,' said Cosmo. 'He belongs to the Band of Blood.'

Bag-of-Bones wriggled free of Lil's embrace and sprang off across the floor.

'He belongs to me more than he belongs to anyone else,' whispered Lil, and she shot a quick smile at Marius.

Cosmo turned to the new arrival. 'You'll have to stay here, of course,' he said. 'It's not safe for you to go outside again tonight.'

'But I can't stay—' began Marius.

'It's not open to debate,' interrupted Cosmo.

Marius's eyes were slowly growing used to the darkness. On a wall was the stuffed and mounted head of an elk. One of the eyes had dropped out and had been replaced by a large green marble. The mouth, once sewn shut, had come unstitched giving the unfortunate beast a lopsided and alarming smile. As Marius watched, moths crawled from between the frayed stitches, buzzing frantically in the candle light. 'What is this place?' he asked.

'You mean, what was it?' said Lil, pointing to an old framed photograph that hung from a panelled wall. 'It was a hotel where rich people stayed.'

'The place was abandoned long ago,' said Cosmo. 'But we live here now. Just us.'

'Will you read us a story, Cosmo?' asked a young girl with auburn hair, taking Cosmo's hand and swinging it backwards and forwards.

'A torture story, Cosmo?' added a small boy with bright green eyes. 'About the evil tyrant Emeté Talbor and his guillotine?'

'Very well,' said Cosmo with a patient nod of his head.

'Will there be much blood, please?' asked the girl, tugging hard on Cosmo's sleeve.

'Of course there will,' said Cosmo with a grin. 'Heads don't come off without a gallon of blood being spilled, do they?'

The girl laughed, chasing the small boy across the floor. 'Emeté Talbor got his head chopped off!' she chanted. 'Emeté Talbor got his head...chopped...OFF!'

'Cosmo always throws more blood into his stories than was ever really there,' said Lil, laughing as the two young children ran off across the lobby floor and disappeared through a doorway.

'How old are they?' asked Marius, his confidence slowly returning.

'Luca's seven,' said Yurgen, jumping up onto the old reception desk and swinging his legs, watching Marius narrowly. 'And Ava's six.'

'They haven't been with us for long,' said Lil. 'Their father fell in front of a tram on Alexis Street. So many people have been killed by the trams, they call them Reapers.'

'Is it safe for them here?' asked Marius.

'Of course it's safe,' said Cosmo. 'We are the Band of Blood.'

'Why don't you tell him all our secrets,' said Yurgen, and Cosmo murmured an apology.

'So...you are the Band of Blood?' said Marius slowly.

'Maybe,' said Cosmo shiftily, and Yurgen rolled his eyes.

Marius took a deep breath. 'Are you murderers?' he asked, fearful that matters might soon take a turn for the worse.

Yurgen gave a spluttering laugh and jumped down from the desk. 'No,' he said. 'We're not murderers.'

It was encouraging to discover that his captors were not cold-blooded killers, but it did not provide any clues as to their actual occupation.

'Gustavo, bring him to the ballroom,' said Yurgen. 'We'll question him there.'

A well-fed boy with an open face and large ears ushered Marius into an enormous room with a vast wooden floor, the walls decorated with plaster cherubs and huge, speckled mirrors. The windows were boarded, but fraying brocade drapes with golden tassels still hung from ornate brass curtain poles.

The Band of Blood gathered and sat on chairs that had been set out in a large circle in the centre of the room.

'Sit down,' said Cosmo, glancing at Marius, as he carried in a brass bell from the reception desk. 'We have to write our names in blood.'

'Why?' asked Marius.

'Because we're the Band of Blood,' explained Gustavo, opening a bag and taking out a large ledger which he placed on a chair. 'We're bonded with blood. Not real blood though.'

'We were going to use real blood,' added Yurgen defensively. 'But Lil faints at the first sight of gore.'

'I do,' admitted Lil. 'I don't like gore much. Especially if it's mine.'

Marius counted twenty-eight members of the Band of Blood seated in the circle. They took it in turns to sign the ledger, writing their names in red ink from a glass bottle.

'Has anyone seen Merla today?' asked Gustavo.

Lil leant from her chair towards Marius. 'Merla never comes down from her room. She lived in a castle before she came here. She got strange.'

'She always was strange,' said Yurgen bluntly. 'She's got stranger over time.'

'Heinrich saw her,' said Lil, nodding to a pale boy with black hair who sat with an accordion on his lap.

'I left food outside her door this morning and I saw her hand when she reached out to get it,' said Heinrich. 'She didn't say thank you. She never says thank you.' He squeezed the accordion moodily and air escaped with a reedy whine like the cry of a dying cat.

'I'll sign for her,' said Gustavo and added Merla's name to the ledger.

'There's no one missing,' said Cosmo with a sigh of relief.

'Then it's a good day,' said Yurgen. He turned to Marius. 'We have to write your name in the book as well. You're a guest of the Band of Blood for tonight. We know you're called Marius, but Marius what?'

'Myerdorf,' said Marius.

'It's blue ink for visitors,' whispered Lil as Yurgen wiped the nib of his pen and dipped it in a bottle of sapphire ink.

'Orphaned or fortunate?' asked Yurgen.

Marius considered the question carefully. He was certainly an orphan; that was beyond question. But as his parents had cared little for him, was it not also fortunate that slavering wolves had put an end to them? He chewed his lip. It was undoubtedly a conundrum to tax the quickest of brains. Deciding at last that dark thoughts are often better thought than spoken, he answered 'orphaned', and kept 'fortunate' to himself.

'Were your Best Beloved kind people?' asked Lil.

'I don't know who my Best Beloved were,' said Marius.

'Best Beloved,' explained Gustavo. 'She means your mother and father.'

'No,' said Marius quickly. 'They weren't kind. They were selfish people. So my tutor, Mr Brunert, looked after me. He was a good man. He gave me nougat.'

'You say you're new to the city,' said Yurgen without looking up from the ledger. 'So what are you doing here? Why did you come?'

Marius hesitated. He felt as though he was standing trial and could not tell whether his evidence was helping or hindering his case.

'Well?' said Yurgen impatiently.

Marius took a deep breath. 'When my parents died I was sent here to live with my great-great-uncle Kalvitas... in his shop on Edvardplatz.'

There was an awed gasp from the assembled children.

Yurgen looked up at the boy. 'Kalvitas the Chocolate Maker?'

Marius nodded and Gustavo leant towards him. 'Really?' he said. 'Your great-great-uncle is M. Kalvitas? My father used to take me there all the time. He makes the best salted caramels in the whole of the Great City.'

'That's enough, Gustavo,' said Yurgen sternly, bringing his hand down on the reception bell.

'But Yurgen—' protested Gustavo.

Yurgen clenched his fists tightly. 'I said, enough.'

Gustavo shut his mouth and folded his arms.

'My great-great-uncle doesn't want me,' said Marius. 'So I don't have anywhere to live now.'

'He could become one of us then, couldn't he, Yurgen?' said Lil.

'The Band of Blood is only for orphans,' said Yurgen, lowering his pen. 'You know that, Lil. And if he's got a great-great-uncle that means he's not an orphan.'

'That's not what it means at all,' said Cosmo, consulting a small red book that he had tugged from his pocket. 'Being an orphan just means no mother or father. There's nothing in the rules about great-great-uncles.'

'But he's got family,' said Yurgen. 'He doesn't need the Band of Blood if he's got someone to care for him.'

'But he doesn't care,' said Marius miserably. 'I think he'd be happier if I drowned myself in the river.'

'He's as much of an orphan as we are, Yurgen,' said Cosmo. 'His parents are just as dead as ours.'

'It's not up to you,' said Yurgen angrily. 'I'm leader of the Band of Blood and it's my decision if he stays or if he goes.'

Gustavo, who had grown bored of sitting silently, pinged the reception bell urgently.

'What is it now?' growled Yurgen.

'I'm hungry,' said Gustavo. 'Can't we eat?'

'All right,' said Yurgen, screwing the lids on the bottles of ink and rising grimly from his chair. 'But this isn't over yet. Nobody becomes a member of the Band of Blood until we know for certain that they're not a spy. Heinrich, take him to the kitchens. Cosmo, you stay here. We need to talk.'

The meeting was abandoned and the hotel was once more alive with noise. Marius let out a low sigh, grateful that for now at least his interrogation was at an end.

'This way,' said Heinrich, closing his accordion and fastening it with a leather strap. He led Marius from the ballroom, across the floor of the lobby and through a maze of narrow passageways to the hotel kitchens. The plaster walls were crumbling and a large copper saucepan in a corner of the room collected water that dripped in through the damp and sagging ceiling. From the holes in the walls and the scattered mounds of sawdust on the tiled floor it was clear that the hotel was at the mercy of rats and determined woodworm.

They found Gustavo there already, busy assembling sandwiches of smoked cheese and garlic sausage.

'Do you live in the hotel all alone?' asked Marius.

'Bad things happened here,' said Lil as she bustled in and emptied a bucket of ice into an ancient copper sink to chill bottles of lingonberry cordial. 'No adult would set foot in this place.'

'What sort of bad things?' asked Marius.

'All sorts,' said Gustavo, sawing through the pile of sandwiches with a murderously sharp knife. 'Killings and suicides and accidents that couldn't be explained. People began to think there was a dark curse hanging over the hotel.'

'Is that's why it's deserted?' asked Marius.

'It's one of the reasons,' said Heinrich.

A scrawny ginger cat prowled into the kitchen, a grey rat squirming and wriggling between its jaws.

'Where do the cats come from?' asked Marius, considering whether or not to free the rat.

'There's a secret entrance they use,' said Gustavo. 'But I can't remember where it is.'

'It's very secret,' grinned Lil.

The cat jumped up onto the counter and dropped the rat on a slice of rye bread.

'We get lots of rats,' said Heinrich, lifting the startled-looking creature from the bread and dropping it gently onto the floor where it bounded off through a hole in the wall.

'Can't you get infections from rats?' asked Marius.

Heinrich shrugged. 'Probably.'

'I want a rat,' said Gustavo with a heartfelt sigh. 'A tame rat. I keep trying to train them but they always bite me.'

'It's because you're so fat and delicious-looking,' said Lil, stirring up a jug of lingonberry cordial. 'That's why.'

'I don't think Yurgen wants me here,' said Marius as he followed Heinrich into a long room with high, boarded windows that had clearly been the dining room of the hotel. There was an enormous table draped with a tablecloth, once white but now stained and moth-nibbled. Two silver candelabra had been placed at either end of the long table and candles burned brightly.

'Yurgen's not so bad,' said Heinrich as he laid the table with porcelain plates from a pantry cupboard, each bearing the eagle crest of Good Prince Eugene. 'It takes a while to get used to him, that's all.'

Gustavo carried the sandwiches in on a silver tray, together with a long pyramid-shaped bar of chocolate praline, wrapped in gold foil. He was followed by Lil with the lingonberry cordial, which she poured carefully into cut-glass goblets.

Gustavo struck a gong with a large silver ladle and the Band of Blood crowded into the room, pulling up chairs at the table. Yurgen entered, dressed for dinner with a tightly-knotted silk tie and a rusting cutlass at his side, Boris the pug yapping and scampering around his feet. Cosmo entered behind him, clutching a journal and a bundle of papers under his arm.

'Why does Yurgen wear the sword?' whispered Marius.

'Why does anybody do anything in this life?' replied Heinrich.

Yurgen took his place at the head of the table, the sides of his mouth twitching into a smile as he surveyed the food laid out before him. There were tins of sardines, a dish of sour cream, cracker biscuits, hazelnut chocolate paste and a large bowl of cold plum streusel. 'Now it is time to eat,' said Yurgen, holding up his goblet and glancing along the table. 'We are the Band of Blood!'

'The Band of Blood!' came the answering cry.

'A very good vintage,' said Gustavo appreciatively, swilling the lingonberry cordial round in his mouth and spitting it back into his goblet.

'Where does all the food come from?' asked Marius, marvelling at the feast.

'That doesn't concern you,' snapped Yurgen. 'That's a secret of the Band of Blood.'

Marius's face reddened. He lowered his head and pushed away his plate.

'You were lucky Bollo didn't get you in the Reformatory van,' said Lil, quickly changing the subject and slurping from her goblet. 'He's always prowling the streets, looking for orphans to cart away. That's why Yurgen rescued you.'

'I didn't think I needed rescuing,' said Marius.

'You're new to the city,' said Gustavo, spreading a slice of rye bread with anchovy and herring paste. 'You get slung into the Reformatory, you never come out again. And that's an end to you.'

'Do you mean the Schwartzgarten Reformatory for Maladjusted Children? My tutor, Mr Brunert, mentioned it once,' said Marius. 'Is it really as bad as that?'

'Worse,' said Gustavo. 'The Superintendent's half mad and half evil.'

Marius laughed. 'They don't let evil people look after children!'

'He means it,' said Lil. 'She was locked up for cruelty to orphans. But then the Schwartzgarten Board for Impoverished Delinquents had her released again.'

'Why?' asked Marius in disbelief. 'If she was cruel to orphans?'

Gustavo snorted. 'Because they couldn't find anybody better.'

'There aren't many worse places than Schwartzgarten to be an orphan,' said Lil, dipping a slice of bread in the hazelnut chocolate paste.

'How long have you been here?' asked Marius, suddenly envious of a life lived in the mouldering grandeur of the old hotel.

'Almost too long to remember,' said Gustavo.

'But not actually too long,' said Cosmo, who was making notes in his journal, his papers spread out on the table in front of him.

'Yurgen has been here the longest,' said Gustavo, piling plum streusel onto his plate.

Cosmo lowered his voice. 'There were more of us once.'

'But Yurgen never talks of it,' said Gustavo. 'Not now.'

'He talks to me,' whispered Cosmo, as Marius watched Yurgen cut slices from the praline pyramid with the blade of his cutlass. 'He tells me all his secrets.'

Boris, who had been running round the room licking up scraps of fallen food, sprang onto the table and began lapping peppermint cordial from Yurgen's goblet.

'Hey, get out!' cried the boy. He stood up, pushed the dog gently away and drained his goblet to the dregs. With a laugh he yanked the journal from Cosmo's hands. 'Can't you even stop working for supper?'

'Give it back!' yelled Cosmo, jumping to his feet and reaching desperately for the book.

Yurgen read aloud from the journal. '"The week passed on wings of lead..." What does that mean, Cosmo?'

'It means we haven't had many adventures this week,' said Cosmo. 'Now give me back my journal!'

Yurgen grinned, ruffled Cosmo's hair and returned the book. 'Then we'll have to make sure we have more adventures next week, won't we?'

'I'm going upstairs to write,' said Cosmo moodily. 'I do not wish to be disturbed.' He gathered up his papers and walked quickly from the room.

Yurgen picked up his spoon and flung a globule of sour cream at the departing boy, which missed narrowly but splattered spectacularly against a peeling portrait of Good Prince Eugene that hung from the wall.

'Show the new boy where to find bedding, Gustavo,' said Yurgen as he stalked off towards the lobby. 'He can share your room.'

'Are you full?' asked Gustavo, scraping up a last spoonful of plum streusel.

'I am,' said Marius. 'Do we have to wash our plates?'

'We don't do that here,' said Gustavo, as he rose from the table. 'We use the laundry chute.' He took Marius's plate and piled it on top of his own. Pulling open a hatch in the wall he dropped the plates down the chute, listening with satisfaction as they crashed into the cellar below. 'And we don't have to clean the tablecloth either. When we're not here the rats come out and eat up the crumbs.'

'Then the cats come out and eat up the rats,' said Lil, leading Marius out of the dining room and across the lobby to the grand staircase. 'This way.'

'We're on the third floor,' said Gustavo. 'It seems a

long way up after a big supper, but it's not that far really.'

The stairs were covered with an ancient red carpet and Marius had to tread carefully to avoid catching his feet in gaping, moth-eaten holes.

The once-grand corridors of the hotel were now lit with dim lantern light, revealing peeling paint and cracked plasterwork. There was noise everywhere; children darted from room to room, running along the corridors and sliding down the staircase on old wooden doors that had been wrenched from their hinges.

'This is it,' said Gustavo at last. 'The third floor.'

'That's Cosmo's room,' said Lil as they passed an open door. 'He writes his books in there. He's got a very brilliant brain.'

'Or so he says,' grinned Gustavo.

Arriving at the end of the corridor Gustavo pushed open a door. 'This is the place. There are good views of the Cemetery. If you like looking at cemeteries.'

Marius glanced around the dark and poky room. There were two beds with ragged and greying linen, and a scrap of faded purple carpet in the middle of the room dotted with black rat droppings.

'That's where I sleep,' said Gustavo, pointing to the bed that stood closest to the window. It was surrounded by heaps of clothes and empty jars of hazelnut paste. 'Yurgen says I live like a pig.' He laughed. 'It doesn't matter though. I like pigs.' He opened the door of a battered wardrobe. 'There are extra quilts and blankets in there. Help yourself.' Getting down on his hands and knees he reached under his bed, dragging out a stack of dog-eared catalogues. 'Do you like motor cars?' he asked. 'I do. My father worked for the Estler-Spitz Motor Car Company.' He turned the pages of one of the catalogues and tapped a coloured illustration with his finger. 'That's the motor car we had. An Estler-Spitz Snubnose Mark II. You can read them if you like.'

'Thank you,' said Marius.

'But first,' continued Gustavo, 'I want you to write in this.' He held up the ledger that the Band of Blood had signed downstairs in the great ballroom.

'Gustavo is Keeper of the Ledger,' said Lil as Gustavo opened up the book.

'At the back it contains the memories of the members of the Band of Blood,' explained Gustavo, taking a pen and a bottle of ink from his pocket and passing them to Marius. 'You have to write your memories too.'

'But Yurgen hasn't admitted me to the Band of Blood,' said Marius.

'He will,' said Gustavo. 'He's got to.'

'You're an orphan like the rest of us,' added Lil. 'Yurgen never abandons orphans. He's not black-hearted like that.'

Gustavo turned to the next clean page of the ledger. 'We have to remember the bad things as well as the good. It makes our Best Beloved more real in our memories that way.' He passed the book to Marius.

'We'll leave you for a while,' said Gustavo, as Marius sat on the end of his bed. 'Come on, Lil.'

Marius carefully read through the list of questions that had been written on the page. He dipped the pen in ink and began to write.

NAME:

Marius Myerdorf

NAME OF PARENTS:

Hermann and Isadora Myerdorf

MOST PLEASANT MEMORY OF YOUR PARENTS:

It was not easy to dredge up pleasant memories. But at last Marius put pen to paper.

They would sometimes give me chocolates.
WORST MEMORY OF YOUR PARENTS:
The first time they forgot my birthday. I was four years old.
MANNER OF DEATH:
Wolves.

Marius blotted the ink with the sleeve of his pullover and closed the ledger.

Gustavo reappeared at the door. 'I'll take that for safekeeping,' he said, gently prising the book from Marius's hands and stowing it away beneath his bed. 'It helps, I think. To write things in ink. Come down if you want more food. I'll eat the whole bowl of plum streusel if nobody stops me.'

Marius waited until Gustavo had disappeared before

stepping cautiously from the room and setting off along the corridor to explore. The door to Cosmo's room still stood open and a feeble fire smouldered in the grate of a marble fireplace. The boy sat cross-legged on the floor, surrounded by bottles of coloured ink. He had changed into a velvet smoking jacket with a red silk cravat secured in position with a ruby pin.

'You can come in,' said Cosmo without looking up, 'but don't touch anything.'

Marius hesitated.

'I won't invite you twice,' said Cosmo.

Marius stepped inside the room. It was wider and taller than he was expecting, much larger than the room he was to share with Gustavo. The walls were lined with bookcases.

'You've got a lot of books,' said Marius, walking slowly around the room.

'Yes,' replied Cosmo, dipping his pen in a bottle of emerald ink and scratching out a line in his journal.

Marius ran his finger slowly along a row of leather book spines. 'Did you steal them?'

'No,' said Cosmo, getting up from the floor as Marius

pulled a book from the shelf. 'Of course I didn't. They were my mother's books. She was a professor at the University of Lüchmünster. I get my intelligence from her.'

'How did you bring them all here?' asked Marius curiously.

'It took time,' said Cosmo, removing the volume from Marius's hands and returning it to its place on the shelf. 'You ask a lot of questions.'

'Do I?' asked Marius.

'You do,' said Cosmo, removing his spectacles and wiping the good lens with his pocket handkerchief. 'I think that's interesting.'

Marius carefully lifted another leather-bound book from a shelf and turned to the front page. It was a history of Schwartzgarten, written by Kristifan Von Hoffmeyer. A small label had been pasted into place on the marbled paper:

PROPERTY OF THE UNIVERSITY OF
LÜCHMÜNSTER: NOT TO BE REMOVED.

'That's a first edition,' said Cosmo with a weary sigh. 'Do you have clean fingers?'

'I think so,' said Marius, wiping his hands on the front of his pullover and presenting them to Cosmo for inspection.

'Very well,' said Cosmo. 'But don't turn the pages of the book too quickly,' he cautioned. 'And never fold the corners down to mark your place.'

'I won't,' said Marius, settling himself in a wingback armchair beside the dwindling fire. By the arm of the chair was a small table on which stood a chessboard with carved marble pieces. A game was already in play.

'I've tried to teach them,' said Cosmo, following Marius's glance. 'But it doesn't do any good. No one wants to learn in this place. Only me. So I have to play the black and the white pieces myself.' He took a chocolate cigar from a box and bit off the end.

'The black queen is undefended,' murmured Marius.

'Do you play chess?' asked Cosmo in surprise.

'In Blatten I did,' said Marius. 'My tutor, Mr Brunert, taught me.'

'Very good,' said Cosmo. He reached out his hand, moving a black rook across the chessboard and sweeping a white knight to one side. He smiled to himself and lifted the cracked glass stopper from a crystal decanter.

'A drink?' he asked.

Marius nodded and Cosmo poured two goblets of peppermint cordial.

The two boys talked long into the night, sipping peppermint cordial and playing chess as they sat beside the dying embers of the fire.

By the time Marius returned to his room Gustavo was asleep in his bed and the lantern had been extinguished. Quietly, Marius pushed the door shut behind him and tiptoed towards his own bed.

Gustavo snorted and rolled over. 'Who is it?' he mumbled. 'Who's there?'

'It's me,' said Marius.

'As long as it's not murderers,' said Gustavo, and rolled over to face the wall. 'I warn you, I snore like a creature from the forest.'

Marius laughed and climbed into bed. 'Good night,' he said.

But Gustavo was already asleep.

CHAPTER SIX

THE NEXT morning Marius was woken by the shutters of the hotel as they creaked and rattled in the wind. Sitting up and rubbing his eyes, he found that he was all alone.

Gustavo had left a wedge of smoked cheese in a corner of the room for the rats to feed on and his plan had evidently been successful. Marius flung his pillow towards the feasting vermin and the creatures scattered, retreating beneath Gustavo's bed.

He climbed out of bed and walked to the window, gazing out through a crack in the shutters. He could see as far as the great forest at the eastern edge of the city and the towering mountains to the north. Blatten seemed further away than ever in the pale morning light.

As he emerged from his room he saw a hand appear from a door at the far end of the corridor. 'Perhaps that's Merla,' he thought. 'The strange girl who doesn't sign her own name in the Ledger.' The hand felt around on the threadbare carpet, as if searching for something. But, failing to find the something that had been expected, the hand withdrew inside the room and the door was slowly closed. 'She's hungry,' Marius mused. He returned quickly to his room. On a table beside Gustavo's bed was a half-eaten bowl of plum streusel from the night before that had been untouched by the scampering rats. He picked up the bowl and walked stealthily back along the corridor. Placing the bowl on the floor in front of the bedroom door he gave a gentle knock and moved quietly away.

As he turned his back and began to retreat, he heard the door creak open behind him. He turned in time to see the hand appear from inside the room, groping around on the floor. Before Marius could call out, the fingers seized the bowl and dragged it inside the room. He ran along the corridor; a grille had been opened in the door and two dark eyes peered out.

'Hello,' said Marius. 'My name is—'

'Don't want to talk,' came a muffled voice from the other side of the door. 'Go away.'

As Marius opened his mouth to speak again the grille slammed shut.

'So you've met Merla,' said Yurgen, appearing at the top

of the stairs with Cosmo and Boris in tow. 'Told you she was strange.'

'Her parents were rich,' said Cosmo. 'Her father was Count Von Hasselbach. There's a statue of him in the cemetery. They had money. Lots of money. Very few people can pay for statues of their Best Beloved. But she was left with nothing when her father died. Not a single thing to remind her of him.'

'Where does that lead?' asked Marius, as he carried on along the passageway towards a door that had been boarded shut. Boris growled.

'You can't go any further!' shouted Yurgen. 'It's not safe. There was a fire here, years ago.'

Marius stopped in his tracks.

'A terrible fire,' added Yurgen, not certain that Marius had seized the enormity of the disaster. 'It's dangerous. No one can pass beyond that door.'

'Are you hungry?' asked Cosmo, quickly. 'There's breakfast downstairs if you want some.'

Marius walked down to the lobby. A few stray beams of light penetrated the shuttered windows. Suddenly he gasped and stopped in his tracks. A man in a dark blue uniform with bright copper buttons stood alone on the floor of the lobby. Though the uniform was unfamiliar to a boy who had spent his life in the mountains, Marius could tell at once that the man was an officer of the police. He held his breath and stepped back behind the old reception desk, but his hand caught against the brass bell which rang out loudly.

The Constable turned suddenly. He was a young man, tall with piercing green eyes and a closely-cropped head of blond hair.

Marius darted out from behind the desk, skidding across the granite floor. He scrambled up the stairs to Cosmo's room, where he found the boy sitting on the floor talking with Yurgen.

'There's a police constable,' he panted. 'He's downstairs!'

As he spoke there were heavy footsteps in the corridor and Marius turned in horror to see the Constable standing outside the door. He stumbled backwards and was preparing to bolt towards the window when Yurgen let out a laugh.

'You're safe,' he said. 'He's a friend.'

'This is Constable Sternberg,' said Cosmo. 'He looks out for us. He's an honorary member of the Band of Blood.'

Sternberg bowed his head in acknowledgement of the

compliment. He held up his left hand, pointing to a gold signet ring on his little finger.

'We gave him the ring,' said Cosmo. 'It's a symbol that he's one of us.'

'Who's this then?' said Sternberg. 'A new member?'

'We don't know yet,' said Yurgen, glancing slyly at Marius. 'Perhaps.'

'Yes,' said Cosmo firmly. 'He's one of us.'

'Come on down to the kitchen,' said Sternberg. 'I've brought you food.'

They followed the Constable downstairs, meeting Gustavo on their way. He saluted to Sternberg, who laughed and saluted back.

'Look what I found,' said Gustavo, holding up Marius's Inspector Durnstein book. 'I told you Marius was one of us.'

'Have you been going through my things?' asked Marius, trying to control his temper.

'I thought there might be chocolate,' said Gustavo with a shrug. 'It's a good book, isn't it? Especially when Durnstein discovers the corpse hidden inside the wardrobe—' He stopped suddenly. 'Have you got to that part yet?'

'I haven't,' said Marius.

'Oh,' said Gustavo. 'Sorry.'

They passed Heinrich, who was sitting on the reception desk, playing his accordion.

'Morning, Heinrich,' said Sternberg. 'Still playing that thing, are you? You'll be performing at the Schwartzgarten Opera House before too long.'

Heinrich beamed.

'You made sure you weren't followed?' asked Yurgen, as they wound through the passageways to the kitchen.

Sternberg laughed. 'Think I'm a fool? Of course I wasn't followed. Now here, this crate's for you. It'll keep you fed for a few days more.'

'What's inside?' asked Gustavo.

'There's rye bread and potatoes, lingonberry cordial, tins of sardines, apples and pears and beetroot,' said Sternberg. He smiled at Marius. 'If I didn't bring them fruit and vegetables they'd make themselves sick on hazelnut chocolate paste.'

'But I like hazelnut paste,' said Gustavo.

'Have this instead,' said Sternberg, throwing Gustavo an apple which the boy caught clumsily. 'If you don't eat your greens you won't grow up to be big and strong like me.' He turned to Yurgen, who was stocking a cupboard with tins of sardines from the crate. 'Does the boy have papers yet?'

'No,' said Yurgen. 'Not yet.'

'What's his last name?'

'Myerdorf,' said Marius, and Sternberg turned quickly. 'I am new to the Great City. I travelled from Blatten to—'

'I don't care where you came from,' interrupted Sternberg, retrieving a piece of paper from his pocket. 'What I care about is this.'

He unfolded the paper and held it out for Marius.

DISAPPEARED: ONE BOY, ANSWERS TO THE NAME MARIUS MYERDORF. FIFTY IMPERIAL CROWNS PAID FOR INFORMATION LEADING TO HIS CAPTURE. WRITE OR TELEPHONE TO THE OFFICES OF THE SCHWARTZGARTEN DAILY EXAMINER.

'Where did this come from?' asked Yurgen urgently.

The Constable refolded the paper and returned it to his pocket. 'It was in every copy of *The Schwartzgarten Daily*

Examiner this morning,' he said. 'Somebody wants the boy, that's clear enough.'

Yurgen advanced on Marius. 'What is it you haven't told us?' he hissed. 'What is it you're keeping from us?'

Marius could feel his heart leaping in his throat. 'There's nothing I haven't told you,' he said.

'There must be something,' said Cosmo gently. 'Nobody offers that amount of money for the return of an orphan.'

'Marius is the great-great-nephew of Kalvitas the Chocolate Maker,' said Gustavo.

'That might be important,' said Sternberg. 'It seems there's somebody going round putting an end to the Chocolate Makers in this city – it's all over the papers. The Guild of Twelve lost three members last month and Helmut Fugard's been killed in his shop – that's another one off to his grave.'

'You think they want Marius dead as well?' asked Yurgen.

Marius's heart seemed to be pounding so heavily in his throat that he held his hand to his mouth so Yurgen could not hear the noise.

'Who knows,' said Sternberg. 'But it's not safe for any

of you if you're seen with a boy that's being hunted out, whoever's doing the searching. He's endangering the Band of Blood. Take him to Duttlinger and get him disguised, then go on to Franz for false papers.'

Yurgen nodded.

———

It was decided that it would be safest to wait until late afternoon before setting out from the hotel, in a small group made up of Yurgen, Marius, Lil and Gustavo, with Boris as ever tugging at his leash.

'We never use the front entrance,' said Yurgen, pointing to a heaped stack of heavy furniture that had been pushed against the old door of the hotel. 'We go out the way you came in, along the alleyway that runs beside this place.'

Heinrich was guarding the doorway that led from the lobby. 'Halt,' he said. 'Who goes there?'

'Us, you idiot,' said Yurgen, giving Heinrich a push that sent him stumbling back and tripping over his accordion.

'Be careful out there,' said Heinrich, picking himself

up from the floor and dusting down his clothes.

'Of course we'll be careful,' said Yurgen. 'We're always careful. Now come on, Marius. Keep close by my side.'

Marius's mind teemed with a surging mass of confused thoughts. Try as he might, he could not fathom a reason that someone might want him, let alone offer fifty Imperial crowns for the pleasure – it certainly wouldn't be his great-great-uncle, he thought. He half-suspected that he might be dreaming, but a sharp punch on the arm from Yurgen reassured him that he was very much awake.

'Don't daydream,' said Yurgen. 'Unless you want Bollo to take you for a one-way trip to the Reformatory.'

Stepping out into the alleyway Marius blinked, though the sun was fast dying in the west.

'We keep to the shadows where we can,' said Gustavo, as they weaved their way through the Old Town, and across the Princess Euphenia Bridge. It was a harsh, cold afternoon with flakes of snow biting at their cheeks, and they passed easily into the New Town without anyone so much as looking at them.

But as they negotiated the crowds on busy Biedermann Street, Marius was alarmed to spot a tall wooden tower in the middle of the street, where a police constable stood staring out through a pair of binoculars. 'They're looking for me,' he moaned.

'Keep your head down,' said Yurgen, and Boris growled. 'If we disappear deeper into the crowds it'll be harder for the police to spot us. If we're separated, go back to the hotel and wait for us there.'

There was a sudden shrill blast of a whistle and Marius turned in horror. 'Stop!' cried the policeman in the tower, waving his binoculars. 'Stop, you!'

'Don't look back,' hissed Yurgen. 'Keep walking.'

'You there!' shouted a voice from the crowd. 'Wait!' A second policeman was forcing his way towards them and his hand clamped down on Marius's shoulder. 'He told you to stop. Something wrong with your ears, is there? Now, show me your papers.'

Marius pulled away.

'Easy now,' said the police constable. 'You won't come to any harm.'

Yurgen took Marius by the arm, turned sharply and ran off down an alleyway, dragging the boy after him, with Gustavo and Lil following behind.

Even the ravens, it seemed, were eyeing them with suspicion, cawing uneasily from the rooftops.

'Now quickly, this way,' whispered Yurgen, leading them into a narrow street off Edvardplatz. He stopped in front of a shop and turned to make certain that they had not been followed.

Marius gazed up at the brightly painted sign above the shop door:

F. DUTTLINGER
THEATRICAL SUPPLIERS
PURVEYOR OF DUTTLINGER'S PATENTED
ARTIFICIAL HAIR

'Sometimes we need to hide in plain sight,' said Yurgen. 'And Duttlinger's the man to hide us.' He opened the door and the bell clattered. 'Duttlinger?' he hissed. 'Duttlinger, are you here?'

A curtain was drawn aside at the very back of the shop and a man appeared. He was peculiar to look at, with a high starched collar, a long white beard and a shock of wiry grey hair.

'That,' said Lil, 'is Duttlinger.'

'The Band of Blood!' exclaimed the man in delight, hurrying forward to welcome his visitors.

'Why not run into the street and scream it?' said Yurgen, a note of exasperation creeping into his voice. 'There's police crawling round outside.'

'Why, have you done something wicked?' asked Duttlinger, his eyes sparkling. 'A robbery? A murder or two? Whatever it is, I shall take your secret with me to the grave.' He leaned down to pat Boris, who snuffled appreciatively.

'They're searching for Marius,' said Yurgen, pushing past the man and dragging the boy behind him. 'We need a disguise so the police won't recognise him.'

'Very well,' said Duttlinger, pulling down the blinds and locking the door of the shop. 'Come into the back room and we'll talk.' He ushered Marius and the others into a musty-smelling room with a gas stove and a dentist's chair. 'Have no fear, I can disguise you so well that your own mothers would hardly recognise you.'

'If we still had mothers,' said Yurgen sourly.

Duttlinger's face dropped. 'What a fool I am. What a

fool! A thousand apologies. I meant no offence.'

'It doesn't matter,' said Marius, peering round the curtain, fearful that the police would burst into the shop at any moment to drag him away.

'It seems it will be my life's work to disguise orphans,' continued Duttlinger. 'Only recently I transformed the niece and nephew of the great Gisela Mortenberg.'

Marius stared blankly at the man.

'But you must know of the Mortenberg twins?' said Duttlinger, his lips pursed and a pained expression glancing across his face. 'Perhaps you read about them in the newspapers?'

'I don't think so,' said Marius.

'About so high,' said Duttlinger, gesturing vaguely with his hand to indicate a child somewhere between the height of a low footstool and a hat stand. He unhooked his beard and lifted the grey hair from his head; beneath, he was entirely bald. 'Ah, Gisela. Dear Gisela. That siren of the silver screen.' He shook his head sadly and lifted a boiling kettle from the stove. 'Now, peppermint tea for all, I think!'

'Yes please,' said Lil, smiling to reveal a sharp set of fangs.

'They suit you,' said Duttlinger. 'They were a favourite set of a customer of mine. He died wearing them.'

Lil coughed and spat out the teeth.

Duttlinger poured the peppermint tea. 'So, your name is Marius?'

Marius nodded.

'Sit in the chair. This won't hurt a bit,' said Duttlinger, with a sly smile. 'So long as I get it right, that is.'

Marius sat back in the chair and took a deep breath.

'What are you going to do to him?' asked Lil, heaping her cup with sugar.

'I'm not quite sure yet,' said Duttlinger, considering matters. 'I could alter his height if that would be desirable?'

'Can you make him shorter?' asked Yurgen.

'Only if I cut off his legs,' said Duttlinger as he sipped his tea.

'I'd rather go to the Reformatory than have my legs cut off,' said Marius, who sensed that Duttlinger was joking but was not prepared to stake his legs on it.

'I will have my little jest,' said Duttlinger with a laugh, waving Yurgen, Gustavo and Lil from the room. 'Now, let us waste not a moment more. Leave me alone with the boy and I'll see what I can do.' He closed the curtain and set to work.

Marius gripped the arms of the chair tightly as Duttlinger took down tins of greasepaint and rolls of crepe hair.

'Try this for size,' said the man, lifting a wig from its block and pulling it tightly over Marius's head. 'A perfect fit. Excellent.' He smeared greasepaint on the boy's face, dipping a sponge in water to carefully smooth the make-up. 'Now which teeth? Which teeth?' he muttered. 'Would bleeding gums be suitable? Or perhaps buck teeth?' He shook his head. 'No, no. I will fatten you up instead.' He added padding around the boy's stomach and filled out his cheeks with swabs of cotton wool.

'Is he nearly finished?' grunted Yurgen from the other side of the curtain.

'A little patience, please,' called back Duttlinger. 'Miraculous transformations take time.'

At last the curtain was drawn back. Marius climbed from the chair and stepped out into the shop.

Lil's mouth fell open and Boris growled. It was a complete transformation; Marius was fatter-looking than before, bulging at the waist and around the cheeks. His face was paler, and his hair had been concealed beneath a short, brown wig.

'I think the effect is satisfactory,' said Duttlinger, as he led Marius to a full-length mirror beside the shop counter.

Marius could not even trust his own reflection and held his hands to his face in disbelief.

'You look as fat as Gustavo now,' laughed Lil.

'I'm not fat,' said Gustavo, slurping his tea. 'I've got heavy bones.'

'I'm not me any more,' whispered Marius.

Duttlinger clasped his hands together and glowed with professional pride. 'Can there be a greater compliment? I think not.' He gave a little bow and giggled in delight. 'Excellent, excellent.'

A police whistle sounded from a nearby street.

'We have to go now,' said Yurgen, clambering up from his chair. 'Thank you, Duttlinger. How much do we—'

'Tut, tut,' said Duttlinger. 'It was my pleasure as always. An act of charity to assist the orphans of Schwartzgarten. You are heading for our friend Franz, I imagine?'

'That's right,' said Gustavo.

'It's supposed to be a secret,' growled Yurgen.

'I won't breathe a word,' said Duttlinger, crossing his heart with his finger. He opened a door at the back of the shop. 'Out this way,' he said. 'It'll be quickest and safest.'

Yurgen led them into the alley behind Duttlinger's shop and along a dark side street. Kneeling down, he pulled back a round iron cover set into the cobbles.

Though the prospect of being captured by the police terrified Marius, the thought of climbing down into a dark hole in the ground did little to lift his spirits.

'After you,' grunted Yurgen.

They felt their way carefully down the iron rungs of an ancient ladder. Yurgen climbed down last of all, with Boris tucked safely under his arm. He switched on his flashlight and pulled the cover closed above them. The tunnel was thick with rat droppings and a sickly-sweet smell of damp hung in the air.

'It's not far now,' said Yurgen, pointing ahead with the beam of his flashlight.

Lil pulled aside a thick veil of cobwebs, leading the way along the passage, which opened out into a dimly illuminated stone chamber beyond.

There was a stained and threadbare rug on the floor and an odd assortment of chairs had been scattered about the place. On a small table in the middle of the room was a dry loaf of rye bread and an opened tin of red cabbage.

A thick-lipped man with rolled-up sleeves appeared through the gloom. He was so pale that blue veins showed beneath the surface of his skin.

'Like a monster from a book,' thought Marius, stepping back behind Yurgen.

'I thought you'd be here before too long,' said the man, cracking a hazelnut between his teeth and spitting a fragment of shell from the corner of his mouth. 'Sit, sit...' he muttered, waving his hand in the direction of a dilapidated leather sofa that stood against a wall of the room. His arms were spattered with ink and he smelled strongly of garlic sausage.

The boys sat down on the sofa with Boris curled up at their feet. Lil sat at the table, thawing her fingers above the flickering flame of a candle.

'You're like ice, girl,' said the man, wrapping a blanket around Lil's shoulders.

'Thank you,' said Lil with a shivering smile.

The man turned his attention to Marius. 'I'm Franz,' he said. 'And you must be the relative of the great Kalvitas.'

'How did you know—?' began Gustavo.

The man raised an inky finger and tapped it against his nose. 'I have my sources.'

'Marius needs papers,' said Yurgen impatiently. 'The police are after him.'

'Money first,' said the man, cracking down his teeth on another hazelnut shell. 'You know my price.'

Lil lifted a purse from the pocket of her overcoat and poured a steady stream of curselings onto the table.

'Count it if you want,' said Yurgen.

'I think I can trust you,' said Franz, flicking another fragment of nutshell across the room.

Boris whined lazily as a rat pressed its way between the sofa cushions and crawled across onto Marius's lap where it sat lazily, waiting to be fed.

'Don't mind rats, do you?' asked Franz.

Marius held his breath and shook his head.

'Not that there's much I can do about it if you're against the creatures,' continued Franz. 'This is a ratty place.' He opened a cupboard door as if to illustrate his point, revealing rats of every shape and colour, as they wriggled their fat and furry bellies over tins and boxes. He lifted an albino rat from a cage beside the sofa. 'Won't do harm to man nor child, this one,' he said, stroking the rat which nibbled appreciatively at his fingers. The rat stared down at Gustavo with sad pink eyes.

'He's beautiful,' said Gustavo longingly. 'What's he called?'

'Rat,' said Franz bluntly, dropping the creature back into the cage and tossing in a titbit of garlic sausage. 'They're all called rat. This one's a sensitive creature and hungry as a wolf. You're hungry as well, I suppose?'

'We are,' said Gustavo quickly. 'We're always hungry.'

Yurgen scowled at the boy. 'Anyone would think you never get fed.'

'Don't worry, Yurgen,' said Franz with a laugh. 'I won't charge you extra for a morsel to eat.' He served up a thick pork goulash from a pan on the stove, seasoning it with salt and a grinding of black pepper. And, as the children ate, Franz set to work on Marius's papers. 'Any distinguishing scars?' he asked.

'I've got a pimple on my arm,' said Marius hopefully.

'That doesn't count,' said Franz.

'I've got scars,' grinned Gustavo, climbing to his feet and rolling up the sleeve of his shirt. 'Do you want to see them?'

'We've seen enough of your scars,' said Franz, waving Gustavo away. 'Now get out of my light, boy, so I can work.'

'Can we think up a new name for Marius to put on the papers?' asked Lil.

'Already done that,' said Franz. 'He's called Leandro Hempler now. Age eleven, from the city of Lüchmünster. Mother's name, Griselina. Father's name, Igor.'

'Griselina,' sniggered Gustavo. 'Sounds like a made-up name.'

'It is a made-up name,' said Franz. 'I like to be creative.'

Franz worked quickly, but even so it took an hour before he had completed his task. He provided Marius with a forged identity card, a library ticket, and a travel permit.

Marius held the documents in his hands, smiling at his new identity and imagining how much nicer than his own parents Griselina and Igor might have been.

There was a heavy pounding of feet from the street above and Yurgen looked up anxiously. 'That'll be the police,' he said. 'They're still looking for us.'

'Very well,' said Franz. 'But you'd better go out another way. If we follow the tunnels along there's a safe place I can take you where you should be able to climb out of the sewers without being spotted.'

'Come on, Boris,' said Yurgen, as Franz unhooked an oil lantern from the wall and guided the children through a narrow and curtained archway, on through a small stone room that was used as a store cupboard and out into a long, dark tunnel. With a grin he raised his lantern to reveal that the tunnel was lined with human skulls.

Marius flinched.

'That's a sight to haunt your dreams, isn't it?' laughed Franz.

'Whose heads were they?' asked Lil, as the lantern light picked out a gold tooth on a shattered skull.

'This was all Talbor's doing,' said Franz. 'Cut off so many heads during his reign of terror that he ran out of places to put them. So they ended up stacked down here. In some of the tunnels they're keeping the ceiling from caving in.'

Yurgen lifted a skull from the pile and held it high. 'Doesn't look well, does he?'

'You shouldn't do that,' said Lil. 'It's not respectful to the dead.'

Yurgen smiled and returned the skull to its ledge.

'The tunnels have been here for over two hundred years,' said Franz. 'Since long before Talbor's rule.' He reached inside his shirt and lifted out a silver medallion that he wore on a chain around his neck. 'This is from Talbor's day. It all gets washed down here. There's riches in sewers.'

The damp walls of the tunnel glittered in the lamp light as they continued their journey beneath the sprawling city.

'Where does this tunnel lead?' asked Marius, his voice echoing strangely along the dripping walls of the sewer.

'Not so loud,' hissed Yurgen, seizing Marius's arm and holding his hand to the boy's mouth.

'The tunnel leads wherever we want it to lead,' said Franz, pointing up ahead to a ramshackle raft made from wooden crates, lashed together with twine. 'We have to go by boat now.'

Boris gave a sharp yap and held back, so Yurgen lifted him into the boat.

'Is it safe?' asked Marius, as he climbed aboard.

'Safe?' said Franz. 'Of course it's not safe. It springs

water like a colander and the parcel twine's coming loose. But what's life if it hasn't got a bit of risk in it, eh?'

Franz untied the mooring rope and pushed away from the sewer wall with a wooden paddle. They slipped slowly along the pitch-black tunnel, with only the flickering flame of the oil lantern to light their way. There was a high-pitched squeal as two fat black rats leapt from a dripping pipe and splashed down into the sewer water in front of them.

'Don't know 'em,' said Franz with a shrug. 'They're not my rats.' He held up his lantern to illuminate the intersection between two tunnels. 'Look, there,' he said, pointing to a rusting sign on the wall above them. 'When they built the sewers they gave each tunnel the same name as the street up above.' He pointed the lantern towards a tunnel that stretched away to the left. 'That's the Street of the Seven Locksmiths. But I'll take you on a bit, it'll be safer.' He guided the boat a little way further along the tunnel, finally stopping beside a stone landing platform that had been built into the wall of the tunnel.

'Follow the steps up,' said Franz as he helped the children from the boat. 'And keep a sharp watch for the police.'

CHAPTER SEVEN

T HE FLIGHT of stone steps from the sewer led up
into the cellar of an abandoned warehouse, with a
small iron grille set high into the wall. The mortar had been
scraped away, and Marius watched as Yurgen removed the
bars and crawled out onto the pavement beyond.

Yurgen took Marius's hand and pulled him up, with
Lil and Gustavo crawling through behind him. Last of
all came Boris, leaping up from the cellar into Yurgen's
outstretched arms.

They found themselves in a deserted side street, close to
the Imperial Railway Station.

Marius made certain that his wig was still in place and
that the padding around his waist was securely fixed. He
was almost hoping that he would be stopped by the police,
so he could prove with the false documents that he was no
longer Marius Myerdorf, but Leandro Hempler instead.

'There's work to do,' said Yurgen as they walked to the
end of the street. 'Gustavo, you go back with Lil, and I'll
take Marius to Sallowman.'

'We'll see you at the hotel later,' said Gustavo, linking his arm with Lil's and heading away towards the Old Town.

'The Band of Blood doesn't beg and we don't steal,' said Yurgen, as he walked with Marius along the Street of the Seven Locksmiths. 'What we get, we earn. You understand?'

'I understand,' said Marius, who was not at all sure that he did understand but was reluctant to draw attention to the fact.

Yurgen opened out a map that had been ripped from an old copy of Muller, Brun and Gellerhund's guidebook. 'These are the friends of the Band of Blood,' he said, pointing to scattered buildings across the city of Schwartzgarten that had been hand-coloured with red ink. 'Keep this with you at all times.'

The old organ grinder from Edvardplatz was walking towards them on the other side of the street, wheeling his instrument behind him. 'It's not safe for you tonight,' he grunted. 'If you know what's good for you then you'll keep to the shadows. Bollo's out and about.'

'Thank you,' whispered Yurgen, and pushed a curseling into the man's hand.

The organ grinder grunted again and wheeled his cart on into the shadows, raising his top hat as he passed.

'One of our friends,' said Yurgen by way of explanation, ushering Marius on towards a shop on the corner of the street, bearing the name:

OSKAR SALLOWMAN
CHICKEN BUTCHER

Boris was yapping excitedly and it was an effort for Yurgen to keep hold of the leash.

'You know where we are, don't you, boy?' said Yurgen. 'You need friends as much as the Band of Blood.' He released Boris from the leash and the dog bounded into the shop, skidding across the sawdust-scattered floor.

A tall hulk of a man stood behind the counter, hanging chicken carcasses from iron hooks in the ceiling.

'Hello, Sallowman,' said Yurgen.

The butcher turned and wiped the sweat from his brow with the back of his hairy hand. 'Yurgen!' he cried.

'How's business?' asked Yurgen.

Sallowman smiled and shook hands with the boy. 'Good

for me, not so good for the birds.' He held out a chicken wing for Boris, and the dog wagged his tail, running circles in the sawdust. The butcher patted him on the head and laughed as Boris dragged the wing into a corner of the shop. 'So who's this you've brought?'

'He's called Marius,' said Yurgen. 'He's new.'

'Is he a worker?' asked Sallowman.

'He will be,' said Yurgen, following as the butcher lumbered out to the back of the shop.

'I work for Sallowman at the end of each day,' said Yurgen. 'I gather up the chicken scrapings and wash down the floor. Unless we can find something else you're good at, Marius, you can help me.'

It was not a job Marius had ever expected to take, and was certainly not an occupation that Mr Brunert had discussed with him. But hard work would earn curselings, and with no one else but the Band of Blood to look after him, curselings would keep him fed.

As soon as the butcher had locked his shop for the night, the boys set to work, scrubbing down the shop counter, sweeping up the sawdust and sluicing the floor with buckets of hot, soapy water. But Sallowman was no tyrant, and he laughed until the tears tumbled down his cheeks as Yurgen chased Marius around the shop, pulling at the tendons of a scrawny chicken leg so the claw opened and closed like the diabolical hand of a reanimated corpse.

'You've worked hard,' said Sallowman, when all traces of blood and chicken fat had been washed away. He took money from the cash register and handed it to Yurgen. 'You've earned your money tonight. There's an extra crown to sweeten things.' He nodded to Marius. 'We'll make a chicken butcher out of the boy yet. Do you want bones for Boris?'

'Thank you,' said Yurgen.

Sallowman laid a sheet of newspaper on the counter and gathered up a bundle of meaty chicken bones.

Marius, who stood leaning over the counter, spotted an advertisement in the corner of the newspaper:

NOTICE IS HEREBY GIVEN OF THE SALE
BY AUCTION OF THE ESTATE AND PERSONAL
EFFECTS OF THE LATE MARIA VON HASSELBACH,
TO BE HELD AT THE SCHWARTZGARTEN AUCTION
HOUSE THIS THURSDAY FROM THE HOUR OF TWO.

'Didn't you say the Von Hasselbachs were Merla's Best Beloved?' asked Marius.

'They were,' said Yurgen. 'Old Maria was Merla's grandmother. She was cruel. She cared more for her jewels than she did for Merla.'

Marius ripped the notice from the newspaper and folded it carefully. 'Maybe if Merla had something to remind her of her family she might be less strange?'

'She might be,' said Yurgen, 'but I wouldn't hold out much hope.'

With the money from Oskar Sallowman weighing down their pockets, Yurgen and Marius bought provisions from a dark shop in the Old Town and returned with them to the hotel.

They found Gustavo kneeling on the kitchen floor, sucking hard on his finger.

'Been bitten again, have you?' asked Yurgen.

'It was a big rat,' said Gustavo. 'It drew blood. They normally just nibble but this one wanted to hurt.' He tied his pocket handkerchief tightly around his finger. 'I'm running out of good fingers.' He turned his attention to the provisions that Yurgen was emptying from a canvas bag.

'Did you buy the food from old Kretzman?'

'Kretzman was closed,' said Yurgen. 'We had to go to Mr Kobec.'

'What did you get?' asked Gustavo.

'Potatoes,' said Yurgen.

'And cake?' said Gustavo eagerly, standing up and rubbing his hands together expectantly.

'And beetroot,' said Marius. 'There's lots of beetroot.'

'But no cake?' groaned Gustavo, lowering himself onto a chair.

'No cake,' said Yurgen.

'But I like cake,' said Gustavo.

'We all like things we can't have,' said Yurgen. He walked out into the lobby and slammed his hand down on the reception bell. 'I hope you've all been working hard for your keep,' he shouted. 'It's time to pay your dues!'

The Band of Blood assembled in the ballroom of the hotel and emptied their earnings into a large brass pot that had been placed in the middle of the floor.

Yurgen frowned as he gathered up the coins. 'It's not enough to feed us for long.'

'I've got something we can sell,' said Lil, holding up

two small paintings in giltwood frames, one of a vase of bright geraniums and the other a view across the rooftops of Schwartzgarten.

'But they're your father's pictures,' said Yurgen.

'We need to eat,' said Lil. 'The print shop in Howmann Street always stays open late. Maybe the old woman will give us money for them.'

'It's very late though,' said Gustavo. 'It'll be risky.'

'The more money we get tonight the better we'll eat at breakfast,' said Lil, and this was enough to convince Gustavo.

———

Lil set out with Gustavo, Marius and Cosmo.

Marius felt confident in Duttlinger's disguise – his stomach padded and his cheeks puffed out – and he grinned as he caught sight of his reflection in the glass door of a small café.

The print shop was a long walk from the hotel – a small, dark building, overshadowed by the glue factory next door. Inside, tables and chairs were stacked with oil paintings and watercolours, and scattered piles of old photographs.

The owner was sitting behind a table at the back of the shop. She was a hunched creature with wiry grey hair and smelled strongly of vinegar and two-day-old boiled cabbage.

'What do you want?' she said, sipping from a steaming bowl of beetroot soup. 'Can't you see I'm busy?'

Gustavo nudged Lil forwards with his elbow.

'Do you buy old pictures?' asked Lil, taking a step towards the table.

'Sometimes,' said the woman, smacking her lips. 'Depends. What've you got to show me?'

Lil opened her bag and took out the pictures. 'They're not stolen,' she said.

'Don't care much if they are,' said the woman, peering beadily at the two paintings. 'How much do you want for them then?'

'We don't know,' said Marius. 'What would you pay?'

'You've got to have an idea,' said the woman, slurping up another mouthful of soup. 'That's how we make a bargain.'

'Five Imperial crowns,' said Lil quickly. But as soon as the figure had escaped her lips she knew it was too low.

The woman pounced greedily, taking out a small black tin and rattling it hard.

'Or maybe six crowns?' said Lil, her fingers tightening around her father's paintings.

'Too high,' rasped the woman. 'Do you want to sell or don't you?'

Slowly, Lil nodded her head.

'Then it's a deal done,' said the woman, pushing the soup bowl away and opening her money tin. 'I haven't got many notes. I'll have to make it up in coins.'

A cold mist was gathering outside and Lil stood shivering as she watched the woman hang the two paintings in the window of the shop.

'Come on,' said Cosmo. 'A cup of peppermint tea will cheer you up.'

Lil smiled. 'Yes,' she said. 'It will.'

They passed a café where a hissing silver coffee machine filled the air with blasts of steam.

'Gustavo, you stay outside with Marius and keep watch,' said Cosmo, holding the door open for Lil and disappearing with her inside the café.

Gustavo paced up and down the pavement, whistling

under his breath. He pulled on a fur hat from his pocket, with flaps that covered his ears. 'Want to see something, Marius?' he said. 'Falkenrath's chocolate shop is along the street from here. It's my favourite shop. Sometimes, if there's money to spare, we buy praline pyramids there.'

Marius was uncertain. 'Cosmo told us to keep watch.'

'We won't be long,' said Gustavo, crossing the street. 'It's just down here.'

Marius followed Gustavo to a shop with red, painted walls. Even from a distance, Marius could recognise the golden cocoa pod of the Guild of Twelve beside the door. The shop sign was a wooden pyramid hanging from a brass hook, coloured to resemble milk chocolate and painted with the words:

ADOLPH FALKENRATH: CHOCOLATIER
PRALINES A SPECIALITY

The lights burned brightly in the windows of the shop and the door stood open.

'That's odd,' said Gustavo. 'He's normally shut for the night by this time.'

Marius glanced through the window. Inside was a chocolate pyramid, almost as wide and very nearly as tall as the room. 'Are his pralines always so big?' he asked.

But Gustavo was not listening; he had stepped inside and was staring in disbelief at the enormous chocolate structure. It was so large that the two could only pass around it by pressing their backs against the walls of the shop.

'Is it real chocolate, do you think?' asked Marius.

Gustavo leant forward, extended his tongue and took a long lick of the pyramid. 'It's real,' he said. 'Delicious.' He stopped. 'There's a hole here. But it's too dark to see in.'

Marius took the flashlight from his overcoat pocket and shone the beam through the hole in the chocolate wall.

'What can you see?' asked Gustavo.

The beam of light had settled on a man lying outstretched inside the pyramid. 'There's somebody in there,' said Marius. He gave a startled yelp as the flashlight revealed the man's eyes, wide open and glassy. 'I think he's dead!'

'Oh, he's dead all right,' said a voice, and Marius and Gustavo swung round in horror. A young police constable stood at the back door of the shop. 'What are you boys doing here?'

'N...n...nothing,' said Gustavo, hardly able to get a word past his lips.

'Let's see your papers,' said the Constable, holding out his hand.

The boys obediently handed the man their forged papers.

'Leandro Hempler and Gunter Guttermund,' said the Constable. 'Not murderers, are you?'

'No,' said Marius. 'We just found the door open and looked inside the shop. We found the hole in the pyramid and—'

'I made that hole,' said the Constable. 'I discovered the dead body. You're not in any trouble.'

'What's this?' asked Marius, lifting a bottle from the shop counter. He removed the stopper and sniffed the sickly-sweet contents.

'Chloroform,' said the Constable, snatching the bottle away from the boy. 'Breathe in too much of that and you'll be out cold on the floor.' He replaced the stopper. 'Whoever the killer was, he used it on Falkenrath. Knocked him out with chloroform then built the chocolate pyramid around him.'

'Couldn't he have eaten his way out?' asked Gustavo, eyeing the pyramid hungrily despite its grisly filling.

'He must have suffocated before he even had the chance to try,' said the Constable, who was now down on his hands and knees examining the contents of a cupboard and searching for clues.

Outside, a pair of headlights shone through the gathering mist and the wheels of a motor van rolled slowly over the cobbles, passing in front of the shop.

Gustavo gave an agonised moan and clutched Marius's wrist. 'That's the Reformatory van. We've got to warn Cosmo!'

'Hey! Wait!' shouted the Constable, as the boys fled from the chocolate shop. 'Don't you want your papers back?' But his words went unheard.

As Gustavo and Marius ran back along the street a voice crackled over the speakers on top of the Reformatory motor van. 'Show yourselves, gutter rats. You can't hide forever!'

Gustavo banged his fist loudly against the window of the café, but there was no sign of Lil or Cosmo inside. 'Where are they?' he groaned. The motor van ground to a halt. 'It's the Superintendent, Marius,' he shouted. 'Run! Save yourself!'

But it was too late. A small woman jumped down from the cab and seized Gustavo by the arm. 'The little poppet's mine!'

'Get your hands off me!' yelled the boy.

'Let him go,' shouted Marius, running to help free his friend.

'I don't think so,' snarled the Superintendent, holding onto Gustavo with a vice-like grip. 'Bollo, get the other one!'

A tall, thick-set man with a red face and balding head stepped forward and grabbed Marius around the waist, dragging him towards the waiting motor van and hurling him inside. The Superintendent pushed Gustavo in behind him, cracking her knuckles with satisfaction as Bollo slammed the doors shut. 'Have a pleasant journey, my precious poppets!'

There were no seats, so Marius and Gustavo sat

huddled together on the floor of the freezing motor van, warmed only by the choking exhaust fumes that filtered in beneath the door, as the vehicle lurched quickly away.

'It was brave of you to try and help me,' said Gustavo.

'You're welcome,' said Marius, his teeth chattering. 'I'm shivering from the cold, by the way. It's not because I'm frightened.'

'I know,' said Gustavo. 'I'm not frightened either,' he added hurriedly.

'Are they taking us to the Reformatory, do you think?'

Gustavo nodded grimly. 'And there's nothing the Band of Blood can do to save us now.'

CHAPTER EIGHT

T HE DOORS of the motor van were flung open and
Bollo dragged Marius and Gustavo from inside.

The Superintendent beat her fist against the wooden
gates of the Schwartzgarten Reformatory for Maladjusted
Children.

'Who is it?' came a man's voice from beyond the gates.

'It's me, you idiot,' growled the Superintendent.
'Another two nuts for the nuthouse.'

The gates were pulled open by the night porter, a small
man with a long beard and a glint of malice in his eye.

The Superintendent walked quickly across the
courtyard and up a flight of stone steps. Bollo followed
along behind, dragging the two boys up the steps
and into a cramped room that was evidently the
Superintendent's office.

'Welcome to your new home,' said the woman.

Bollo sniggered.

Marius had not yet had the chance to look at the
Superintendent closely and this he now did. She was

hardly taller than he was, with a harsh slit of a mouth and a sharply pointed nose. Her hair was a dirty yellow, plaited tightly on either side of her round head: the roundest that Marius had ever seen.

'What are you staring at?' snarled the Superintendent. 'Show me your papers.'

Marius reached towards his pocket but stopped, his hand hovering in mid-air. 'We don't have our papers,' he said. 'We gave them to the police. But my name is Leandro and this is Gunter.'

'A likely story,' said the Superintendent. 'Bollo, search their pockets.'

Bollo rummaged through the boys' overcoats, taking out Marius's flashlight, guidebook and the folded notice announcing the auction of Maria Von Hasselbach's possessions.

'Going to an auction, are you?' sneered the Superintendent. 'Got money to burn, have you? I'll take the flashlight, I can sell that. The guidebook's worth nothing to me,' she said, thrusting the book back into Marius's hands.

Bollo was extracting a sticky tangle of nougat, praline

and melted chocolate from Gustavo's pockets. 'Filthy little toad,' he muttered.

'I was saving that for later,' said Gustavo hopelessly.

The Superintendent felt the cloth of Marius's coat between her finger and thumb. 'Nice cut to the jacket... and those shoes would fetch a curseling or two.'

'But...but they're my clothes,' said Marius.

'For now,' said the Superintendent. 'But if something unfortunate happens to you, then they'll belong to the Reformatory, won't they? Now, follow me. You're just in time for supper.' She led the two boys out of the office, bumping into a small girl with pigtails of blonde hair who was hurrying along the corridor. 'Stop right there, gutter rat!' said the Superintendent, holding her finger to the girl's head. 'What's this? A little toy bear?'

The girl pulled back.

'Hand it over,' said the Superintendent, clawing the bear away from the girl. 'What have I taught you?' She twisted the bear's head from its shoulders and thrust the decapitated body back into the girl's hands. 'You must always share your toys.' Leaving the girl sobbing in her wake, she pocketed the head and dragged Marius and

Gustavo on towards the Reformatory canteen, where more than a hundred children stood waiting to be fed.

'Dinner time, my poppets!' announced the Superintendent. She passed a bowl each to Marius and Gustavo and turned the tap of a large soup urn.

A thick green liquid bubbled out into Gustavo's bowl. 'That looks disgusting,' he whispered.

'It's cabbage soup and stewed potato peelings,' said a girl quietly as they took their bowls to the enormous table that ran the length of the cavernous space. 'Breakfast, lunch and supper. We call it sludge. Because it tastes like sludge.'

Marius observed the girl with interest. Her long dark hair hung about her face in greasy clumps and it was not impossible to believe that she had been raised on a diet of sludge from birth. 'I'm Magda,' said the girl. She nodded towards a boy with close-cropped brown hair who had already taken his place at the table. 'That's Anolfo.'

The boy gave a nod of greeting.

'There's something crawling in mine,' said Gustavo, his nose crumpling in disgust as he prodded his spoon into the bowl.

'Count yourself lucky you've got a bit of roughage,'

snapped the Superintendent, who was prowling around the room, listening out for any murmurs of discontent among the miserable diners.

'I'd rather die than eat this,' said Gustavo under his breath.

The Superintendent lowered her head and whispered into the boy's ear. 'That can be arranged,' she hissed, like steam escaping from a burst pipe. She stroked Gustavo's hair with the back of her hand. 'I could eat you up and spit you out, my little poppet.' She gave a sudden bark of a laugh and continued on her way, offering threats to the inmates and doling out physical punishment with indiscriminate pleasure.

A tall, thin boy with a scowling face passed by on the opposite side of the table, dribbling sludge from his bowl onto the head of a smaller boy.

'That's Olof. You want to steer clear of him,' whispered Anolfo. 'Don't do anything to make him mad.'

Olof drew up a chair and sat down, flanked on either side by two sturdy girls with pug noses and short, red hair.

'Who are the two girls?' asked Marius.

'Henrietta and Helga,' said Magda. 'They're even worse than Olof.'

It was hard for Marius to eat with Duttlinger's cotton swabs still in place padding his cheeks, so he slipped them out into his hand. He took a small mouthful of the sludge. It tasted even more revolting than it looked.

'Imagine it's plum streusel,' said Gustavo. 'That's what I'm doing.'

Marius screwed his eyes tightly shut. But the vile flavour of cabbage and stewed peelings was far more powerful than the boy's imagination. He even tried to imagine that he was eating liver and onions, but it was hopeless.

Gustavo slurped up the last of his sludge and sat back in his chair.

'Hungry, were you?' asked the Superintendent. 'Never worry, my poppet. There's a never-ending supply.' She clicked her fingers and Bollo took Gustavo's bowl and ladled out more of the green sludge.

'There now,' said the Superintendent. 'All the nourishment you could ever want. Greedy wart!'

'Never eat all your food,' whispered Magda as the Superintendent walked on. 'She'll punish you for that.'

A door opened at the far end of the canteen as a warder wheeled away the soup urn.

Gustavo suddenly stood up, shaking like a caged beast that has been shown the path to freedom.

'What are you doing?' whispered Marius.

'You can stay if you want but I'm getting out of here,' said Gustavo. 'I'm not going to spend the rest of my days locked away in this place eating sludge.'

He raced towards the open door and the Superintendent beat the soup ladle loudly against the table. 'Catch him!' she screamed.

The door was slammed shut and there was nowhere for Gustavo to go. Like a trapped rat, he ran back towards the table, darting between the approaching warders.

'Bollo,' shrieked the Superintendent. 'Fetch the straitjacket!'

Full of sludge, Gustavo soon ran out of breath and was easily captured. He did not even have the energy to struggle as the warders seized his arms and legs.

'Thought you could get away, did you?' laughed the Superintendent as Bollo fastened the straitjacket, tying Gustavo's arms securely across his chest. 'There's no way out. You're wasting your breath even trying to escape.'

Gustavo sighed brokenly and his head slumped forward.

'And now perhaps you'd like to see your rooms?' smirked the Superintendent, leading Marius and Gustavo up a winding spiral staircase. 'I've got a nice cell set aside for troublemakers.' A cockroach scuttled in front of their feet. 'Don't mind the bugs, my poppets. If we didn't have cockroaches then what would the rats eat?'

'Are there rats?' asked Gustavo hopefully.

'Of course there are rats,' said the Superintendent. 'What do you think we eat for special treats? Along here, this is your cosy little cell. With Anolfo next door for company if you get lonely.' She unlocked a door with a key from the bundle she wore around her waist. 'Now get in, the pair of you.'

It was a miserable room, hardly large enough to take the two iron bedframes in which Marius and Gustavo would sleep.

The door clanged shut and the boys could hear the rattle of the Superintendent's keys as she walked away along the corridor.

'Not even a single rat for company,' said Gustavo, glancing around the room before sitting heavily on the end of his bed.

'I've seen a dead body and been locked up in a reformatory in the same night,' said Marius, lying back on his mattress, his mind swimming. 'Things were never like this when I lived in Blatten.'

Gustavo frowned. 'Kidnapped children and murdered Chocolate Makers. It's like an Inspector Durnstein mystery. I liked Falkenrath. But he must have crossed somebody to end up dead in his shop like that.'

The mattress was so thin that Marius could feel the springs poking into his back. He climbed off the bed and paced up and down the cell.

'Are you going to do that all night?' asked Gustavo. 'You're making me dizzy.'

Loudspeakers crackled and whistled along the corridors of the Reformatory and Marius hurried to the door of the cell. 'What's that noise?'

'It's the Superintendent,' called Anolfo from the neighbouring cell. 'Every night she does it. She drags her fingernails down an old blackboard in her office. They say some people have been driven out of their minds by the noise.'

Marius shuddered.

'I don't mind it so much now,' continued Anolfo. 'I don't think I'd be able to get to sleep if she stopped doing it. It's like a lullaby. But horrible.'

CHAPTER NINE

MARIUS COULD not sleep; his mind was foggy with overthinking. As a dirty scrap of morning sunlight lit the cell, he slipped out of bed and walked across to the window, staring out through the bars and down onto the courtyard below.

Gustavo snorted in bed and Marius shook him awake.

'Is it time for breakfast already?' groaned Gustavo. 'I don't think I can eat another mouthful of sludge.'

'It's not breakfast,' said Marius. 'We've got to think of a way out of this place.'

'Get out?' said Gustavo, sitting up in bed with some difficulty, his arms still securely fastened inside the folds of the straitjacket. 'How? I can't even get my arms out of my sleeves.'

'There has to be a way,' said Marius. 'What would Inspector Durnstein do?'

'He wouldn't be in a reformatory for maladjusted children in the first place, would he?' said Gustavo. 'Can you scratch my nose?'

Marius sighed and reached out his hand.

'Lower...lower. You've got it.' Gustavo let out an appreciative moan. 'That's better.'

The door to the cell was suddenly wrenched open and Bollo glowered in at Marius and Gustavo.

'Sleep well, did you, my little poppets?' grinned the Superintendent, her head appearing around the door behind Bollo.

'It was too cold to sleep,' said Marius.

'I never find it cold in this place,' said the Superintendent. 'And do you know why?' She did not wait for a reply. 'I'll tell you. It's your misery that warms me.'

Bollo untied Gustavo's straitjacket and the boy gasped with relief as he was finally able to free his arms.

'Perhaps next time you'll think twice before trying to escape, my sweet one,' said the Superintendent, striding from the cell. 'Now, it's time for your breakfast. Sludge is at its best when it's hottest.'

Marius and Gustavo joined the line in the vast canteen, surrounded by their fellow inmates. Breakfast was another bowl of the thick, lukewarm sludge served with dry slices of rye bread.

'Do you recognise anybody?' asked Marius, as their bowls were filled. 'Any of the missing members of the Band of Blood, I mean?'

Gustavo glanced along the line of children. 'Nobody,' he said. 'Not a single one. And we've lost three this past month.'

This was puzzling to Marius. 'If the lost members aren't here, then where are they?'

A swarm of roaches scuttled across the floor and Marius stepped back, bumping into Olof.

'Watch where you're going,' grunted the boy.

'I'm sorry,' said Marius. 'I didn't mean—'

Olof was staring strangely at Marius. 'Why are you so pale?' he asked. 'Are you ill? Is it contagious?'

'He's from the mountains,' explained Gustavo, trying to distract the boy before he could discover that Marius's face was still smeared with Duttlinger's greasepaint. 'He's from the town of Blat—'

'Nobody asked you, did they?' said Henrietta and Helga in unison.

Olof took a step forward, so he was nose-to-nose with Marius. 'He's so pale I can almost see right through him to where his brains should be. White as a lily.'

Henrietta and Helga laughed.

'That's what I'll call you,' said Olof. 'Lily. Lily and his fat friend.'

'Quieten down for Mama, my little poppets,' said the Superintendent, appearing behind Olof and stroking his hair, her long red talons scratching his face. 'That's no way to welcome new visitors to our happy home, is it?'

After breakfast the inmates of the Reformatory were led outside into the stone courtyard. Marius stared up at the high, grey walls that surrounded them.

'See what I mean?' said Gustavo. 'How can we ever get away from here? It's more like a fortress than a reformatory.'

Bollo was herding the children through a doorway into a long gymnasium with a polished wooden floor. High up, a gallery with a mesh screen stretched from one end of the room to the other, and Marius had the distinct impression that they were being watched.

The Superintendent appeared at the door, striding into the centre of the gymnasium, a long wooden stick in her hand. 'You know why you're here, my poppets,' she shouted. 'To run and jump and make Mama proud.' She blew a whistle and the inmates began to dart around the room, running from wall to wall.

'I never liked exercise,' panted Gustavo as he struggled to keep pace with Marius.

'Run faster!' bawled the Superintendent, hammering on the floor with her stick.

'I think I'm going to be sick,' moaned Gustavo. 'I've got a stitch.'

'Don't think about it,' said Marius. 'It'll go away.'

'But it hurts,' groaned Gustavo.

The Superintendent wheeled a leather vaulting horse into the centre of the gymnasium. 'Now jump!' she barked, nodding up to the gallery as each child in turn took a run-up and vaulted the horse. 'Good, good! Mama has trained you well!'

Marius cleared the horse easily, landing safely on the other side.

'Well done, Lily,' said Olof sarcastically. 'Now it's the fat one's turn.'

Marius looked up towards the gallery and watched

intently as two figures passed behind the screen. 'Someone's spying on us,' he whispered.

Gustavo glanced upwards.

The Superintendent beat her stick against the polished floor. 'No talking!' she screamed. 'Jump!'

Gustavo was already out of breath, but again the Superintendent pounded her stick against the floor and he knew he had no choice but to attempt the jump. He ran as quickly as he could but his legs failed him; he slammed hard into the vaulting horse and was knocked backwards by the force. 'My ribs!' he wimpered, writhing round on the floor. 'I think I've broken my ribs!'

'Take him to the infirmary,' snapped the Superintendent. 'And let this be a lesson to all of you. The less you eat the higher you jump.'

———•———

Gustavo had not broken his ribs, but dark bruises had already begun to bloom across his chest as a warden examined him in the infirmary. The suggested remedy to ease the pain was another bowl of sludge.

Marius went to collect his friend and the two boys

made their way from the infirmary back towards the canteen. They were almost there when they encountered Olof, standing with Henrietta and Helga outside the Superintendent's office.

'Here they come,' said Olof, barring their way. 'Little Lily and his fat friend.'

'We're going to the canteen,' said Marius patiently, trying to push past the boy.

'But you can't go,' said Olof. 'We haven't finished talking yet.' He seized Gustavo by the scruff of his shirt and dragged him into the office. 'I don't think the Superintendent will mind if we have our little chat in here.'

'Let go of him,' said Marius, but Helga and Henrietta held him back.

'Don't like running round the gymnasium, do you?' continued Olof.

'No,' replied Gustavo. 'I don't.'

'Maybe you don't want to be rescued from this place, but some of us do,' spat Olof. 'And if running round the gymnasium is the only way to impress new parents, then that's the way it's got to be. Do you understand?' He tightened his hold on Gustavo's shirt. 'That's why they come to watch us from behind that screen. To see if they want to take us. But they're only going to want healthy children, aren't they, you fat lump? It'll put them off all of us if you're wheezing and complaining like a girl.'

In unison, Helga and Henrietta gave a nasal snort of a laugh.

Olof turned to Marius. 'And what about you, Lily? They'll think they're visiting a sick house with you as white as a cemetery statue.' He opened a drawer in the roll-top desk and took out a large bottle of rubbing alcohol and a box of cotton wool balls that the Superintendent used to strip the scarlet nail polish from her long fingernails. 'Let's see if we can rub some colour into those cheeks of yours,' continued Olof, lifting up the bottle and swirling the contents within. 'Hold him down.'

'No,' cried Marius, as Henrietta and Helga pinned him to the floor. 'Let me go!'

Olof dipped a ball of cotton wool in the rubbing alcohol and wiped it hard across Marius's face.

Marius kicked out, the alcohol stinging his face.

Gustavo reached out to help his friend, but his ribs still ached and he did not have the strength to fight.

'What's this?' said Olof, as the layer of Duttlinger's greasepaint was wiped away to reveal Marius's pink face beneath. 'He's wearing make-up!'

Suddenly the door burst open, and the Superintendent lurched into the room, cracking her knuckles loudly. 'What's going on in here?' she barked.

'Nothing,' said Olof innocently.

The Superintendent sniffed the air. 'What's that smell?' she growled. 'Have you been drinking my rubbing alcohol?' She seized the bottle, which Olof was attempting to conceal behind his back.

'Little Lily's wearing make-up,' said Olof with a sly smile.

'Clear out!' said the Superintendent. 'And you can take the fat one with you.'

Helga and Henrietta marched Gustavo from the room, with Olof grinning as he followed behind.

Marius tried to escape with the others but the Superintendent held him back. 'Not you,' she purred, squinting hard at the boy's make-up-smeared face. 'I thought something wasn't quite right.' She smoothed Marius's hair and the wig came away in her hands. 'So, you've come in disguise, have you?' she said, with a surprised laugh. 'Are you wearing false teeth as well?' She reached inside Marius's mouth and pulled hard at his teeth. 'They seem real. But what's this?' She pulled out the cotton swabs that had padded the boy's cheeks. 'Who are you hiding from?' she growled. 'What have you done?'

'I haven't done anything,' protested Marius.

The Superintendent took a sheet of paper from her desk. 'They're looking for a boy that's run away,' she said. 'Offering fifty Imperial crowns for his capture. Marius Myerdorf. That wouldn't be you, would it, my little poppet?'

'I told you,' said Marius. 'My name is Leandro.'

'I know what you told me,' replied the Superintendent, taking pen and ink from a drawer. 'But I'm not the trusting sort. I'll write to *The Schwartzgarten Daily Examiner.* Then we'll find out what's what and who's who. You might be worth your weight in gold to me.'

There was a knock at the door and Bollo entered, panting. 'It's the Schwartzgarten Board for Impoverished Delinquents,' he said. 'The Chairman's here!'

'He came last month,' said the Superintendent irritably, putting down her pen. 'Maybe he should run his own reformatory if he likes children so much.'

'His motor car's approaching the gates,' said Bollo. 'The inmates are lining up in the courtyard.'

'You'll keep,' said the Superintendent, pointing a sharp red talon at Marius. 'Bollo, take him outside with the rest of the gutter rats.'

The Chairman's car, a sleek Estler-Spitz Diabolo, rolled into the courtyard, driven by a chauffeur with a black peaked cap.

'All alive?' asked the Chairman as he stepped out onto the cobbles.

'All alive that should be alive,' replied the Superintendent. She cracked her knuckles gleefully and the Chairman winced at the noise.

'This could be our chance to get out,' whispered Marius as he took his place in line beside Gustavo. 'But the gates are guarded, and the walls are too high to climb.'

'We could get into the trunk of the Chairman's motor car,' offered Gustavo. 'But we'll need a diversion.'

'Are you trying to escape?' asked Magda.

'No,' said Marius firmly, fearing that the girl was a spy planted by the Superintendent.

'You can trust me,' said Magda with a wink. 'I want to help.' She slipped her hand into the pocket of her coat and pulled out a small bottle of Van Bendick's Effervescent Liver Salts.

The Superintendent and the Chairman were slowly making their way along the line of children. The Chairman pulled Anolfo from the row, staring into the boy's ears and making scribbled observations in a notebook.

Magda carefully unscrewed the lid of the liver salts and tipped the contents into her mouth. She quickly began to foam and froth, bubbles dribbling from her chin.

'What's this?' demanded the Chairman, hurrying over and taking Magda to one side. 'What's wrong with the girl?'

'Nothing's wrong with her,' said the Superintendent, hurrying to keep up with the Chairman. 'She gets like that sometimes. It's quite normal.'

'Quite normal?' snorted the Chairman. 'Quite normal for a girl to foam at the mouth?'

'Take my advice,' said the Superintendent confidentially. 'She likes the attention. Don't make a scene of it or she'll be foaming at the mouth every day of the week.'

But the Chairman paid no attention to the Superintendent. He marched Magda from the courtyard and towards the infirmary.

'Quickly,' said Marius, choosing his moment. He backed away from the line of children and ran towards the Chairman's motor car, with Gustavo walking as quickly as his aching ribs would allow.

The trunk was not locked and it opened easily. Marius helped Gustavo to climb inside.

'What if we suffocate like Falkenrath?' whispered Marius, as he hauled himself in beside his friend.

'We won't suffocate,' said Gustavo, as they pulled the lid closed. 'I know these motor cars inside out. My father worked for Estler-Spitz, remember?'

They waited in silence for many minutes until at last they heard the engine splutter into life.

'We did it!' said Gustavo as the motor car bumped across the courtyard and out onto the street beyond the Reformatory gates.

'But how will we get out again?' asked Marius.

'Let's solve that problem when we come to it,' said Gustavo.

CHAPTER TEN

EVENTUALLY THE Chairman's motor car came to a halt and Marius and Gustavo lay still, too scared to breathe in case it gave away their hiding place.

They heard the chauffeur get out, then footsteps as he hurried round to open the door for the Chairman. Then two sets of footsteps moved away from the motor car and receded quickly into the distance.

Gustavo heaved a sigh of relief.

'How do we get out now?' whispered Marius. 'What if we're trapped here?'

'We're not trapped,' said Gustavo. 'I know a trick. This isn't the first time I've been locked in an Estler-Spitz! Three little knocks...that's what you have to do.' He tapped his fist close to the lock. 'And one thump.' He hit the lock hard with the flat of his hand and the lid of the trunk popped open. 'Freedom!'

Marius laughed as the afternoon sunlight streamed in.

Gustavo climbed out of the trunk, dropping quietly onto the cobbles. He peered in through the window of the

Chairman's motor car. 'Pigskin leather seats,' he murmured. 'And the dashboard is polished spruce. I'll have a motor car like this one day, Marius. My own Estler-Spitz. And I'll travel around in the driver's seat, not in the trunk.'

'There'll be time for that later,' said Marius, jumping down beside his friend and slamming the trunk closed. 'But now we've got to get back to the hotel. We have to tell Yurgen that we're safe. Where are we, do you think?'

'Near the Schwartzgarten Opera House,' said Gustavo, glimpsing the large glass dome above the rooftops. 'We'll head for Marshal Podovsky Street, then over the Princess Euphenia Bridge.'

Quickly but cautiously they pressed through the crowds on their way to the Old Town. Suddenly Marius came to an abrupt halt and pointed ahead.

'What have you seen?' asked Gustavo urgently. 'Is it Bollo? Is it the police?'

It was neither. Marius was gazing up at an imposing edifice of tall marble pillars, above which a banner fluttered and billowed in the breeze:

AUCTION HERE TODAY:
THE ESTATE AND PERSONAL
EFFECTS OF THE LATE
MARIA VON HASSELBACH

'We've got to get inside,' said Marius. 'Don't you remember? Maria Von Hasselbach was Merla's grandmother. This should all be hers, rightfully.'

'I know all that,' said Gustavo. 'It's in the back of the Ledger. Now come on, Marius. We've got to keep moving.'

But Marius would not be led. He climbed the steps to the auction house and Gustavo hurried behind him.

The auction room had attracted a large crowd and the bidding was well under way.

'What are we doing here?' asked Gustavo. 'We haven't got any money.'

'Merla doesn't have anything to remember her Best Beloved,' said Marius.

'I know that too,' said Gustavo. 'I do read the Ledger, you know.' He took the hat from his head and passed it to Marius. 'You'd better wear this,' he said. 'People might recognise you without your wig.'

'That's your number,' said a woman in the booth beside the door, handing Gustavo a wooden paddle.

'What do we do with these?' asked the boy, waving the paddle in the air.

'Be careful,' said Marius. 'If you keep flapping that thing around the auctioneer will think you're bidding for something.'

The auction lots had been laid out on tables at the back of the enormous room. There were paintings, marble busts and diamond jewellery in velvet cases.

Marius reached out for an emerald-encrusted ostrich egg, resting on the back of three carved, golden elephants.

'Don't touch,' said a porter, gently plucking the egg from its stand and placing it on a shelf just beyond his reach.

'Lot eighty-seven, ladies and gentlemen,' cried the Auctioneer, standing at a lectern at the front of the room, 'is a jewelled tiara, once worn by the late Maria Von Hasselbach. Who will start the bidding at fifty Imperial crowns?'

A fat man with a moustache raised his paddle.

'I have fifty crowns,' said the Auctioneer. 'Do I hear sixty?'

'I'll give you sixty!' cried a tall woman in a velvet hat.

'Excellent, madam,' said the Auctioneer. 'Do I have seventy?'

Once more, the fat man with the moustache raised his paddle.

'Seventy crowns,' said the Auctioneer. 'The bid is with you, madam.'

An elderly woman with hair as white as alabaster held up her hand. She was sitting between two women who Marius recognised at once as the thin woman and the fat woman from his train journey to Schwartzgarten.

'Baroness Smelteva,' said the Auctioneer, with a respectful bob of his head. 'You are most welcome. Do I hear any advance on eighty crowns? No? Selling once, selling twice—'

Gustavo turned suddenly to look at the woman, his wooden paddle flailing in the air.

'A new bid from the young gentleman,' announced the Auctioneer. 'Ninety Imperial crowns. Any advance?'

Gustavo gasped and lowered his paddle. But it was too late. 'Selling once. Selling twice. Sold to the boy for ninety crowns,' cried the Auctioneer, as he brought down his gavel.

'How are we going to pay for it?' whispered Marius.

Gustavo stared apologetically at the Porter who glared back at him. 'I don't have ninety crowns,' he confessed.

'Mis-sale,' called the Porter, and the Auctioneer irritably struck the bid from the records.

'Then Baroness Smelteva's bid of eighty crowns stands. Do I hear ninety? Ninety crowns? No? Then the diamond tiara is sold to Baroness Smelteva of Offelmarkstein for eighty Imperial crowns.'

There was polite applause and the Baroness bowed serenely.

Marius sat in watchful silence as each lot in turn was auctioned off. He did not have a plan, except perhaps a vain hope that an item would be discarded or lost in the crowded room so that he could then take it as a gift for poor Merla.

Gustavo fidgeted in his seat, anxious to return to the Band of Blood as quickly as was possible.

At last the auction came to an end and the crowds slowly departed.

Marius picked up a small plaster bust that had been left on a table.

'That's the Count Von Hasselbach,' said the Porter.

'Why wasn't it sold?' asked Marius.

'It was broken on the way here from the old woman's house,' said the Porter. 'See how chipped it is.'

'Can we have it?' asked Marius, who felt sure that Merla would treasure this memento of her Best Beloved.

'Go on,' said the Porter in a hushed voice. 'Hide it away in this box before anyone notices.'

Marius smiled gratefully as he took possession of the box.

The sun had already set as Marius and Gustavo emerged from the auction house, but a beam of light dazzled them as it cut through the gloom.

'Halt!' bellowed a voice. 'Not another step, if you know what's good for you!'

Parked at the foot of the auction house steps was the Reformatory motor van.

'So you thought you could escape, did you?' growled the Superintendent.

Marius and Gustavo stepped backwards, but Bollo was waiting in the shadows. He seized the two boys and dragged them down the steps.

'You're hurting my arm,' shouted Gustavo.

'Count yourself lucky he's not breaking it,' said the Superintendent, as she opened the doors of the van.

'What are you going to do to us?' asked Marius, his voice hoarse and rasping.

'Oh, I've dreamt up punishments especially for you, my poppets,' laughed the Superintendent. 'And punishments, and punishments, and punishments. And when I've run out of ideas I'll claim my fifty crowns for your capture.'

At that moment a tram rounded the corner from Alexis Street. The driver rang the bell in warning and Bollo released his grip on Gustavo's arm.

'Run!' screamed Gustavo, leaping across the tram rails.

'Get them, Bollo!' bawled the Superintendent.

Marius followed Gustavo across the tracks. They took a sharp right into a side street that passed beside the auction house and ran full-pelt into a man – an elderly man, with leathery skin and hair as white as mountain snow.

The man was Kalvitas.

'Marius?' he hissed. 'Marius, is that you?'

Running into the arms of Kalvitas seemed hardly better than running into the arms of the Superintendent, and

Marius twisted and wriggled as he attempted to shake himself free.

'My boy!' cried Kalvitas, and he hugged Marius so tightly that the boy feared his bones would crack. 'I've been searching everywhere for you.'

'You have?' gasped Marius in bewilderment.

'And who is your friend?' asked Kalvitas. 'Or were you the one that kidnapped my great-great-nephew? I'll cut your gizzard out if you did!'

'This is Gustavo,' said Marius quickly. 'He's not a kidnapper.'

'We can't stay here,' said Gustavo. 'We have to go before Bollo catches up with us.'

'Who is Bollo?' asked Kalvitas.

'He works for the Reformatory,' explained Marius. 'He's trying to catch us.'

'He won't try anything if I'm with you,' said Kalvitas, guiding the boys along the street. 'You're under my protection now.'

'Where are you taking us?' asked Gustavo. 'Not to the police?'

'No,' said Kalvitas. 'Not to the police.'

The street opened out onto Edvardplatz, and they crossed the cobbles to Kalvitas's shop.

'Let's shut out the dark,' said Kalvitas, unlocking the door and shepherding the boys inside. He lit the gas lamps and pulled the blinds down at the windows.

Gustavo was staring silently about him, his mouth wide open.

'What's wrong with the boy?' whispered Kalvitas. 'Is he sick?'

'I haven't been here since my father died,' said Gustavo. 'He brought me every Friday to buy Pfefferberg's Nougat Marshmallows.'

'I'll make a pan of caramel hot chocolate,' said Kalvitas, 'and you can both tell me your tales.'

But Gustavo glanced anxiously at the door of the shop. 'I have to get back,' he said, 'to tell Yurgen that we're safe. He'll be worried.'

'Then take some chocolate with you,' said Kalvitas. 'It's deathly cold outside and you'll need provisions if you've far to go. Run up and fetch him down another pullover and a scarf, Marius.'

Kalvitas heaped Gustavo's outstretched arms with

salted caramels and Pfefferberg's Nougat Marshmallows, enough to fill the boy's pockets, as Marius returned from upstairs with the warm clothes.

'Are you coming, Marius?' asked Gustavo, and Kalvitas's face dropped.

'I'll come tomorrow,' said Marius.

Gustavo nodded, and a smile spread across Kalvitas's wrinkled face. The old man opened the door a crack and peered out. 'It's safe,' he said. 'There's nobody around.'

'Don't let Bollo catch you,' whispered Marius.

'I won't,' said Gustavo, slipping out through the door and keeping to the shadows as he crossed Edvardplatz on his way back to the hotel.

Kalvitas locked the door. 'Well,' he said. 'You're home at last.'

'Home?' said Marius, and found that the word was pleasing on his tongue. But he shook his head, and glanced out between the blinds. 'That doesn't mean I'm safe,' he said. 'Somebody's hunting for me. There's a reward of fifty Imperial crowns.'

'That was me,' said Kalvitas. 'I offered that reward for your safe return'

'You?' said Marius. 'But why?'

The old man smiled. 'We didn't start off well, did we, boy? I think we can change all that. If you want?'

'What about the Superintendent?' asked Marius, grateful that his ancient relative seemed more kindly than before but suspicious of the miraculous transformation.

'I told you what I do to kidnappers,' said Kalvitas, lifting his silver cutlass from the wall. 'I cut out their gizzards!' It took all the old man's strength to pull the sword from the scabbard and raise the blade into the air. 'But I'm hungry now; I'll save my gizzard-cutting for later.' He shuffled off into the kitchen and Marius followed behind. 'Now, tell me of your adventures.'

Marius told the old man of his capture by Bollo and the Superintendent, but he made certain not to give away any secrets of the Band of Blood. The old man listened keenly, nodded his head at the right moments and observed that things were even blacker now than they had been in the days of the tyrant Emeté Talbor.

'Though there are stories that the Vigils are walking the streets again,' said Kalvitas. 'As they did in Talbor's day.'

'What are the Vigils?' asked Marius.

'They were Talbor's private army,' explained Kalvitas. 'They wore hooded cloaks and long-beaked masks and struck fear into the hearts of all who crossed their path.'

'Will you tell me a story from the old days?' asked Marius, as Kalvitas set to work preparing supper.

'Oh, I know stories and stories,' said Kalvitas, taking a plate of liver from the cold box. 'What manner of story is it that you'd like?'

'A story about heads coming off, perhaps,' said Marius, as Kalvitas sliced up the liver. 'How many heads did you chop off in battle, Great-great-uncle?'

'Too many to remember,' answered Kalvitas. 'More than five hundred and less than ten thousand. Either way, that's a lot of heads. It's a messy business though. There's spurting blood and dribbling gore. But if your sword's sharp enough it's like slicing through warm butter.' He fried up the liver and onions in a pan. 'The sharper the blade, the cleaner the cut.'

Marius leant his elbows on the table and rested his head in his hands. 'Tell me your best story,' he said.

'They're all good,' said Kalvitas. 'It's hard picking

one from another. I could tell you the tale of how I helped to free Schwartzgarten from the wicked tyrant Talbor—'

'And how he had his head cut off by the blade of his own guillotine?' interrupted Marius.

'Ah, you've heard that tale before,' said Kalvitas.

'My friend Cosmo told me,' said Marius. 'Were you there to see it when it happened?' he asked, sitting up eagerly in his chair.

'Of course I was there,' said Kalvitas. 'You think I'd miss a thing like a beheading? Because I wouldn't.' He stopped and shook his head, muttering under his breath. 'But all that was a long time ago.'

'But you do remember,' said Marius, wide-eyed and eager for tales. 'Don't you?'

Slowly, Kalvitas nodded his head as he served up two plates of the liver. 'As if it was yesterday,' he said.

Marius stared at the plate of steaming, grey liver and his heart sank. It was better than a tepid bowl of sludge, but that was hardly a cause for celebration. Was he to be served a plate of liver and onions every night until his dying day? He sighed as he picked up his spoon, daydreaming of hazelnut chocolate paste and pyramids of praline.

'What is it, boy?' asked Kalvitas, as he took his place at the table. 'Is something troubling you?'

'I don't really like liver and onions,' said Marius.

'Nor do I,' said Kalvitas. 'My mother used to make it and I cook it out of habit now. I loved her dearly, but it was my father that had the gift in a kitchen.' He pushed away his plate. 'What do you like?'

Marius shrugged.

'That's not an answer,' said Kalvitas with a smile, hauling himself up from the table. 'But I know what you will like.'

The old man disappeared from the kitchen and Marius waited with growing curiosity.

Kalvitas returned with two bars of chocolate, wrapped in golden foil. 'My finest milk chocolate,' he said, taking milk and cream from the ice box and emptying the bottles into a copper pan on the stove.

Marius watched, fascinated, as Kalvitas removed the foil from the bars of chocolate and snapped them into pieces, stirring them into the pan until the milk and cream became a rich and velvety brown. He whisked vigorously to froth up the bubbling mixture, which he poured into a cup, stirring in a spoonful of buttery caramel and piping on peaks of whipped cream. He added a grating of chocolate and a sprinkling of cinnamon and set the cup down in front of Marius.

Marius took a sip. The chocolate was smooth and delicious and his teeth seemed to sting from the sweetness.

'Is that good?' asked Kalvitas.

Marius grinned and nodded, wiping his mouth with the back of his hand.

'A telegram came while you were...away,' said Kalvitas, holding up a small envelope.

'Why would anybody want to send me a telegram?' asked Marius.

'If you don't open it you'll never know, will you?' said Kalvitas. 'Here,' he smiled and sliced the envelope open on the tip of his sword, passing the telegram to Marius.

'It's from Mr Brunert,' said Marius, who had quite forgotten that he had written to the man. 'My old tutor.'

'Well?' said Kalvitas, as Marius silently read the message. 'What does it say?'

'He says he's coming to Schwartzgarten,' said Marius,

his heart jumping. 'He's catching the overnight express from Blatten.'

———

It was early the next morning, with the blinds not yet raised at the windows of the chocolate shop, that Mr Brunert arrived and knocked at the door.

Kalvitas unlocked the door and opened it wide. 'Yes?' he said. 'Who is it?'

'I've come to speak with Marius Myerdorf,' said Mr Brunert removing his hat and combing his fingers through his hair.

Marius ran to the door, hardly able to believe that Mr Brunert had actually arrived when he had wished for it for so long. 'Great-great-uncle,' he said, 'this is Mr Brunert. My friend.'

'Hello, Marius,' said Mr Brunert. 'I thought you and I might go for a walk.'

———

Mr Brunert and Marius walked slowly together beside the River Schwartz, sharing a packet of chocolate diabolotines that the boy had brought with him from Kalvitas's shop.

'Are you happy, Marius?' asked Mr Brunert, chewing hungrily on one of the fiery cinnamon chocolates. 'Your great-great-uncle hasn't attempted to murder you, has he?'

Marius stared at his former tutor. 'No,' he replied.

'Excellent,' said Mr Brunert.

'Why?' asked Marius. 'Were you expecting him to try?'

'I'll confess, it was a thought that has troubled me,' said Mr Brunert. 'It is so easy to poison children these days without the police being any the wiser. I had wondered if that was the reason for your letter.' He stared hungrily at the bag of diabolotines and Marius offered him another chocolate.

'Have you been paid yet?' asked Marius.

'Neither crown nor curseling,' replied Mr Brunert. 'I had to sell my second-best shoes to travel here today.'

This was hard for Marius to take in. 'If I ever become rich,' he said, 'I'll pay you back everything you were owed by my parents and a thousand crowns more.'

Mr Brunert smiled gratefully. 'I shall probably be so poor that I'll take it,' he said. 'Now, I have news for you, Marius. I have located a distant aunt. A great-great-great-aunt who is barely hanging onto life in a remote village in the distant mountains and—'

'Stop!' bellowed a hoarse voice from behind them. 'You can't take him!'

Marius and Mr Brunert turned to see Kalvitas hurrying along the pavement towards them, a long knitted scarf wound many times around his neck. 'You want to take him away from me, don't you?' cried Kalvitas. 'That's why you've come. Did you write to him about me, Marius? Did you say I was cruel to you? That I was a monster of a man?'

'Not quite that exactly,' said Marius. 'But you did say you didn't want me here.'

'I say a lot of things,' said Kalvitas. 'You shouldn't listen to me. I'm an old fool.' He gripped Mr Brunert by the arm. 'I don't want you to take the boy,' he pleaded.

'And I don't want to go now,' added Marius, taking Kalvitas's hand and giving it an encouraging squeeze.

'Then all is well,' said Mr Brunert with a smile.

CHAPTER ELEVEN

THAT AFTERNOON, as soon as Mr Brunert had departed to catch his train, Marius paid a visit to Adalard Frobe, the Antiquarian Bookseller next door to Kalvitas's chocolate shop. His head was filled with his great-great-uncle's tales of battle and warfare and he was burning to know more.

Pushing open the door, he breathed in the sweet-sour smell of old paper and cardboard. Books were stacked in tottering piles on tables and chairs and against every wall of the shop.

'Are you friend, or are you foe?' cried an old man, rising from behind a desk at the back of the shop, almost hidden by a stack of encyclopaedias.

'Friend!' called Marius.

'Come in, come in!' said the man. 'Adalard Frobe at your service. I shan't be more than a moment...no, I've taken a wrong turn there. Ah, yes...this way.' He laughed. 'One day there will be so many books that I won't be able to get out again and they'll find my withered corpse starved to death in a corner of the shop, or crushed beneath the weight of fallen dictionaries.'

'That would be sad,' said Marius.

'There are worse ways to go, I imagine,' said Frobe, as he finally managed to escape from the maze of books. He was grey-haired and hunched, dressed in a shapeless, moth-eaten cardigan and wearing half-moon spectacles that sat low on his beaky nose. 'Boiling to death would be a bad way to die, for example. Or being chopped into tiny, bloodied pieces in a strudel factory. Now, how may I help you? Are you lost or are you a customer?'

'I might be a customer,' said Marius. 'I'm looking for a book.'

'Then your feet haven't guided you wrong,' said Frobe, puffing at a carved wooden pipe that filled the tiny shop with clouds of tobacco smoke. 'If you were looking for hats then I'd say most definitely that you were mistaken in arriving at my door. But books? Books we have in abundance.' A strand of tobacco dropped from his pipe and fizzled and sparked on his cardigan, until he patted it out with the palm of his hand. 'Forgive me, pipe smoking is a filthy habit. Now, is it books of adventure you're after? Or poetry? Or zoology? Or algebra? Or—'

'Do you have a copy of Von Hoffmeyer's *A History of Prince Eugene?*' interrupted Marius, before the man could list every variety of book for sale in the shop.

'I should think I do,' said Frobe. 'Now let me see...' He lifted a small leather volume from a crowded shelf and raised the spectacles from his eyes so he could better read the writing. 'Yes, this is the most recent edition of the book.'

'I might not be able to buy it though,' said Marius, who had become aware of a large sign on the wall which read:

THIS IS NOT A LENDING LIBRARY

'My father put that sign up many years ago,' said Frobe. 'Ignore it, my dear boy. Pay it no heed. Nobody buys anything these days. I expect I will go to my grave without a sorry curseling in my pockets. I'm only grateful for the company when a visitor comes my way.' He returned his spectacles to his nose and peered down at Marius. 'You're old Kalvitas's nephew, aren't you?'

'His great-great-nephew,' corrected Marius.

'Ah,' said Frobe and a curious smile played on his lips. 'You want to read up about your great-great-uncle? Is that it? See what manner of man he truly is?'

'Is it true that he was a great hero?' asked Marius.

Adalard Frobe sat down heavily in his chair and was lost for a moment in a cloud of dust. 'Oh yes,' he said. 'He was a hero, sure enough. If it were not for your great-great-uncle, Emeté Talbor may never have been defeated. It is all in the book.' He climbed to his feet again and lifted a stack of papers and books from a step ladder, dusting the wooden treads with his handkerchief so Marius could sit down. 'Read, read,' said the old man. 'I wouldn't begrudge you an education, even though I may not profit from it myself. It gladdens my heart to see a boy with a book in his hands.'

Marius sat down on the stepladder and opened the book, as Frobe returned to his desk. The light was dim in the shop and he had to hold the book so close to his eyes that his nose almost touched the pages. He read for more than half an hour, revelling in the adventures and battles that Kristifan Von Hoffmeyer related. Flicking forward to the end of the book, he was puzzled by an error on the final page:

Kalvitas makes chocolate in his shop to this very day,
though he is more than ninety years of age.

'But Great-great-uncle Kalvitas is only eighty-eight years old,' he thought, as he closed the book and stood up.

'I think I would like to buy the volume, please,' said Marius, approaching Frobe's desk.

But the Bookseller had fallen asleep in his chair. The pipe had tipped from an old marble ashtray, spilling smouldering tobacco across a pile of ancient papers.

Marius extinguished the smoking documents by dropping a heavy encyclopaedia on top, and returned the pipe to the ashtray. Placing a heap of curselings on the desk he left Adalard Frobe to his dreams.

—◦—

As Marius had promised Gustavo the night before, he made his excuses to Great-great-uncle Kalvitas and returned to the Band of Blood, carrying the plaster bust of Merla's father, Count Von Hasselbach. Bag-of-Bones was slinking along the alleyway beside the hotel and he followed the cat through the secret entranceway and into the lobby.

'You've come back then, have you?' said a voice. 'I thought you'd left us for good.'

Marius turned to see Yurgen sitting on the reception desk, holding a long piece of wood studded with iron nails. 'So your great-great-uncle didn't want you to drown yourself in the River Schwartz, after all?'

Marius could feel his face redden. 'I thought he did,' he said. 'I thought he didn't want me. But I'm still a member of the Band of Blood, even if I don't sleep here at night.'

Yurgen lifted up the piece of wood, swinging it down against the desk so hard that splinters flew.

Gustavo and Cosmo ran out from the dining room.

'I thought there were attackers,' said Gustavo.

'No,' said Yurgen. 'Not attackers. Just the traitor.'

'Leave him, Yurgen,' said Cosmo, carefully prising the weapon from Yurgen's hands. 'Marius is no traitor. He's done nothing wrong.'

Yurgen snorted.

'What's happened?' demanded Marius.

'It's little Luca and Ava,' explained Gustavo quietly. 'They were taken last night.'

'Was it Bollo?' asked Marius. 'Did he catch them—'

Yurgen held out his hand to reveal a small copper button, shaped as a pumpkin. 'That's the only clue we've got. We found it close to the hotel, where they were last seen. Not much to go on, is it?'

'Gustavo says you were the only members of the Band of Blood in the Reformatory,' said Cosmo.

Marius nodded.

'It doesn't make sense,' Cosmo continued. 'We've lost six members of the Band of Blood in the past three months. They can't all have been adopted from the Reformatory that quickly, can they?'

'So if they aren't in the Reformatory, where are they?' asked Marius. 'Who's taken them?'

'We've mounted a search,' grunted Yurgen. 'Scoured the streets for any sign of the missing members of the Band of Blood. But we found nothing last night.'

'What's in the box, Marius?' asked Cosmo curiously.

'It's for Merla,' said Marius. 'It's a plaster bust of Count Von Hasselbach. From the auction of her grandmother's belongings. I have to give it to her.'

'We don't have time for that now,' said Yurgen, but

Marius was already hurrying up the stairs.

Cosmo and Gustavo walked with Marius to Merla's room, with Yurgen following reluctantly behind.

'You're safe then, Marius,' said Lil, approaching along the corridor.

'Marius has a new girlfriend,' said Yurgen. 'He's brought Merla a present.'

Marius tapped gently at the door. 'We've got something for you, Merla.' There was no answer. He knocked again, harder than before. To his surprise, the door was not locked and swung open.

Marius entered the room. It was a strange place, with a bare boarded floor and no curtains at the window. The room was without furniture, except for a pile of eiderdowns and cushions in the corner. It was more like a nest than a bed. The walls of the room had been defaced with scrawled words and illustrations depicting Merla's short and unhappy life. There was hardly a patch of wall that had not been decorated.

Merla was sitting on the floor by the window, peeling strips of wallpaper with her fingernails. She was a small girl, with skin the colour of porcelain and short, black hair tied with a ragged pink ribbon. She turned her head slowly, observing her visitors mournfully through pale, grey eyes.

'What is it?' she said. 'Is it a trick?' She crumbled a stick of charcoal in her hand and watched transfixed as the pitch-black ash trickled through her fingers.

'She's always worst at this time of year,' said Yurgen. 'She gets mournful the closer we get to the Festival of the Unfortunate Dead.'

Merla peeled back a long strip of rotting wallpaper. 'I can hear you, you know,' she said. 'It's rude to talk about people as though they're invisible.'

'What are the drawings of?' asked Lil, staring curiously at the walls.

'Dead things mostly,' said Merla blankly. 'I've seen a lot of dead things.'

Cosmo's attention had been seized by a picture of an unfortunate-looking animal, with long and mangled limbs. Above the illustration, in long and mangled letters, were two words:

ded Kat

The eyes were drawn as crosses to indicate that the cat was, indeed, no more.

Cosmo fought the urge to correct Merla's spelling. Instead he said, 'It's very...dark.'

'Some days I find it impossible to drive the dark thoughts from my mind,' replied Merla. She gave a chilling smile. 'Want to hear something interesting?' she said. 'I know eleven different ways to kill someone with a pencil.'

'How do you know?' asked Cosmo. 'Did you read about it in a book?'

Merla's eyes narrowed. 'I just know,' she said. She glanced across the room to Marius. 'Do you like the pictures? I make the charcoal myself so there's a never-ending supply.' She gestured to the fireplace where a heap of wood smouldered in the grate.

'What did you burn this time?' asked Yurgen, stirring the wood with the tip of a fire poker.

'My bed,' said Merla. 'I didn't need it. Or anyway, I needed charcoal more.'

Cosmo whispered to Marius. 'She keeps burning her furniture,' he said. 'It's lucky the hotel doesn't burn down. We'd all roast to death in our beds.'

Merla crumpled a long strip of wallpaper in her hands. 'I want a table.'

'You burned the last table,' replied Yurgen.

'I didn't like that table,' said Merla. 'I want another table. A table that's made out of lots and lots of wood.'

Marius had followed the illustrations from wall to wall and now stood staring up at a drawing of a man, lying sprawled out on the ground, beneath which Merla had written:

A KORpse i FouNd

'I suppose he might have been drunk,' said Marius. 'How do you know the man was dead?'

'Because I prodded him with a stick,' said Merla. 'That's how.' She turned to Cosmo. 'I think this is some of my best work. Don't you?'

'Corpse is spelt with a "C",' said Cosmo at last.

Merla wrung her blackened hands together. 'I knew you wouldn't like them.'

'It's not that,' said Cosmo hurriedly. 'It's only...it's very bleak, that's all.'

'My life is very bleak,' replied Merla. 'You said you've got something for me. What is it?'

Marius approached slowly, like a zookeeper approaching a wild bear. He placed the box on the floor.

Merla grasped the box greedily and her grey eyes sparkled. 'Is it something to eat? Is it chocolate?' She lifted the lid and pulled out the bust of Count Von Hasselbach. She gave a startled moan and Marius took a step back.

'Father?' whispered Merla. 'Father, is that you?' She cradled the plaster head in her arms and burrowed down in the bedding, curled up like a frightened forest creature. 'You can go now,' she murmured.

Silently the visitors departed, and Yurgen pulled the door closed behind them.

The grille slid open and Marius turned.

'You did this for me?' asked Merla, her eyes seeming brighter than before through the narrow slit in the door.

Marius nodded.

'Why?'

'Because I knew you didn't have a memento of your Best Beloved,' said Marius.

'Oh,' said Merla, and slammed the grille shut.

CHAPTER TWELVE

SEBASTIAN MONTELIMAR had locked his chocolate shop for the night. He was preparing to make his way home when he encountered a thin woman in a fox fur, pacing uncertainly by the lamppost at the corner of the street.

'Are you in distress, Madam?' asked Montelimar.

'I am a visitor to Schwartzgarten,' explained the woman. 'I have been staying with my elderly aunt, but it seems that I can't open the door. The key will not turn in the lock, and I'm afraid to call out as my aunt is ill in bed.'

'Might I be of assistance to you?' asked Montelimar, twisting the tips of his moustache.

'I could not think of asking for the help of a stranger,' said the woman tearfully, lowering her head.

'My name is Montelimar,' said the man, raising his top hat and bowing to the woman. 'There. Now I am no longer a stranger!'

'The apartment is this way,' said the woman, as she led the Chocolate Maker down a dark alleyway across the street from his shop. 'It is most kind of you to come to my aid.'

'It is my pleasure,' said Montelimar with another small bow. 'I would never abandon a lady to her fate. You need not worry.' He pulled a large, white handkerchief from his breast pocket. 'Wipe your tears with this.'

'You are too kind,' said the woman, dabbing at her eyes.

'Now, lead on, dear lady!'

'This way,' said the woman, guiding Montelimar towards a darkened apartment building on Beckmann Street. As they entered there was hardly a glimmer of light in the lobby and no concierge behind the desk.

'One could almost believe that the building had been abandoned,' said the Chocolate Maker. 'Are you quite certain that this is the place?'

'Yes, yes. Please hurry,' said the woman, leading Montelimar along a narrow corridor that led from the lobby. At the very end of the passageway there was a door, and here she stopped. She reached into her purse and produced a small silver key.

Montelimar pressed his cheek against the door. 'Help is on the way!' he called, to reassure the woman's sickly aunt.

He held out a gloved hand to take the key.

'You are a charitable gentleman indeed,' said the woman, as Montelimar twisted the key in the lock; it turned easily.

'Brute force was all it needed,' murmured the Chocolate Maker, pushing the door. It swung open on squeaking hinges. He entered the room, the floorboards creaking beneath him. It was a curious place and it unsettled Montelimar; there was no furniture in the apartment, no pictures on the walls. No sign of life at all.

Montelimar frowned. 'But the place is empty.'

'Not empty,' replied the woman from the doorway, giving the man a firm push in the small of the back which sent him stumbling into the centre of the room. 'Because you are in it.'

Montelimar turned furiously. 'What is the meaning of this?' he demanded. 'Is it a joke?'

'A joke in deadly earnest,' said the woman with a smile that sent the Chocolate Maker's heart lurching in his chest.

'What is that smell?' asked the man, his nostrils aquiver. 'It smells like—'

'Like poison gas,' said the woman, and she pulled the door shut.

'Madam?' cried Montelimar, and beat against the door with his gloved fists. 'Madam!' There was no answer, but he could hear footsteps moving swiftly away.

He held his hand to his mouth as a cloud of noxious gas swirled around him.

'Help me!' he shrieked. 'I'm choking!'

But the building was deserted, and cry as he might, there was no one to come to his aid.

———⚬———

'Montelimar is dead!' cried Kalvitas the following morning, hurrying into the kitchen, where Marius sat stirring a cup of caramel chocolate. 'Murdered!' He brandished a rolled-up copy of *The Schwartzgarten Daily Examiner* in his hand, swiping at the air as if to fight off an invisible assailant. 'They found him lying face down in an abandoned apartment.' He unrolled the newspaper and read from the front page. 'His eyes were bloodshot and his lips were blue.'

'How did he die?' asked Marius, taking a deep slurp of the chocolate.

'They say it was poison gas,' said Kalvitas, turning the pages of the newspaper with trembling fingers. 'Another member of the Guild of Twelve murdered. There's a price on my head, Marius. If they wanted Montelimar dead then they'll want me dead as well.'

———•———

That afternoon the surviving members of the Guild of Twelve gathered in the Governor's Palace.

Kalvitas arrived with Marius at his side.

'But he's only a boy,' said the Private Secretary as the Guild members were ushered into the Governor's presence.

'That may be so,' said Kalvitas, 'but he is a Chocolate Maker all the same.'

The Guild of Twelve had shrunk considerably and there were only four surviving Chocolate Makers in attendance: Mr Hirsch, Bertold Becklebick, Mr Biddulph and Kalvitas himself.

The Governor sat at his desk, eating plump, dried apricots enrobed in dark chocolate and sipping from a large glass of schnapps.

'Something must be done,' insisted Becklebick, casting an accusatory glare at the Inspector of Police who sat miserably in the corner of the room. 'I am a highly respected member of the Guild of Twelve. Consider the unfortunate consequences for a man in my position if the killer is not caught. The financial burden. Already, customers are staying away from my shop. They don't want to end up entombed in chocolate like Falkenrath.'

'Stop gassing, you bloated air bag,' muttered Kalvitas. 'It's no worse for you than it is for the rest of us.'

Marius bit his lip and tried not to laugh.

Pacing the marble floor, the Governor dictated a reward notice, to be placed in that evening's edition of *The Informant*. 'For too long,' he began, 'this killer of Chocolate Makers has held our fair city in his clutches. Whomsoever shall provide information leading to the arrest, trial and inevitable execution of this fiend or fiends...' He stopped briefly at his desk, picked up another chocolate apricot, popped it into his mouth and resumed his pacing. His Private Secretary stood patiently, pencil in hand. 'Then something about a reward, etcetera, etcetera...is that sufficient?'

'No,' said Becklebick.

'No?' squealed the Governor.

'You have the audacity to question the Governor?' gasped the Private Secretary, and Marius watched as he palmed a chocolate apricot and concealed it in his waistcoat pocket.

'I merely ask this,' continued Becklebick. 'Where will the killer turn next? Will he target another member of the Guild of Twelve, or does he have other plans in store?'

'Other plans?' echoed the Governor.

'Perhaps he'll grow weary of slaughtering Chocolate Makers. He may very well turn his attentions to those in power,' mused Becklebick. 'Who knows. Could be me, could be you.' He smiled. 'Couldn't it?'

'Kill me?' croaked the Governor.

'It's a thought to ponder,' replied Becklebick.

'Maybe the Anarchists have returned,' cried the Governor. 'Maybe they've come to finish me off in the very same way they despatched my brother!' He stared up at the high shelf above his desk. There, in a row, were seven plaster busts of the Governors who had preceded him. 'In one month alone they blew up three Governors. My own dear brother went up like a fountain,' he cried emotionally. 'Bits of him dripping from the walls of the Palace like scarlet goulash.' Agitated, he beat his fist on the desk, upsetting his glass of schnapps, which his secretary mopped up with a sheet of blotting paper. 'This must not continue,' said the Governor, barking at the Inspector of Police, who shrank back into a corner of the room like a startled rat. 'Something must be done.'

'My feeling is this,' said the Inspector. 'The murderer is someone who hates chocolates.'

'Who in their right mind hates chocolates?' demanded the Governor.

'That's just it,' said the Inspector. 'Who said the murderer is in his right mind?'

—————

The sky was pewter-grey and snow was falling fast as Kalvitas and Marius walked the streets from the Governor's Palace on their way back to Edvardplatz.

'That fool of an Inspector won't solve anything,' grumbled Kalvitas. 'He couldn't find his own moustache if he peered down his nose at it. The Guild of Twelve... what's left of them...meet tomorrow to discuss the art of Chocolate Making, as they do every month. I'll take you with me, Marius.'

'Can I bring my friend Yurgen as well?' asked Marius.

'He knows lots of people on the streets and he's got a good head for solving mysteries.'

'Very well,' said Kalvitas, turning up the collar of his overcoat against the driving snow. 'I feel quite sure that two boys would do a better job of solving this mystery than the Department of Police.'

CHAPTER THIRTEEN

A LONG TABLE spread with a crisp, white tablecloth had been erected in a private room above the Emperor Xavier Hotel. The four surviving members of the Guild of Twelve each arrived with boxes of chocolates, which were laid out on the table. Kalvitas brought an Augustus Torte, a rich chocolate cake named in honour of the Grand Duke of the same name.

Marius invited Yurgen to the gathering and the boy came willingly, his curiosity piqued. The two boys sat side by side at the table, observing the Chocolate Makers with interest.

The Chocolate Makers talked about the Governor's offer of a reward and the Inspector of Police's uselessness at rounding up suspects. They eyed each other suspiciously, as if fearing that the killer was one of their number.

Biddulph was sitting apart from the other Guild members, staring wistfully at a full-length portrait of a Chocolate Maker in white apron and hat, which hung from the wall in an impressive gilt frame.

'Who is that, sitting by the painting?' whispered Yurgen.

'That's Biddulph,' said Marius. 'The man talking to Great-great-uncle Kalvitas is Mr Hirsch, and the scowling man is Bertold Becklebick.'

'Who is the painting of?' asked Yurgen. 'Do you know?'

Marius leafed through his guidebook and read from the entry about the Emperor Xavier Hotel:

The portrait is of the late Maxim Caffard, the finest Chocolate Maker that ever lived in the Great City. He is depicted in his chocolatier's uniform, proudly displaying his gold medal, the highest honour ever awarded by the Guild of Twelve. When Caffard died, many went into deep mourning for the man. Three women, dressed in grey and wearing black armbands, climbed to the parapet at the top of the Emperor Xavier Hotel, where they jumped to their deaths on the pavement below.

Marius turned to his great-great-uncle who was sipping from a cup of cinnamon chocolate. 'Is it true that if you stand above Caffard's grave on a hot day you can still smell the aroma of sweet cocoa rising from the ground?'

'Whoever's been filling your head with that nonsense?' asked Kalvitas.

'It's in my guidebook,' said Marius.

The old man laughed. 'They put that in for the visitors,' he said. 'But Caffard's death caused ripples, you might say.' He cut Marius and Yurgen two thick slices of the Augustus Torte. 'The day he died his recipes were stolen. Poor Biddulph never recovered from the shock. He had a hunger for Caffard's cakes and pastries, you see.'

Biddulph shook out his white napkin and laid it carefully on his lap. He took a single chocolate from a silver dish.

'I don't understand it,' said Mr Hirsch, who was sitting beside Kalvitas. 'My chocolate shop is opposite Biddulph's, I see him in his kitchen at night; he never eats more than a scrap of meat. But look at the size of him. More like an airship than a man.'

'There's something devious in the man's eye,' whispered Yurgen. 'He needs to be watched closely.'

After eating a second chocolate and dabbing his mouth with his napkin, Biddulph staggered to his feet. 'You must excuse me, gentlemen,' he wheezed. 'I do not feel well and I must return home to my shop at once.' With a perfunctory nod of his head, he gathered up his overcoat and hat and headed for the door.

'Follow him,' said Yurgen. 'See where he goes. I'll stay here and follow Becklebick when he leaves. Tomorrow we can follow Hirsch.'

Kalvitas and Hirsch were talking animatedly about the rising price of cocoa beans and Marius was able to slip away without being noticed, following Biddulph down the staircase to the entrance of the hotel. He watched as the man hurried across the street, narrowly avoiding a passing tram.

Marius followed Biddulph to a dark corner of Beckmann Street. It was a painfully slow walk, as the Chocolate Maker was so fat that he had to stop every few paces to catch his breath.

Arriving at last outside his shop, Biddulph unlocked the door and entered the building, glancing suspiciously through the glass pane as he pulled the door shut behind him.

Marius stepped into the doorway of a café across the

street so he could not be seen, then crossed over and crept along a dark alleyway at the side of Biddulph's shop. A small window was open in the wall, and by climbing up onto an air vent he was able to wriggle through, jumping down from the sill onto a tiled floor.

The building was silent. Had Marius not known that Biddulph was inside he would have imagined the place to be entirely empty.

A staircase led to the next floor, and Marius slowly mounted the steps. On the landing a door led into a small kitchen. The blind was still raised at the window and the moon cast enough light for Marius to find his way around the room.

There was an indistinct noise from above: a rasping, grating sound that Marius struggled to make sense of. Could it be snoring? It was. It seemed that Biddulph was so exhausted from the exertions of the day that he had returned home and fallen asleep. Marius smiled and looked around. It was a spotlessly clean room, but surprisingly empty. From the window Marius could see across the alley, into the apartment of Mr Hirsch, who had just returned to his chocolate shop from the Emperor Xavier Hotel. Marius kept his head down so he would not be seen and continued to explore the kitchen.

In a provisions cupboard there were jars of pickled beetroot, the crust of a loaf of bread, and a scrap of boiled ham under a meat cover. It was not enough to keep a skeleton alive, let alone a man of Biddulph's great girth.

There was a loud creak from above. Biddulph had clearly been roused from his slumbers and was slowly descending the staircase.

Marius could not run for freedom without being seen, his only chance was to hide. The cupboard was too obvious a place to conceal himself and there was every danger that he would be discovered.

As the footsteps drew nearer, Marius glanced quickly around the room. Beneath the sink was a curtained alcove and this seemed the safest place to hide. He clambered in and held his breath as the kitchen light was switched on and Biddulph shuffled into the room. Through the gap between the curtains, Marius watched as the man approached the cupboard, took out the bread and the scrap of ham and walked to the table.

'Hello again to you, Mr Hirsch,' he chuckled under his breath, waving his hand to the man, who stood watching from his window across the alleyway. 'You'll never know my secrets, you sly old wolf.'

Biddulph drew up a chair at the table and sat down. He cut a thin slice of bread, which he buttered, and laid the ham on top. He took a mouthful, chewing slowly. Removing the napkin from his shirt collar, he shuffled his way across the floor to the window and closed the blinds. He was so close to Marius that the boy could have reached out to touch the Chocolate Maker's kneecaps. Biddulph switched out the light and opened the kitchen door. But instead of leaving the kitchen, he walked back into the room.

Biddulph approached a shelf of recipe books which lined the kitchen wall. His hand lingered over one particular book:

AN ILLUSTRATED HISTORY
OF SCHWARTZGARTEN'S
COCOA QUARTER

Biddulph pulled the spine of the book towards him;

there was a click, and the bookcase receded into the wall, revealing a tiny room beyond.

Marius clapped his hands to his mouth to prevent a gasp from escaping his lips.

The ceiling of the concealed room was so small that Biddulph, who was short himself, had to lower his head before entering. It was a second kitchen, but on a minute scale. Biddulph lit a candle, which cast a flickering light in the secret chamber. There was a stove and oven, an enamelled sink, a store cupboard and a table and chair, all of the most exquisite quality. And there, on the table, was a recipe book. It was leather-bound, with a gold clasp and gilded pages. As Biddulph unfastened the clasp, Marius could make out writing on the spine, embossed in gold leaf. It was a name:

MAXIM CAFFARD: MY LIFE IN CHOCOLATE

It was the stolen recipe book, taken from the Grand Emperor Xavier Hotel all those years before.

Biddulph found his place in the book and set to work, placing a copper pan of butter on the stove and lighting the gas. He stood patiently, waiting for the butter to melt, whistling quietly to himself.

Marius watched as Biddulph lifted the butter from the stove. He melted in chocolate, sifted in flour and sugar, and tipped the mixture into a greased torte mould before sliding it carefully, lovingly, into the oven.

And then he waited. For a very long time. So long in fact that Marius's eyes began to grow itchy, his head grew heavy and he slumped forward, fast asleep.

He suddenly jolted awake, conscious of a warm, wet sensation on his cheek. His eyes flickered open. He looked up above him, but there was no dripping of water. He slowly became aware that he was not alone behind the curtain. Two eyes stared directly into his. They were the eyes of a large, black rat that had settled itself on his shoulder. The self-same rat that had evidently been licking his face.

Forgetting for a moment where he was, Marius let out a short, piercing yelp, and the rat jumped from his shoulder and scuttled out under the curtain. By a happy coincidence, Marius's yelp coincided with another loud noise from the other side of the curtain, in the tiny secret kitchen. It was the sound of an ancient alarm clock that Biddulph had placed on the table beside him.

Peering from beneath the sink, Marius saw the man splutter, snort and open his eyes. Marius checked his pocket watch; he had been hidden for over an hour.

Biddulph stretched and rubbed his hands. He climbed up from his chair and walked to the oven. He opened the door and removed the torte pan. Turning the cake onto a wire rack, Biddulph coated the torte with a mirror-smooth glaze of chocolate.

It was the most beautiful thing Marius had ever seen.

Without even waiting for it to cool, Biddulph placed the chocolate torte on the little table, tucked a crisp white napkin into his shirt collar and began to eat. He did not move until he had consumed every last morsel. He did not even throw a crumb to a half-starved mouse that dropped onto the table from a hole in the ceiling.

The Chocolate Maker washed the dishes in the sink and blew out the candle. Quietly and carefully he stepped from the secret chamber. He closed the concealed door behind him, making sure it was securely fastened, and walked from the kitchen.

Marius waited until he could hear Biddulph snoring

from upstairs before he climbed out from under the sink. His muscles ached and his bones clicked as he stretched his arms and legs. He made his way stealthily from the kitchen, down the stairs, through the silent building, and stepped out into the moonlit street.

Unseen by Marius as he slipped away, a hooded stranger with a raven's beak appeared from the shadows, passing noiselessly along the alleyway and into Biddulph's chocolate shop.

Chapter Fourteen

'WHAT IS it you want?' said the man at the newspaper kiosk on Alexis Street the next day, as Marius, Gustavo and Cosmo crowded round. 'Come to rob me blind, is that it?'

'Have you got the new Inspector Durnstein mystery?' asked Gustavo.

'I've got it all right,' said the man. 'But have you got the curselings to pay me for it? That's my question.'

'We have,' said Gustavo, taking money out of his pocket and tipping it onto the counter.

'Here you are then,' said the man, lifting down the book and holding it out for the boy.

INSPECTOR DURNSTEIN:
THE MYSTERY OF THE
REAPPEARING CORPSE

Gustavo held the book tightly in his hands, as if it had suddenly become his most prized possession.

'Look at this,' said Marius urgently, taking a newspaper from the stand. 'It's Biddulph. He's dead.'

'Biddulph the Chocolate Maker?' said Cosmo. 'How can he be dead? He was alive when you left his shop last night, wasn't he?'

Marius lowered his voice. 'I didn't murder him if that's what you mean.'

'What happened to him?' asked Gustavo.

'It says Mr Hirsch found him,' said Marius, reading from the newspaper. 'His shop is across the street from Biddulph's.'

'Get to the good stuff,' said Gustavo. 'How did he die?'

'He'd been tipped out of the kitchen window, onto his head,' said Marius. 'He was a short man, but I suppose he's even shorter now.'

'If you're buying the paper it's another curseling,' said the newspaper seller. 'If not, clear off.'

Marius placed the newspaper back on the stand.

The four boys returned to the hotel with the new Inspector Durnstein mystery, Gustavo taking sly glances at the pages of the book whenever he had the chance. It was a slow journey as Marius insisted on walking to Edvardplatz to make quite certain that Kalvitas was safe.

Over supper that night the Band of Blood discussed Biddulph's murder.

'Maybe Hirsch killed the man,' said Marius. 'Maybe he was eaten up with jealousy that Biddulph had stolen Caffard's recipe book. Inspector Durnstein says it's often the person who discovers the body that turns out to be the murderer.'

'What do you think, Heinrich?' asked Gustavo.

Heinrich didn't answer. He was staring blankly into his bowl of goulash, pushing a piece of meat with the end of his fork.

'What's wrong?' asked Yurgen. 'Aren't you hungry?'

Heinrich looked up. 'What did you say?'

'I said, aren't you hungry?' repeated Yurgen.

Heinrich shook his head and stared back into the bowl.

'I don't think it was Hirsch,' said Marius. 'I don't think he's strong enough to tip Biddulph out of a window all on his own.'

'Maybe he wasn't on his own,' suggested Gustavo, helping himself to Heinrich's uneaten goulash. 'He could have been working with someone else, couldn't he?'

'It's possible,' said Marius. 'I just don't know.'

As soon as supper was finished, Cosmo disappeared upstairs for a few minutes, then returned to the dining room, dressed in his smoking jacket, the Inspector Durnstein book in his hands. The Band of Blood had gathered at one end of the room, and Yurgen threw wood onto the fire to make a blaze.

There was a murmur of expectation as Cosmo settled himself in an old leather armchair beside the fire.

'He always reads the Durnstein books to us a chapter at a time,' said Gustavo to Marius. 'He likes to ration it out so it lasts longer.'

'Ssh,' said Lil, as Cosmo glared at Gustavo and cleared his throat. 'He's about to start.'

'*The Mystery of the Reappearing Corpse*. Chapter One,' began Cosmo. 'Inspector Durnstein stepped from his motor car and crossed the street with Constable Mandel at his side. The sky was gravestone-grey and a distant rumble of thunder warned of danger to come...'

'He reads it well, doesn't he?' whispered Gustavo, as Cosmo kept his audience enthralled, altering his voice to play a dozen different characters.

'He does,' said Marius.

'I like the voice he does for the Inspector best,' continued Gustavo. 'Close your eyes and you'd think he was as old as forty.'

Marius was indeed impressed by the voice that Cosmo had chosen for Inspector Durnstein. It was a throaty growl much like that of Franz the forger.

'We'll read the next chapter tomorrow,' said Cosmo at last, closing the book.

There was an anguished howl from Gustavo. 'Can't you read until you get to the first dead body, Cosmo?'

But Cosmo was firm. He stood up and tucked the book safely inside the pocket of his smoking jacket.

The assembled children slowly began to get up and make their way to their rooms. But Heinrich, who was still sitting on the floor, slumped forward and lay motionless.

'Get up, Heinrich,' laughed Gustavo. He turned to Yurgen. 'Heinrich thinks he's a dead body!'

'Come on, Heinrich. It's not funny any more,' said Yurgen, shaking Heinrich by the arm.

But the boy did not move.

'Something's not right,' said Marius, kneeling down

beside Heinrich and holding his hand to the boy's forehead.

'What's wrong with him?' asked Lil. 'He's not dead, is he?'

'No,' said Marius. 'But he's very hot. We need to take him upstairs to his room.'

Yurgen and Gustavo took Heinrich's arms and Marius and Lil took his legs. They carried the boy upstairs to his room and lifted him onto the bed.

Heinrich opened his eyes.

'He's awake!' said Lil, sitting on the edge of the bed and holding Heinrich's hand. 'Where do you feel bad?' she asked gently.

Heinrich attempted to sit up, but the effort was too great and he fell back against the pillow with a low moan. His shirt was wet from perspiration.

'Is he going to die?' asked Lil.

'I don't know,' said Marius. 'But he's got a very high temperature.'

A small boy barrelled into the room, panting for breath. 'The Constable's here,' he said. 'I told him Heinrich's bad.'

Constable Sternberg appeared at the door, his face grey and an anxious look in his eyes. 'What happened to him?' he asked. 'Did somebody hurt him?'

'No!' said Lil. 'Cosmo was reading to us, then Heinrich fell over. We thought he was pretending to be dead...then we thought he was really dead—'

'I didn't think he was dead,' said Cosmo.

Sternberg leant over the bed. 'Heinrich?' he whispered. 'Can you hear me?' Heinrich groaned. His eyes flickered open then closed again. 'Has he been eating? You know the boy's fragile. He's been ill before.'

'We tried to get him to eat,' said Lil. 'But he wouldn't.'

'How long has he been like this?' asked Sternberg angrily. 'You have to look after him. He's precious.'

'He wasn't hungry at supper,' said Gustavo. 'He normally is.'

Heinrich opened his mouth to speak but no words came out.

'He needs to see a doctor,' said Sternberg.

'Doctors ask too many questions,' growled Yurgen.

'But we've got to do something,' insisted Marius. 'What if he dies?'

'I'm not a doctor,' said Sternberg, lifting Heinrich from the bed. 'I don't know what's wrong with him. But he's sick, Yurgen. I know that. He's got the sweats. If you keep him here he'll get sicker and sicker.'

'Where are you taking him?' demanded Yurgen, following the Constable along the corridor and down the staircase.

'We need somebody who won't ask awkward questions,' replied Sternberg as he carried Heinrich through the hotel lobby. 'I'll take him to the pharmacy in Dagmar Street.'

'What is the matter with the boy?' asked the Pharmacist as Heinrich was carried in through the door, with Marius and Yurgen at his side.

'He's got a fever,' said Sternberg. 'Feel his head. He's burning up.'

'For how long?' asked the Pharmacist, laying his hand to Heinrich's forehead.

'He wasn't hungry at supper,' said Marius.

'He's sick,' said the Pharmacist. 'This boy needs a doctor.'

'He won't need a doctor,' said Sternberg firmly. 'I can take care of him.'

The Pharmacist glanced uncertainly at the man. 'He'll need to be kept warm until the fever passes. I can give you medicine to bring down the temperature.'

'Give me whatever he needs,' said Sternberg. 'It doesn't matter how much it costs. The boy has to get well again.'

Returning Heinrich to the hotel, the Constable heaped the boy's bed with blankets and eiderdowns.

'Here you are, Heinrich,' said the Constable, opening a tin of pork goulash which he pulled from his bag. 'This is what you need. A nice bit of meat to put some flesh on your bones. Build you up to be a big, strong boy.'

Suddenly Gustavo burst into the room, his face pale and his eyes staring.

'The Ledger has gone!' he cried. 'It's been stolen!'

'What do you mean it's been stolen?' said Yurgen.

'I mean, it's vanished,' said Gustavo. 'It was in my bag this afternoon and now it's not. I've searched everywhere for it.'

'You're always losing things,' said Sternberg with a laugh. 'Maybe the rats got it.'

'Maybe it fell out of your bag,' suggested Lil.

Gustavo considered this possibility. 'It might have done,' he said. 'Sternberg's right, I do lose things sometimes. I caught a tram today, so maybe the Ledger *did* fall out of my bag.'

'You want The Bureau of Forgotten Things,' said Sternberg, settling down in an old, three-legged armchair in a corner of the room. 'But it won't be open until the morning. I'll take you there myself. I'll stay here tonight and look after Heinrich.'

'He's right, Gustavo,' said Yurgen. 'There's nothing we can do now except wait.'

CHAPTER FIFTEEN

CONSTABLE STERNBERG was true to his word and stayed through the night, administering medicine every four hours in accordance with the Pharmacist's instructions. By the morning, Heinrich's temperature was going down and he was even able to try a mouthful of the goulash.

Gustavo had not slept and spent the night searching through the hotel again for the lost ledger, but in vain. When the time came to leave for The Bureau of Forgotten Things, his nerves were a-jangle.

'If someone's stolen the Ledger then they'll be able to pick us off one by one,' said Gustavo, suddenly more anxious as he hurried along the streets of the New Town towards Borgburg Avenue, with Marius, Yurgen, Lil and Cosmo at his side. 'It will give away all our secrets.'

'None of you will be safe,' agreed Sternberg, who was escorting them on their journey. 'We've got to find the Ledger and quickly.'

Gustavo uttered a moan of despair, but nothing could be said to comfort him as the Band of Blood descended the stone steps to The Bureau of Forgotten Things.

'Who is it?' came a voice, and the Attendant shuffled out from his room, flossing his teeth with violin string. 'Oh,' he said, 'it's you, is it?' He peered over his spectacles at Lil. 'Ah, my favourite,' he said, smiling to reveal a row of gold teeth. He leant forward and reached out his hand, pulling a brass curseling as if by magic from behind Lil's ear, which he presented to the girl with a bow of his balding head.

Marius gazed about him. Many hundreds of umbrellas dangled from an iron rail in the ceiling. There were bags and cases, walking canes, snow shoes and skis, and enough books to fill the shelves of a library. Every object imaginable had been gathered, even a large stuffed alligator, hanging from three brass hooks fixed high in the ceiling.

'We need to start searching,' said Gustavo urgently, rummaging through a large box.

'We've lost an...an item,' said Lil, choosing her words carefully.

'An item?' said the Attendant with a frown. 'A valuable item?'

'Not valuable exactly,' said Marius hurriedly.

'Well nothing disappears forever,' said the Attendant. 'It'll all turn up here, whatever you're looking for. Hats and musical instruments, shoes and gramophones, fur coats and ear trumpets, stuffed animals and scientific paraphernalia, glass eyes—' He stopped abruptly. 'You want false teeth? I've got false teeth.' Slipping his hand into his pocket he pulled out a set of teeth and flung them across the room to Marius, laughing loudly as the boy yelped in surprise and the teeth fell clattering to the floor.

Cosmo had become engrossed in sorting through books in an old wooden tea chest. 'So many wonderful books,' he murmured.

'You're not here to read,' said Yurgen, snatching a volume from Cosmo's hands. 'You're here to search.'

Suddenly Sternberg held up a large book. 'Is this what you're looking for?' he called.

Gustavo rushed across and seized the ledger, clutching it tightly to his chest. His legs were trembling so violently that he had to sit down. 'Yes,' he whimpered. 'This is the Ledger. It's safe. We're all safe.'

Marius had joined Cosmo at the box of books, his eyes alighting on a copy of Von Hoffmeyer's *A History of Prince Eugene*, the very same book he had bought from Adalard Frobe. He held up the volume to show his friend. 'I have a copy of the book, but this is a first edition,' he said. He thumbed through the pages and was surprised to find a chapter he had never read before:

THE DEATH OF THE DARK COUNT

'Who was the Dark Count?' asked Marius.

'General Akibus,' said Cosmo. 'He was Talbor's second-in-command.'

'This chapter isn't in my copy of the book,' said Marius.

'No,' said Cosmo. 'It's only in the first edition. I don't know why. My mother had a copy, but they're very rare.'

Marius leant against a shelf and began to read:

And what, you may be asking, of General Akibus? How did the Dark Count meet his end, if meet his end he did?

In the days and weeks that followed Good Prince Eugene's triumphant return to Schwartzgarten, there were those who remained faithful to Emeté Talbor. It seemed to the citizens of the Great City that the Vigils, Talbor's feared private army, had vanished, as if into thin air – but this was wishful thinking. Though the gauntlets, capes and raven masks had been discarded, many a heart and many a head were still turned to darkness.

The Dark Count was well protected by those who had once served Talbor, staying first in one house and then another, moving from place to place through the web of sewers that ran beneath the city. But even the most faithful of men can have their loyalty bought for the right price, and the youngest son of the House of Koski betrayed Akibus to Prince Eugene, for the princely sum of ten Imperial crowns and a barrel of beetroot schnapps.

'Burning to death would seem a fitting end for the

Dark Count,' declared Prince Eugene, who had feared the man greatly since facing him on the field of battle. 'Ottoburg, my Court Inventor, will design a wooden box, in which the Dark Count will be imprisoned, like a rat in a cage. The box will be filled with gunpowder and Akibus will burst like a shooting star above the city, a sign that darkness has been banished from Schwartzgarten forever.'

Kalvitas, Prince Eugene's closest friend and advisor, was dispatched to visit the Dark Count in his cell, taking measurements of the man in order that Ottoburg's box would fit snugly. But Akibus, it seemed, was a changed man; he swore to Kalvitas that he had seen the error of his ways, and he was the very picture of misery and apology when reminded of his bloodthirsty exploits in battle. Kalvitas, who was fast growing weary of Prince Eugene's lust for revenge and who was kind of heart, took pity on Akibus and a deal was struck; Kalvitas would assist the man to escape on the binding promise that he would never return to Schwartzgarten.

'Here is a dagger,' said Kalvitas, passing a stiletto

blade to the prisoner. 'Hide it in your boot, then as I transport you to Edvardplatz for your execution tomorrow, pull out the blade and nick me slightly so there is blood drawn, and I can tell the Prince that I was overpowered.'

The next evening came. A heaving crowd had gathered on Edvardplatz, and Ottoburg made the final adjustments to the engine of Akibus's destruction, a wooden case with padlocks which he had named the Star Box, filled with enough gunpowder to blow the Dark Count into many millions of glittering pieces.

As Akibus was transported by armed carriage through the streets of Schwartzgarten, with Kalvitas beside him, the plan for escape was put into motion. But the darkness of Akibus's heart was greater than the goodness of Kalvitas's intentions.

'You fool!' cursed Akibus. 'Never make a deal with your enemy. I shall do more than draw blood. I shall drain every drop in your body and then I will slay the fat prince!'

The Dark Count fought like a man possessed.

Kalvitas, who was as agile as a cat, parried the blows and soon subdued his treacherous assailant, but not without much blood being spilled. The Dark Count's blade had cut deeply into the boy's right arm, a gaping wound which ran from the tip of his elbow very nearly to the back of his hand...

Marius looked up in surprise. 'It says that Great-great-uncle Kalvitas had his arm sliced by the Dark Count,' he said.

'By Akibus,' said Cosmo. 'That's right. But few people know about that these days. Only historians like me.'

Marius turned to the front of the book. Inside the cover was a paper label:

If this book should become separated from its owner, return it at your earliest convenience to Kristifan Von Hoffmeyer at the Library of Schwartzgarten.

Marius gasped. 'This book belonged to Kristifan Von Hoffmeyer himself!'

'Very likely,' said the Attendant. 'He's always losing

things. That man must be the most forgetful citizen that Schwartzgarten has ever known.'

'Even worse than Gustavo?' laughed Sternberg.

Gustavo gave a half-hearted twitch of a smile.

'You mean Von Hoffmeyer still lives?' said Cosmo. 'I thought he must have died long ago.'

'He's alive all right,' said the Attendant, lifting down a wooden crate from a shelf. 'He lives in rooms above the Library of Schwartzgarten. This whole box is full of his books.'

'We should go now and see how Heinrich is feeling,' said Sternberg. 'You've got the Ledger back.'

'Not so fast,' said the Attendant, waving a hand. 'That book is property of The Bureau of Forgotten Things. What have you got to deal for it?'

'Nothing,' said Gustavo miserably.

'And nothing gets you nothing,' said the Attendant, tugging the ledger from the boy's hands.

'We could return the box of books to Kristifan Von Hoffmeyer for you?' suggested Cosmo. 'He would probably reward you for it.'

'He probably would,' said the Attendant thoughtfully.

'Very well then. I will give you the box to return, but mind you come back with the reward if you ever want anything else from me again.'

'Spit on it?' said Gustavo.

'I don't want a handful of spit,' replied the Attendant. 'Now take your Ledger and be off with you.'

———◆———

It was agreed that Cosmo and Marius would return the box to Kristifan Von Hoffmeyer straight away, and the two boys slowly made their way from The Bureau of Forgotten things, across the city. The Library of Schwartzgarten was a towering building of red bricks and dark wooden beams, jewelled with intricate windows of stained glass. Pushing open the large mahogany doors, Marius and Cosmo carried the box inside, into the main hall of the library. Long tables with electric reading lamps were set out in rows, and librarians hurried backwards and forwards with trolleys of books.

With a meaningful cough, a tall librarian with greasy black hair alerted the boys' attention. 'Your reading ticket, please,' he said.

'We're not here to take books,' said Marius. 'We're here to return them. We have to speak with Kristifan Von Hoffmeyer.'

Cosmo lifted the wooden box onto the desk.

'And what is this?' asked the Librarian.

'From The Bureau of Forgotten Things,' said Cosmo. 'This box of books belongs to Kristifan Von Hoffmeyer.'

'Very well,' said the Librarian, lifting a speaking tube from the wall. He blew sharply into the mouthpiece and after a long pause there was an answering whistle. 'Two boys are downstairs to see you,' he said. 'They have brought a box with them from The Bureau of Forgotten Things.' There was a pause as the Librarian listened to the response from above. 'Yes, I shall tell them.' He turned to Marius and Cosmo. 'Kristifan Von Hoffmeyer thanks you for returning his possessions and wishes you both a good day.'

'But we want to speak to him,' said Marius.

The Librarian tutted and shook his head. 'That will not be necessary.' He was about to return the speaking tube to its hook when Marius said:

'Tell him that the great-great-nephew of Kalvitas the Chocolate Maker is here and wishes to speak with him.'

The Librarian sighed impatiently as he relayed the message, then leant close to the earpiece to hear the reply. With a look of surprise, he replaced the speaking tube and turned to Marius.

'Von Hoffmeyer will see you.'

CHAPTER SIXTEEN

K RISTIFAN VON Hoffmeyer's office was high above the Library of Schwartzgarten and was reached by way of a winding and rickety wooden staircase. It was difficult to manoeuvre the box up the steps and it was many minutes before Marius and Cosmo arrived at a large room with dark panelled walls. The long windows were of stained glass and illustrated the founding of the Great City by the Hungry Seven, many hundreds of years before. Light filtered in strangely and Marius was forced to squint. Across the floor from the window was a desk and a brass lantern.

Marius and Cosmo lowered the box to the floor.

'I have few visitors and that is how I wish it,' said a scratchy voice, and Marius swung round.

An old man sat huddled up before a fire at the far end of the room. He rose slowly from his chair, wrapping a woollen rug about his shoulders. 'There is a slight chill in the air and I am prone to disease. My health is fragile, you understand. Man is at war with the germ unseen and his only defence is the pocket handkerchief.' He blew his nose. 'I have seen bacteria under the microscope...how they swarm and multiply. Hundreds of millions of assassins...invisible to the naked eye.' He slowly approached the children. 'Which one of you is kin of the great Kalvitas?'

Marius took a deep breath and stepped forward.

Von Hoffmeyer looked the boy up and down. 'And what is your name?' he asked.

'Marius Myerdorf.'

'That is a mountain name,' said Von Hoffmeyer.

'My parents were from Blatten,' said Marius. 'But they are dead now.'

Von Hoffmeyer did not meet Marius's eye; he turned towards the fire and reached up to wind the mantel clock.

Cosmo dragged the box of books across the floor towards the historian. 'These are all yours,' he said. 'We thought you would like them back.'

Von Hoffmeyer bent down and retrieved his *A History of Prince Eugene* from the box. 'Ah,' he said, 'I wondered what had become of this.'

'The attendant at The Bureau of Forgotten Things thinks you might give him a reward,' said Marius.

'Then the man is a fool,' said Von Hoffmeyer.

'Do you live here?' asked Cosmo, staring around the book-lined walls of the room in awe.

'Yes,' said Von Hoffmeyer. 'This is where I live and this is where I write.'

'What is the best part of being a historian?' asked Cosmo.

'Once a year I am rewarded for my scholarly diligence, in accordance with the Old Ways,' said Von Hoffmeyer. 'I am presented with a crate of anchovy paste. And what is the worst part, you might ask? I will tell you.' He took a cracker biscuit from a tin on his desk. 'There are never enough jars of anchovy paste to last me the entire year.'

'Don't you get sick of fish?' asked Marius.

'I do not eat meat,' said Von Hoffmeyer, smearing anchovy paste sparingly onto his cracker biscuit as he spoke. 'I prefer animals to humans and it would seem quite incorrect to eat them. But fish are joyless creatures. Hardly more intelligent than grass.'

'We wanted to ask you about Akibus,' said Marius. 'The Dark Count.'

'I know who Akibus was,' snapped Von Hoffmeyer.

'Why did you leave the story of his attack on my great-great-uncle out of the later editions of your book?' asked Marius.

Von Hoffmeyer's eyes darted anxiously. 'There is doubt about Akibus's fate,' he said. 'His story is inconclusive and that is why I removed it from my book. I believe the man fled the city, but there is no evidence to support that.'

Cosmo was examining an old print in a black frame that hung from one of the bookcases. 'This is a picture of Prince Eugene's mechanical horse,' he said.

'That is so,' replied Von Hoffmeyer.

'I read the description in one of your books,' said Cosmo. 'My mother was a professor of history so I know all about it.'

'Do you?' said Von Hoffmeyer, taking another bite of the cracker biscuit. 'Do you indeed?'

'What happened to the mechanical horse, Sir?' asked Cosmo.

'The fat Prince's horse still exists,' said Von Hoffmeyer.

'Really?' said Cosmo. 'Then where is it?'

'It is where it has always been, a rusted hulk in a shed beside the Imperial Railway Station.'

'Can we find the place?' asked Cosmo, who could imagine nothing better than uncovering an artefact from the days of Good Prince Eugene.

'Its tracks still run across the city, set between the tram lines.' Von Hoffmeyer blew on his hands to warm them. 'Now, enough. Be off with you. I am tired from too much talking.'

As soon as the visitors had left Von Hoffmeyer's office, the old man rose from his desk and grasped the speaking tube from the wall. He blew into the mouthpiece to alert the Librarian below.

'Can I help you, Von Hoffmeyer?' came a voice. 'More crackers, perhaps?'

'I don't want crackers,' snapped Von Hoffmeyer. 'Get a message to Kalvitas. A problem has arisen. It's the boy, Marius. I think he's close to discovering the truth.'

Cosmo's head was full of mechanical horses as he said goodbye to Marius and made his way back to the hotel to see Yurgen.

Marius walked slowly around Edvardplatz. As he

approached a fountain close to Kalvitas's shop, he read the relevant entry from his guidebook:

Carved into the ornate fountain is the figure of a young man riding a pony. This is the celebrated battle hero M. Kalvitas, loyal friend to Good Prince Eugene and liberator of the Great City.

Marius climbed onto the fountain to get a better look at the figure sitting atop his pony. He reached up and ran his hand slowly over the carved right arm of the young Kalvitas. A long, wide scar ran from the figure's wrist to the tip of its elbow, just as Kristifan Von Hoffmeyer had described in the first edition of his *A History of Prince Eugene*. 'But Great-great-uncle Kalvitas doesn't have a scar on his arm,' he whispered.

'What are you doing up there?' shouted a voice, and Marius almost slipped from the statue in alarm. A police constable stood at the foot of the fountain.

'That's the hero Kalvitas you're climbing all over!' shouted the man. 'Not a respectful way to treat the great and the good, is it?'

'I am his great-great-nephew,' said Marius.

'And I'm Emeté Talbor,' called the man sarcastically. 'Now get down from there before I have to come up and drag you down.'

Marius slowly climbed down from the fountain.

'Show me your papers,' said the Constable.

'I don't have them with me,' said Marius. 'But I really am Kalvitas's relative. Only I don't want to go home. Not yet.'

'There's one way to sort this out,' said the Constable, seizing Marius by the scruff of the neck and marching him across the cobbles to Kalvitas's chocolate shop; it was closed and the blinds were drawn.

The Constable knocked at the door, which swung open instantly.

'Yes?' said Kalvitas. 'What do you want?'

The Constable gave an embarrassed cough. 'Apologies for disturbing you, sir,' he said, 'but this little gutter rat has the nerve to claim that he's your great-great-nephew.'

'He might be,' said Kalvitas with a flickering trace of a grin. 'Yes, I think this boy does belong to me.'

Kalvitas sat at the kitchen table counting out the day's takings from the shop, which he spread out on an opened sheet of newspaper. All the time he watched Marius keenly. 'What's wrong, boy?' he asked. 'Is something troubling you?'

But Marius did not answer. He sat silently, sipping from a cup of chocolate.

Kalvitas observed the boy curiously from the corner of his eye. 'That chocolate will sort you out.'

But even though he drained the cup, Marius did not feel better. Something about Great-great-uncle Kalvitas no longer rang true and he was determined to get to the bottom of matters.

Cosmo set off from the hotel that evening with Yurgen, Gustavo and Lil in search of Prince Eugene's mechanical horse.

'What use is an iron horse to the Band of Blood anyway?' asked Yurgen sceptically, as they walked along Marshal Podovsky Street. 'It's hardly a way to travel around

Schwartzgarten without being seen by anyone, is it?'

But Cosmo would not be put off. 'Look!' he cried, dropping to his knees, and scraping madly at the ground. 'Between the tram tracks, just as Von Hoffmeyer said.'

'Here,' said Yurgen, taking the grappling hook from his belt and handing it to Cosmo. 'Use this.'

Cosmo scraped away the grime and caked horse dung that had collected over the decades. 'Now all we need to do is follow the tracks and find where it goes.'

The tracks let them through the city to an abandoned goods shed beside the Schwartzgarten Imperial Railway Station. The doors were stiff but they were able to create a wide-enough gap to slip inside.

'It looks like no one's been here in years,' said Yurgen.

At the very back of the goods shed, standing on the rails, was a dark shape, hidden beneath a large canvas sheet.

Cosmo pulled back the cover and through a cloud of thick, black dust, the great hulk of the mechanical horse was revealed, its head hanging loose at the neck. He laughed triumphantly. Boris barked and backed away.

'It looks like we're the first people to see it in a hundred years,' said Lil.

'Not a hundred, only seventy,' said Cosmo. 'It was used in the days of Good Prince Eugene. I read about it in Kristifan Von Hoffmeyer's history of the Prince. He ate so much food and became so fat that his own horse was killed by his enormous weight.'

'I never knew that,' said Lil.

'Because you never read anything,' said Cosmo, a pained note in his voice. 'That's why. If you read books you'd learn about history and then I wouldn't have to explain everything to you all the time.'

'Don't tell us if you don't want to,' said Gustavo with a sly wink to Lil.

'The mechanical horse was designed for the Prince by Ottoburg, the Court Inventor,' said Cosmo quickly. 'As you can see, the neck of the horse is riveted, so that the head could be raised and lowered by pushing or pulling at a lever.'

Gustavo opened a small metal hatch set into the horse's rear. 'What's this for?' he asked.

'It's most probably for the used coal,' said Cosmo, pushing past Gustavo and reaching inside the horse with his hand. 'Yes,' he said, 'there's a boiler inside its belly.' He pulled out a fistful of black dust. 'See? It's spent coal.'

'How does it work?' asked Lil. 'Was it pulled by horses along the tracks?'

'No,' said Cosmo. 'It's like a steam engine. The horse is fed with coal, which builds up steam, which powers the pistons, which move the legs of the creature and drive it forwards or backwards along the rails.'

Yurgen pulled himself up into the iron saddle and sat astride the great mechanical horse. He pushed and pulled at three ebony-topped levers. 'It's rusted solid,' he said. 'These levers won't move at all.'

'I think it could be made to work again though,' said Cosmo, walking into a corner of the shed, where a heap of coal had evidently not been disturbed in years. 'There's fuel enough here to start up the fire. Gustavo understands about motor cars and I have my books on engineering.'

'But this isn't a car,' said Gustavo. 'It's an old rusty horse.'

Cosmo was not listening. 'Every joint must be oiled if we're to get the creature moving.'

'Why would we want to get it moving?' said Gustavo, who felt certain that it was best to leave the horse beneath its canvas shroud.

'The Band of Blood might have need of it one day,' said

Cosmo. 'It would be better to have a mechanical horse than not have a mechanical horse.'

Yurgen sighed and ran his fingers through his hair. 'Then tell us what we need to do, Cosmo.'

———

As soon as Kalvitas had finished totting up the day's takings in the chocolate shop, he rose from the table and pulled on his overcoat and gloves.

'Are you going out?' asked Marius.

'To visit Mr Hirsch in his shop,' said Kalvitas. 'I'll be gone for a good few hours.'

Marius watched from the kitchen window until Kalvitas had disappeared from sight, then ran quickly to his room and snatched up the flashlight from his nightstand. Stealthily he made his way upstairs to the attic.

He was surprised to find the door ajar. Switching on the flashlight, he entered the room and cast the beam around him. It was clear that Kalvitas had never thrown anything away. There were stacks of rusted chocolate moulds, an ancient armchair that had split its seams, and countless boxes and trunks, covered with old oilcloths. The eaves were so low that he had to crouch as he explored the room. His head hit against a bronze medallion hanging from a nail, and he lifted it down and examined it closely.

IN COMMEMORATION OF
THE LIBERATION OF
SCHWARTZGARTEN

Beside the armchair was a long wooden trunk with dull brass handles. Marius swept away the dust with his hand. He gasped and leapt back. It was not a trunk at all, but a coffin. His heart was beating hard and it felt as though his ears were ringing.

Screwed to the lid was a tarnished brass plate, engraved with the name: M. KALVITAS

Marius was certain that he had at last uncovered the truth; the man he had thought was his great-great-uncle was a fraud, a murderer. The real Kalvitas had been killed, his corpse hidden away in the attic where nobody would ever find it. Even Inspector Durnstein would have been shocked by such a discovery.

Extending a trembling hand, he was about to lift the

lid of the coffin when he heard footsteps on the creaking wooden staircase. He switched off the flashlight and crouched down behind the armchair, his heart pounding harder than ever.

But there was no way out and it was futile attempting to hide.

'Let me see you, Marius,' demanded Kalvitas, appearing at the attic door. 'I know you're up here, boy.'

Marius remained silent.

'I won't ask you again,' growled the old man.

Marius climbed shakily to his feet. 'Are you going to murder me?' he stammered. 'Are you going to keep my body up here as well?'

'Body? There's no body in there.' Kalvitas leant down and lifted the lid of the coffin. 'You see?' he said, picking out old papers and scraps of uniform.

'You're not my great-great-uncle at all, are you?' whispered Marius. 'You're an imposter.'

'An imposter? That's such a hard word,' said Kalvitas, snatching the bronze medallion from the boy's hands. 'But then I suppose it's true, up to a point.'

'What do you mean?' asked Marius. 'Up to a point?'

'I might not be your great-great-uncle, but I am a Kalvitas all the same. And we're still blood, boy, you and I.' He stared hard at Marius. 'You don't believe a word I say, do you?'

Marius did not answer.

'Come on,' said Kalvitas, leading the boy from the attic, down the stairs past the squawking budgerigar and into the kitchen.

Marius sat at the table, as close to the door as was possible, fearing that the old man might suddenly become murderous and he would be forced to flee. His head was swimming, he felt lost and bewildered. The man who had taken him in and cared for him was suddenly a stranger again.

Kalvitas tied on his apron. He took a bar of chocolate from a shelf and offered it to Marius.

'No,' said Marius. 'It might be poisoned.'

Kalvitas snapped off a square of the chocolate and chewed it slowly. 'Your great-great-uncle died,' he said at last.

'Then who are you?' asked Marius, laying his palms flat on the table to control his trembling arms.

'I'm his son,' said Kalvitas. 'I'm only your great-uncle. A young man of seventy and not a day more.'

It took Marius a moment or two to absorb this information. 'Then what happened to Great-great-uncle Kalvitas?' he asked. 'Did you kill him?'

'Kill him?' laughed Kalvitas. 'Of course I didn't kill him. He was my father.'

'That doesn't prove anything,' said Marius. 'A lot of people have killed their fathers. Emeté Talbor killed his father.'

'Well, I didn't kill mine,' replied Kalvitas snappishly.

'If you didn't murder Great-great-uncle Kalvitas, then what did happen to him?' asked Marius.

'He was seventy-seven years of age when he died,' said Kalvitas, his voice dropping to a whisper, as though he feared someone might be listening at the door. 'It was many, many kilometres from Schwartzgarten. Far beyond the forest outside the old city walls.' He reached up to a shelf and took down a cardboard tube which contained a tightly rolled map. 'We went on a tour of chocolate shops of the Northern Region and my father was taken sick.' He unrolled the map on the table, holding it in place with two heavy copper chocolate moulds. 'He died at Mannen, a small village outside Lüchmünster. Here,' he said, pointing to a place on the map. 'My poor dear mother died of a broken heart the very next day and I was left all alone. I had her bones brought back to Schwartzgarten to be laid in the cemetery.'

'It's a sad story,' said Marius, who was still not sure whether to believe a single word that came out of the man's mouth.

'It is,' agreed Kalvitas. 'The saddest of all stories.'

'Tell me about your father,' prompted Marius.

'We were as alike as two chocolate truffles in a box,' said Kalvitas. He took a photograph from his waistcoat pocket to illustrate his point. The picture was yellowed with age and showed two men standing side by side outside the chocolate shop. 'He was the finest of all men – good, and wise and brave. He was more friend than father and he taught me all I know about chocolate making. His death was like a stabbing in my poor heart.' Tears were now coursing down the man's craggy face and he wiped his eyes with the hem of his apron. 'It's not easy to lose your parents, however old you might become.'

'You won't lose me,' said Marius, certain now that the man was speaking the truth.

Kalvitas patted his great-nephew's hand. 'You're a good boy,' he said. 'This will be our secret, won't it?'

Marius nodded his head. 'Why do you keep all his belongings locked up in a coffin?' he asked.

'It was the coffin that earned my father his name,' said Kalvitas. 'He jumped into the River Schwartz to flee the tyrant Talbor and that coffin was a life raft to him. He was swept away from the Great City towards the Summer Palace, where he was taken in to work as Pastry Chef to Prince Alberto and his son, Good Prince Eugene. It was an empty coffin, but engraved with the name M. Kalvitas – a name my father took as his own. He kept it hidden beneath his bed in the Summer Palace. It had been smashed to pieces by the rocks, but he brought it back to Schwartzgarten and rebuilt it. And it's been there in the attic ever since.'

Marius stared hard at his great-uncle. For a man of eighty-eight Kalvitas was in remarkable health, but for a man of seventy he had gone to seed early; his cheeks were sunken, his skin was age-mottled and his eyes were a watery blue. A thought suddenly dawned on the boy.

'Have you chopped off any heads?' he asked.

Kalvitas shook his head sadly. 'Not a one. Throw more coal on the fire, my bones are gnawed by the cold tonight.'

'How did you know that I would go up into the attic?' asked Marius as he stoked the fire.

'Von Hoffmeyer sent a message to warn me,' said Kalvitas. 'I know that you went to visit him today.'

'So Von Hoffmeyer knows your secret as well?'

Kalvitas nodded.

'But how did he discover the truth?'

'That,' said Kalvitas, 'is a long story.'

'I want to hear it,' said Marius, who felt that the time had arrived for the full tale to unravel.

Kalvitas settled back in his chair, toying with the strings of his apron. 'After my father and mother died I stayed on in the village of Mannen for several years. And the older I became the more like my father I looked. And this was all to the good. He was a hero, he had lived the life I always wanted to lead. When I arrived back home on the cobbles of Edvardplatz...well, everyone thought I *was* my father. You have to understand, Marius, his story is part of the history of Schwartzgarten. I could not let his legend die.

I had to become him. I told a tale that my wife and son had died in a tragic accident and that was why I had returned alone.'

'But Von Hoffmeyer knew that it was a lie?'

'One day in my shop he saw that there was no scar on my arm,' said Kalvitas.

'Has he been blackmailing you?' asked Marius.

'No,' said Kalvitas with a shake of his head. 'It was nothing like that. The man's kept my secret faithfully these long years gone. He removed the Akibus chapter from his book and I've kept my arms covered ever since. Kalvitas is worth more to him living than dead. Every year I sign a thousand copies of his books for him.'

'It's sad that you're not a hero after all,' said Marius.

Kalvitas frowned. 'Bravery runs in my blood,' he said. 'I'm my father's son. A man can't have all that heroism gurgling through his veins without some of it being handed down. It's only that I haven't had a chance to prove it yet.' He sighed and turned the medallion over and over in his hand. 'I tell you this much, Marius. One day I'll win a medal all of my own.'

Chapter Seventeen

———❖———

For the next three days Marius worked with Kalvitas, helping to prepare chocolates in readiness for the Festival of the Unfortunate Dead. For two nights in a row, the whole city would be out on the streets, to celebrate the Festival and to commemorate their dead. It was Kalvitas's busiest time of the year, and the old man was grateful to have Marius beside him as he turned out the vast quantities of chocolates and caramels that added sweetness to the sombre celebrations.

When he was not working, Marius walked the streets with Yurgen, searching for any clue that might lead them to the missing members of the Band of Blood. But nothing more than the pumpkin button had been discovered. And no other children had gone missing.

Cosmo was busy too, working on the mechanical horse with Heinrich and Gustavo. They scraped back the rusting metal, coated the cogs with grease and oiled the joints in the creature's iron neck. They worked late into the night until their candles had burned to pools of wax.

On the eve of the Festival of the Unfortunate Dead, stalls and tents were erected on Edvardplatz. And still Marius and Kalvitas worked, preparing vast trays of chocolate ravens, caramelised marzipan skulls and Pfefferberg's Nougat Marshmallows.

As the sky grew dark outside and the crowds began to gather, Kalvitas shooed Marius outside to enjoy the festivities, with a bag of chocolate diabolotines to share with Cosmo and Lil, who had made arrangements to meet the boy on Edvardplatz.

While Marius waited, he read from his guidebook:

Once a year, on the Eve of the Festival of the Unfortunate Dead, an old tradition is reinstated. A man in a raven mask walks the streets of the city, knocking at doors to gather the souls of all those who have died in the previous year. 'Any dead this year?' he cries. 'Not this year,' is the answering call. 'Come again next year.' But if there has been a death, then the owner of the house is presented with a coffin of caramel, in commemoration of the deceased...

Marius jumped as the guidebook was tugged from his hands. There stood Lil, grinning at him with Cosmo at her side.

'I'm surprised your eyes haven't dropped out of your head from too much reading,' said Lil, returning the book.

'Learning about the Festival, are you?' said Cosmo.

'Yes,' said Marius. 'Were you both given caramel coffins after your parents died?'

'I was,' said Cosmo. 'My father and mother died the same year, so I had two. But Lil was already living with the Band of Blood at the time of the Festival.'

'Gustavo made me a coffin out of bread and hazelnut paste,' said Lil. 'I think I would have preferred caramel.'

The three friends set off to explore the darkened streets of the New Town, searching out the parade that marked the beginning of the Festival celebrations. On the corner of Alexis Street and Marshal Podovsky Street, they pushed through the heaving crowds to watch as an enormous effigy of Death made its way slowly through the city, with puppeteers draped in black working the figure's skeletal arms with long wooden poles. Drummers followed behind, their faces shrouded with black hoods.

Children and their parents scattered as a bony finger swung towards them; there were shrieks of laughter and cries of horror.

'If the finger points at you, then you're the next to die,' said Cosmo. 'It's all superstition, of course.'

Lil laughed as the looming figure of Death crossed the cobbles towards them, his robes billowing as an icy wind whipped along the street. The finger was pointing directly at Marius, and the bony skull leered out at the boy with glowing gas-lantern eyes from beneath its black, hooded cloak.

'It's you, Marius!' laughed Cosmo. 'He's pointing at you!'

The skeletal finger swung away and Death moved on.

They followed the crowds as the deathly procession wound through the streets of Schwartzgarten and ended up back on Edvardplatz.

Marius stopped at a stall selling rows of beaked raven masks such as the Vigils once wore. He took down a mask and held it to his face. He turned to Cosmo. 'What do you think?'

'Very sinister,' said Cosmo with a laugh.

'Don't touch if you're not going to buy,' snarled the stallholder, snatching the mask away from Marius and hanging it back on its hook. 'Now scamper off or I'll call for Bollo in his motor van.'

A thin woman with a collar of fox fur stepped through the crowds and leant down to face Lil, who was standing on her own at a neighbouring stall, watching with wide eyes as customers queued for sweet apple dumplings. 'A curseling for the orphans?' said the woman and rattled her collection tin.

Lil turned. 'But I am an orphan,' she said.

A fat woman approached. 'An orphan,' she said. 'And so young and pretty. My heart aches for you, child.'

'How fine her hair is,' cooed the thin woman. 'Like strands of spun copper.'

'And all alone,' said the fat woman, opening a small, velveteen box and offering it to Lil. 'Whenever I'm lonely, I seek the companionship of chocolate.'

'Hello again,' said Marius, walking over to join Lil.

The thin woman stepped back. 'Again?' she said.

'We met on the train,' said Marius. 'I was on my way to the Great City. I gave you a curseling for the orphans.'

'He's an orphan too,' said Lil.

'Then I won't ask you for a curseling more,' said the thin woman. 'You are a good boy.'

'Take care,' said the fat woman. 'There are evil people on the streets of Schwartzgarten tonight.'

The women smiled and pushed on through the crowds, the thin woman rattling the collection tin as they went.

Marius, Lil and Cosmo returned to Kalvitas's shop, which had now been shaded red on the map of Friends of the Band of Blood. Storm clouds were gathering and the sign above the shop door creaked in the breeze.

Kalvitas was preparing a chocolate head of Emeté Talbor, which was to be displayed in the window for the Festival of Prince Eugene the following week. He smiled as he pulled back the brass hinges and eased the head from the mould.

The eyeballs were shaped from white chocolate. The irises of Emeté Talbor's tar-black eyes were cast from dark chocolate mixed with caramelised chestnut paste, and each and every blood vessel had been painted with infinite care from a bottle of scarlet cochineal.

Marius was entrusted to push the eyeballs into position

inside the head, and he secured them with a putty of finest almond marzipan. Kalvitas placed the chocolate death mask in the window of the shop on a cushion of black velvet. Beside it sat an edible replica of Talbor's dark heart, moulded from bitter chocolate, glittering with diamonds carved from sugar crystals.

Returning to the kitchen, Kalvitas served up a plate of toasted milk bread and praline paste for the children and shovelled coal on the stove. Marius, Lil and Cosmo ate hungrily.

There was a knock at the kitchen door and Mrs Kurtz entered, untying her apron and folding it neatly.

'That's the last customer for tonight,' she said. 'We sold enough Pfefferberg's Nougat Marshmallows to fill the Schwartzgarten Opera House. I've sent Miss Esterhart home.'

'I'll lock up presently, Mrs Kurtz,' said Kalvitas, who was searching through a shelf of old recipe books. 'Goodnight. I wish you a joyful Festival.'

Mrs Kurtz nodded her head to the children and closed the door behind her.

'Ah,' said Kalvitas at last. 'This is the book.' He leafed

through the pages and jabbed excitedly at a recipe. 'There!' The recipe was illustrated by a line drawing of a towering chocolate torte. 'We can make this together, Marius. You can take it to the Band of Blood for your Festival feast tomorrow night.'

'I could never make anything like that,' said Marius.

'It's easy,' said Kalvitas with a laugh. 'Your mind works and your hands obey.'

Marius glanced out through the window just in time to see a figure flash past the glass. Not trusting his eyes, he peered out onto Edvardplatz, where a breeze swirled the falling snow. On the cobbles stood a man in a black hooded coat with a raven mask.

Marius staggered back from the window.

'What is it, boy?' asked Kalvitas. 'What have you seen?'

'A Vigil,' said Marius. 'With his raven mask.'

'Then I'm the next Chocolate Maker to die!' gasped Kalvitas.

No sooner had he spoken than there came a clattering of the bell from out in the shop.

'Quick,' said the old man. 'Follow me. We need to

hide.' They hurried from the kitchen and into the mould room. 'Up the ladder,' Kalvitas whispered, and he quickly climbed up towards the dark rafters of the high and narrow tower, Cosmo, Lil and Marius following behind him. They peered down as the Vigil entered the room.

Cosmo flinched, knocking his elbow against a large copper mould in the shape of a swan. He reached out to catch the falling mould as it dropped from its hook, but he was too late; it crashed to the ground.

The Vigil stopped in his tracks. He turned and gazed up into the rafters, a smile bleeding slowly across his lips. He grasped the ladder and began to shake it. Marius clung desperately to the rungs. The clatter of copper moulds was deafening. Lil gasped and her hands slipped. Marius reached out and caught her by the arm, and with Cosmo's help pulled her back up onto the ladder.

'Get out!' bellowed Kalvitas, shaking a high swinging beam backwards and forwards so the tin and copper moulds rained down on the Vigil. He held up his hands to shield himself.

'Help!' screamed Lil, adding to the din of falling metal. 'Murder!'

The Vigil turned and fled from the mould room and out of the shop.

'That was close,' said Kalvitas grimly as they slowly climbed down from the ladder. 'They nearly got me that time. But they'll be back. You can count on that.'

CHAPTER EIGHTEEN

⬥⬦⬥

THAT NIGHT, a police guard stood watch outside Kalvitas's shop, and this seemed to lift the old man's flagging spirits, though Marius was not quite convinced that his great-uncle was out of danger.

The day of the Festival of the Unfortunate Dead dawned cold and bright, and Kalvitas and Marius set to work early on the chocolate torte, greasing cake pans, mixing batter, moulding decorations from marzipan and chocolate. It was not until early evening that the cake was assembled: a towering confection of almond sponge cake and chocolate meringue, decorated with chestnut icing and nests of spun sugar. Kalvitas packed the torte in a large, wooden cake box just as Yurgen, Gustavo and two other larger boys arrived at the shop to transport the dessert across the city for the Band of Blood's Festival feast.

The gong was struck and the children took their places at the table, each with an object in front of them that served as a reminder of their Best Beloved. There were headless dolls, saggy and hairless cloth animals and pieces of jewellery. Gustavo had a clockwork polar bear and Lil had a lozenge-shaped piece of cut glass, taken from the chandelier that her mother and father had once owned.

But there was nothing at the head of the table as a memento of Yurgen's lost family.

'He never talks about his Best Beloved,' whispered Lil to Marius. 'He's the only one we don't know anything about.'

A place had been set for Marius between Heinrich and Gustavo. Heinrich, who had now recovered from his fever, held a carved wooden box in his hands.

'Was the box a present from your Best Beloved?' asked Marius as he sat down at the table.

'No, it's not the box,' said Heinrich. He opened the lid and lifted out a crumpled paper chocolate wrapper which he carefully unfolded on the table. 'It was the last thing my father ever gave to me. This wrapper is the most precious thing I own.'

'Do you have anything, Marius?' asked Gustavo.

Marius took the photograph of his parents from his pocket and propped it against his goblet.

Yurgen took his place at the table, as the Band of Blood helped themselves to beetroot soup with sour cream and dill, served from a cracked china tureen. He stared approvingly at the enormous chocolate torte.

Lil had tight hold of Bag-of-Bones, trying hard to tie a silk ribbon around the cat's head.

A silence fell on the room as Merla entered slowly, her eyes cast down towards the floor. There were gasps and murmurs of surprise from the Band of Blood and Gustavo's spoon slipped from his hand, dropping into his bowl and spattering the tablecloth with beetroot soup.

'Sit next to me,' said Lil, pulling out a chair.

'I had a cat once,' said Merla, patting Bag-of-Bones on the head. 'It died.' Without another word she sat down, placing the bust of Count Von Hasselbach carefully on the table in front of her.

Yurgen struck the table twice with the handle of his knife. 'Gustavo will speak now.'

'But I'm eating,' said Gustavo, helping himself to a wedge of smoked cheese. 'Can't I speak later?'

'You're always eating,' said Yurgen.

Gustavo sighed and stood up, taking a crumpled piece

of paper from his pocket. He coughed and began to read. 'Midway along the path of our life we come to a dark wood where the straight way is lost—'

He stopped abruptly. Merla was climbing unsteadily to her feet, holding onto the edge of the table as if to keep herself upright. Boris yapped excitedly.

'I've had enough of speeches,' said the girl and Gustavo sighed and sat back down. 'I want to talk about my family now.' Merla's voice was hardly more than a whisper and at first Marius had to strain his ears to hear her speak. 'I will begin by telling you about my father, Count Von Hasselbach.' She smiled down at the plaster bust. 'Father always wore smart clothes. I remember that. A jacket and a waistcoat. And he had a gold fob watch in his waistcoat pocket. His suit was steam-pressed. My room was in a turret of the castle—'

'It was only a small castle,' whispered Gustavo to Marius.

'It might have been small, but it was still a castle,' said Merla. She smiled wickedly. 'Did you live in a castle? No,' she said. 'I didn't think so.'

Gustavo scowled and cut another wedge of cheese.

'The shutters at the windows were dark green,' continued Merla quickly, as though the words were now bubbling out of her. 'I was woken at seven o'clock each morning when Sofia brought me my tea...in the Lüchmünster porcelain tea cups with the blue pattern—'

'You're showing off now,' said Gustavo, his mouth full of cheese.

Merla ignored him. 'There were three servants...no, four. There was Sofia...she cooked...she cooked and sang and brought me food on a tray.' The longer Merla spoke, the more confident she seemed and the louder her voice became. 'Then there was Kurt...he drove Father's motor car. There were two others; I don't remember their names. I don't remember what they did.'

'And then something interesting happened, did it?' said Gustavo, who was fast growing bored by the story but had not given up hope that it might still become exciting.

'I remember them leaving...one day they were there and the next...' Merla stopped and her expression darkened. 'I looked out of the window...I saw them through the trees, wearing their smart clothes, carrying bags...Sofia and

Kurt and the other two...Kurt had a suitcase...' Her legs seemed to buckle and she held on to the table more tightly than before. 'They didn't even say goodbye...I was sitting on a chair. Some sort of chair with a cushion the colour of...I can't remember...'

Lil put her hand gently on Merla's arm but it was shaken away.

'I don't even remember what the chairs looked like,' mumbled Merla, lowering herself back onto her seat. 'Why can't I remember the chairs?'

'She's not right in the head,' whispered Gustavo, and Lil slapped him on the arm.

'I think Bag-of-Bones should be yours now,' said Lil, passing him across to Merla, who took the cat distractedly, all the time gazing at the plaster bust beside her goblet of lingonberry cordial.

'Poor Father,' she murmured.

———

After supper, dressed in their finest clothes, the Band of Blood assembled in the lobby of the hotel, holding lanterns which Heinrich and Cosmo lit with long tapers.

'We'll leave in small groups,' said Yurgen. 'Keep moving and be watchful. It's the worst of all nights to be caught out by Bollo or the police.'

'Why the worst of all nights?' asked Marius curiously.

'People get caught up in their thoughts when they remember their Best Beloved,' said Yurgen. 'It makes us vulnerable to capture.'

A yellow moon was high in the sky, wreathed in freezing mist, as the Band of Blood made their way along the alleyway beside the hotel and across Bone Orchard Street to the Gate of Skulls.

'A lot of people eat beside the graves, to pay homage to their Best Beloved,' said Yurgen, as he walked with Marius along the winding cemetery paths. 'It's a tradition in Schwartzgarten.'

Families had spread rugs on the snow beside the tombs of their Best Beloved, and were picnicking by lantern light. Rich families feasted on pastries and champagne, while poorer families made do with goulash and rye beer.

'This way, Marius,' said Yurgen. 'I want you to meet somebody.'

They passed through Poisoner's Row and Marius stopped, distracted by one tombstone in particular.

HERE LIE THE SINFUL REMAINS OF OTTO ESTRINBURG,

WHO CHOPPED UP EIGHT MEMBERS OF HIS FAMILY

AND DISSOLVED THE PIECES IN HYDROCHLORIC ACID.

ERECTED BY HIS IDENTICAL TWIN DAUGHTERS, WHO WERE

FORTUNATE ENOUGH TO ESCAPE THEIR UNHINGED FATHER

'How did your parents meet their end, Yurgen?' asked Marius, unable to contain his curiosity.

'They got ill,' said Yurgen simply, and waded on through the snow. 'Now hurry up.'

They walked to a small, squat building of grey stone at the very heart of the cemetery.

'The Sexton lives here,' said Yurgen, rattling a locked iron gate. 'He takes care of the cemetery. He's more wild creature than man, and never does the Band of Blood a good turn unless there's money to pay for it. But there's an old saying that on the Day of the Festival, a favour asked must be granted, or else the dead come knocking.'

'But that's just superstition, isn't it?' said Marius.

'Maybe,' said Yurgen. 'But would you chance it if you lived in a cemetery?'

'Who is it?' cried a husky voice from deep inside the building. 'Go away, or I'll set the cats on you!'

'What good are the cats going to do?' shouted back Yurgen.

An old man with long grey hair shuffled forward from the shadows, wearing a pair of fingerless woollen gloves. 'Oh, it's you,' said the Sexton. 'What do you want?'

'It's the Day of the Festival,' said Yurgen. 'And I demand my favour.'

The Sexton's face contorted as though the very thought of helping the boy caused him pain. 'You'd better come in then,' said the old man sullenly as he unlocked the gate.

Marius and Yurgen followed the man down a dark flight of stone steps, to a small chamber where a fire burned in the grate. 'They all come down here,' said the man, as countless cats pushed past Marius's legs, 'for the warmth. That's what they like. Not the company.' He laughed so hard that he began to cough: a wretched hacking that sent the cats springing for cover. 'They think you've brought them something to eat. Have you?'

'Maybe,' said Yurgen, slipping a tin of sardines from his pocket and peeling back the lid. He crouched down and fed a ginger tom a sardine from the palm of his hand.

'Don't waste it all on the cats!' cried the man. 'They're not the only ones with appetites!'

Yurgen offered the sardines to the Sexton, and the man snatched the tin from him. He dropped a sardine onto a rye biscuit, and swallowed it down hungrily. 'Well,' said the man, wiping his oily mouth on the back of one of his gloves. 'What is it you're here for?'

Yurgen held out the pumpkin button.

'What's this?' asked the Sexton.

'We need to find out where this came from,' said Yurgen. 'It's important.'

'Very well,' said the man. 'I shall put out the word.'

Marius and Yurgen left the Sexton and crossed the cemetery. They found Gustavo, Lil and Cosmo standing with Merla by a slate tomb, above which stood a life-sized marble statue of a bearded man with his arms outstretched.

'That's my father,' said Merla proudly. 'He looks kind, doesn't he, Marius?'

'He does,' replied Marius softly.

Merla smiled and produced a folded piece of paper from her pocket.

'Every year she writes a note to her father,' said Lil as Merla tucked the note between her father's cold, stone fingers. 'And every year she gets worse in her brains. Last Festival she was so scared to leave the hotel that Constable Sternberg had to come and stand watch by the graveside.'

Yurgen lit a candle for Merla, which the girl placed carefully on the tomb.

'Parents are fickle,' said Cosmo, sucking on a chocolate cigar. 'One minute they love you, the next they're dead.'

'What about your parents, Marius?' asked Lil, as they moved slowly away from the tomb. 'Is their grave in Blatten?'

Marius shook his head. 'Wolves, you see. There was nothing left to bury.'

'That was bad,' said Gustavo.

'But tidy,' said Marius. 'It would have been worse if the wolves had left bits and pieces.'

'We shouldn't linger here,' said Cosmo. 'If we stay too long it makes it easier for someone to catch us.'

'No...don't go,' said an old woman, who stood alone by a moss-covered grave. She stretched out her hand as Merla passed and clutched hold of the sleeve of the girl's overcoat.

Merla pulled away.

'My poor weak heart couldn't bear the shock of losing you a second time,' said the woman.

'I don't know who you are,' said Merla. 'You're not my mother.'

'I kept your room empty for a year, exactly as you left it,' wailed the woman, 'and every night these past twelve months I glanced from the window as I closed the shutters, hoping to see you trudging home to me. Only last week did I finally give up hope and let your room to a blind woman and her sickly daughter...but now you're home I'll throw them back out on the street where they belong.'

'She's mad,' whispered Gustavo. 'She's grieving for somebody else. There are ghouls that lurk around the cemetery at this time of the year. The Festival of the Unfortunate Dead does peculiar things to some people. We have to be on our guard.'

Yurgen took Merla by the hand and hurried her on through the cemetery.

'Why's everyone always got to be in a hurry these days?' shrieked the woman. 'Take it along quick or take it along slow, we all end up cold in our coffins soon enough!'

CHAPTER NINETEEN

⬥⬥⬥

THE NEXT day, as Marius sat eating breakfast with Gustavo in the dining room of the hotel, Merla made an unexpected appearance. She shuffled into the room, wrapped in a charcoal-blackened eiderdown, and sat at the table.

Gustavo watched as Merla picked up a jar of hazelnut praline paste, which she spread thickly on three slices of rye bread toast. 'Hungry, are you?' he asked.

'I'm not eating because I want to,' said Merla, taking a defiant bite of the toast. 'It's just so I don't die.' She smiled at Marius. 'I like you,' she said. 'You brought me Father's head.'

Marius smiled back.

'My father talks to me,' continued Merla, licking praline paste from her fingers. 'He sends me letters.' She fixed Marius with her eyes and dropped her voice to a whisper. 'I'm going to see him soon, but it's a secret.'

Gustavo tapped a finger against the side of his head.

'Cuckoo,' he whispered.

After breakfast, Marius found Yurgen pacing in the lobby.

'Come on,' he said. 'I want to show you something.' He led Marius up the staircase to the third floor and along the corridor. He stopped at the door to the forbidden floor and unhooked a skeleton key from his belt.

'I thought it wasn't safe?' said Marius.

'It's safe enough,' answered Yurgen, and turned the key in the lock.

Beyond the door, the hotel corridor was entirely untouched by smoke or fire.

'Nobody comes along here now,' said Yurgen, locking the door behind them and surveying the deserted passageway ahead. 'Only me.'

'You mean there wasn't a fire?' said Marius in surprise.

'These were the suites,' said Yurgen. 'The finest rooms in the hotel.' He opened the first door along the corridor.

It was a curious room, almost twice as large as the room Marius shared with Gustavo. Murals illustrating myths and fables from Schwartzgarten had been painted on the walls.

'This was Izak's room,' said Yurgen, watching Marius closely. 'He was the first one to go.'

'The walls are very strange,' said Marius, stopping to stare at a picture of a tall, spindly-legged creature with a waxen face rising from a pumpkin patch.

'Izak was a painter,' said Yurgen. 'All these murals are his. I keep it exactly as he left it. I keep all the rooms safe for them. In case they ever come back.'

'And has anyone ever come back?' asked Marius quietly.

Yurgen turned away, slowly running the flat of his hand over the wall painting.

'No,' he said at last. 'Eleven have gone but no one has ever come back.'

'Why are you showing me?' asked Marius.

'I wanted you to see,' said Yurgen. 'You're clever, you understand the way things are. If the others knew how many children had been taken, they'd give up hope.'

'There was a message for you,' said Gustavo, as Marius and Yurgen walked back down to the lobby. He reached up to a pigeonhole behind the reception desk and retrieved a small and grubby envelope.

Yurgen tore open the envelope and read the message in silence.

'Well?' asked Marius. 'Who is it from?'

'It's from the Sexton,' said Yurgen. 'We have a clue to follow now! We need to travel to Offelmarkstein at once. The pumpkin button came from a factory there.'

———◆———

The hooded statues of the Twin Travellers were obscured by icy mist as Yurgen and Marius arrived outside the Schwartzgarten Imperial Railway Station, with Gustavo and Cosmo following behind at a distance.

Although Marius was in possession of a crisp bank note from Kalvitas, it was still not enough to buy more than two return tickets on the express train to Offelmarkstein. So it was decided that Marius and Yurgen would make the journey alone.

'We don't have enough money to sit in a carriage,' said Marius with a smile. 'But I'm used to travelling like luggage.'

Cosmo and Gustavo stood leaning against a pillar, pretending to read from railway timetables while they surreptitiously watched out for spies.

A voice boomed over the crackling station speakers. 'The Overland Express to Offelmarkstein will be departing shortly from platform eighteen.'

Marius and Yurgen ran across the concourse and headed for the luggage wagon at the back of the train.

'Hello, young sir,' said the Guard. It was the same man who had travelled with Marius on the train from Blatten. 'So you're travelling as a parcel again, is that it?'

'You know him?' whispered Yurgen suspiciously, as the Guard pulled the wagon door shut.

'He's a friend,' said Marius. 'You can trust him.'

'Make yourselves at home,' shouted the Guard as the pistons hissed. 'And as soon as I've labelled up these cases I'll pour you out some hot beef broth.'

Yurgen leant back against the mail sacks, while Marius took out his guidebook and perched on the edge of a large leather trunk.

'Don't you ever stop reading?' asked Yurgen. 'You're getting as bad as Cosmo.'

'There's a castle in Offelmarkstein,' said Marius, ignoring Yurgen. 'A duke used to live there, but he went mad and jumped to his death from one of the turrets.'

'Jumped or was pushed?' said the Guard, affixing a paper label to a steamer trunk. 'The Duke's family was always a bit troubled in the brains, as they say.'

'The principal industry in the region is marzipan manufacture, and pumpkin growing in the autumn season,' continued Marius. 'Pumpkin schnapps is a great delicacy and a prized—'

'Are you a talking encyclopaedia all of a sudden?' interrupted Yurgen.

'No,' said Marius, looking up from the book.

'Then shut up and let me think,' said Yurgen. 'We want to search for clues in Offelmarkstein, not marzipan.'

'Sorry,' said Marius. He returned the guidebook to his pocket and said no more.

'Can't this train go any faster?' grunted Yurgen.

'I'd be in no hurry to arrive in the Duchy of Offelmarkstein if I were you,' said the Guard, his lips pursed. 'It's gone bad there.'

'What do you mean?' asked Marius.

'It's always been a strange place, but it's terrible now,' continued the Guard, filling two mugs with hot beef broth from the kettle. 'There was a brewery built, then a factory, then another factory. The chimneys smoke day and night and the river runs as black as treacle. They're strange folk that live there.'

'As strange as the people in Schwarztgarten?' asked Yurgen.

'Worse,' said the Guard. 'They don't like outsiders there, so you best keep yourselves to yourselves.'

It was another two hours before the train pulled into the station at Offelmarkstein and rattled to a standstill.

Yurgen and Marius made their goodbyes to the Guard, who wished them well.

They climbed down from the luggage wagon. Grey salt had been scattered on the station platform to melt the ice, and the soles of their shoes scraped noisily as they walked.

Yurgen clutched Marius's arm and pulled him to one side, behind a pile of suitcases. 'We have to be careful,' he whispered. 'We need to find clues. Something that might lead us to Ava and Luca.'

They kept their heads down as they walked from the station and on towards the town. Passing over a bridge that crossed the swiftly flowing River Offel, they found that the Guard had been quite correct in his description.

'There's nothing living in there, that's for certain,' said Yurgen, looking down into the greasy waters. 'It's as black as the grave.'

Further upstream, factories lined the river banks, spewing out a fog of acrid, black smoke.

They crossed the bridge and journeyed on into the heart of Offelmarkstein. It was a small town and eerily silent; the only noise to be heard was the snap of the awnings above the shops as they flapped in the wind.

'I don't like this place,' whispered Marius.

'Something is very wrong here,' agreed Yurgen. 'I can feel it in my bones.'

They gazed in through the window of a pastry shop. There was a large tray of miniature pumpkins shaped from orange marzipan, with stalks of green icing. Marius could feel his stomach growl.

Suddenly Yurgen caught sight of a reflection in the glass.

'I know that face,' he said, swinging round and pointing to a boy who stood on the opposite side of the street.

There was something unnatural about the boy: his black hair was too neat, his cheeks were too red, his eyes were too blue. He reminded Marius strongly of the mechanical figures above the chocolate shop of Akerhus and Hoffgartner.

'How can you know him?' said Marius. 'You said you've never been to Offelmarkstein before.'

'I'm not going to hurt you,' said Yurgen, ignoring Marius and stepping from the pavement. 'I want to talk to you, that's all.'

The boy stared hard at Yurgen. It seemed he was about to take a step forward when a woman appeared at the end of the street and hurried along the pavement. She tugged the boy by the sleeve of his pullover and turned quickly into a side street.

'We have to follow them,' said Yurgen, crossing over the street. 'We can't let them out of our sight.'

'What about our plan?' whispered Marius urgently. 'We're supposed to be searching for Ava and Luca.'

'We're here to find clues, aren't we?' said Yurgen. 'This might be the clue we're looking for. Now, hurry or we'll lose them.'

Marius quickened his step to keep up with Yurgen. The woman was hurrying too; she knew she was being followed and was trying hard to shake off her pursuers.

The boy stopped and turned but the woman pulled him onwards, through a stone archway at the end of the street.

'Quickly,' said Yurgen, running on ahead. 'We can't let them get away.'

Reaching the archway, Yurgen turned back to Marius in dismay. 'They've gone,' he said. 'There's no sign of them.'

A man emerged from a café across the street and stood, staring at the two boys. Marius stared curiously at him.

'Stop gawping,' hissed Yurgen. 'You look like you're guilty of something.' He pretended to look in a shop window, all the time watching the man's reflection in the glass. 'He's not moving.'

'Maybe he's waiting to meet somebody,' suggested Marius.

'Then why is he watching us?' said Yurgen.

Suddenly the man turned and stepped into a telephone kiosk at the end of the street. He pushed a coin into the slot, picked up the receiver and dialled, his eyes fixed on the two boys.

'I think he's calling the police,' said Marius.

'I expect so,' said Yurgen. 'Turn around and walk slowly. We've got to get away from here.'

The two boys walked away as quickly as they could without breaking into a run. They were expecting to hear the sound of police bells, but there was nothing.

It was a small town and the street quickly gave way to a dirt track that led out across fields of pumpkins.

'Where are we going?' asked Marius, as he struggled to follow Yurgen across the field.

'How should I know?' said Yurgen. 'I've never been here before, have I? But the railway station was over that way.' He pointed out across the field. 'We can lay low here until nightfall then make our way to the station to catch the express back to Schwartzgarten.'

'Who was he?' asked Marius. 'The boy we were following?'

'He reminded me of someone, that's all,' said Yurgen quietly, hanging his head and staring down at his boots.

'One of the Band of Blood?'

'Of course one of the Band of Blood,' answered Yurgen moodily. 'Dolf, he was one of the first to go. After Izak, who painted the murals.'

'Was it long ago?' asked Marius.

'Three years,' said Yurgen. 'He was only eight. He got

lost in the crowds on Edvardplatz and never came back.' With a sudden fit of anger he kicked out and his foot struck a large pumpkin on the ground in front of him. But instead of turning to pulp, the pumpkin shattered into pieces.

'It's made of china!' cried Yurgen, bending down to gather up fragments of the smashed pumpkin. 'It's not a real pumpkin patch at all.'

He gazed about him in disbelief. 'They must be mad in this place. Why would anybody fill a pumpkin patch with china pumpkins?'

'They're not all china,' said Marius, tapping his hand on another pumpkin. 'This one's real, at least.'

Yurgen searched around him. 'Here's another china one.'

Marius pulled at the stalk of the pumpkin and found that it lifted away to reveal an empty chamber inside. 'There's something in here,' he said, reaching in and taking out a wax figure, so small that he could hold it in the palm of his hand. The figure had dark hair, tied with a bow of ragged pink ribbon. Marius gasped; around the figure's waxen neck was a small brown luggage label with the words: *Merla Von Hasselbach.*

Suddenly, Yurgen grabbed Marius's sleeve and the wax figure dropped from the boy's hand. 'Get down!' he hissed, pulling Marius behind a wooden water butt.

A motor van was approaching, bouncing along the dirt track that bordered the pumpkin patch. On the side of the van Marius could make out bright orange lettering:

SCHWARTZGARTEN PUMPKIN IMPORTERS INC.

The van stopped and the door opened.

'It's Bollo!' said Marius in surprise, as a man climbed down from the cab.

Bollo left the engine running and opened the back doors of the motor van. He lifted out a wooden crate and slowly approached, stepping carefully around the china pumpkins.

'What's he carrying in the crate?' whispered Marius.

'More pumpkins,' answered Yurgen. 'Now keep quiet or he'll hear you.'

Bollo took three china pumpkins from the ground, which he replaced with three from the crate. He frowned, and scrabbled around in the dirt – his fingers closed around the wax figure of Merla and he returned it to its pumpkin and replaced the lid. He carried the crate away, loaded it into the back of the motor van and slammed the door shut.

'It's safe now,' said Yurgen, as the van started off along the track.

'This is serious,' said Marius, climbing to his feet and brushing the dirt from his knees.

Yurgen was already making his way over the pumpkin patch. 'We can't stay here any longer,' he said. 'We have to get back to Schwartzgarten as quickly as we can. Merla's in danger.'

CHAPTER TWENTY

THE SNOW was falling like needles as Merla walked slowly towards the Schwartzgarten Municipal Cemetery. Passing a parked motor car, she scooped her hand across the bonnet, crushing the powdery snow in her palm until it formed a glass-like nugget of ice.

The Gate of Skulls was locked and chained for the night, so Merla squeezed between the iron bars and waded through the snow on her way to her father's tomb.

Arriving at the graveside, Merla gasped: on the slate slab stood a toy fairground carousel, with a red and white striped roof.

'Father?' she whispered. 'Are you here?' She looked around her; there was no one to be seen and no sound but that of snow falling between the branches of the trees.

Turning the handle of the carousel, she watched, enraptured, as music began to play and light glowed from within.

As the carousel turned, the striped roof slowly opened and a glittering platform appeared from inside, studded with chocolate lollipops wrapped in cellophane and tied with bows of sapphire blue ribbon.

Merla lifted a lollipop from the carousel. Iced upon the chocolate in green sugar piping were two words: SWEET DREAMS.

She tugged gently at the ribbon and the bow unravelled. She bit into the chocolate; the flavour was sickly sweet and unfamiliar.

'Chloroform,' said a voice quietly.

And that was the last Merla remembered.

—◆—

There was a different guard in the luggage wagon, so Yurgen and Marius talked quietly as they travelled from Offelmarkstein to Schwartzgarten.

'There was a story I used to read when I was young,' said Yurgen. 'Pumpkin Boy. It's the tale of a childless couple who make a figure of wax with blood from the husband and hair from the wife, and when they place that figure in a pumpkin patch...well, the figure becomes real. Did you never read *Woolf's Tales*?'

'I read algebra mostly,' said Marius.

'Don't you see though?' said Yurgen. 'I think somebody's brought the old story to life.'

Marius frowned. 'You think children are being kidnapped and brought to Offelmarkstein?'

'I do,' said Yurgen. 'And now they want Merla.' He took a small slab of peanut praline from his pocket. 'Hungry?' he asked. 'You want some?'

Marius nodded, deep in thought.

Yurgen snapped off a chunk of the praline and passed it to Marius.

They ate in silence.

'That's what I like about you,' said Yurgen, pulling a globule of praline from his mouth. 'You always eat like you don't know where your next meal is coming from.'

Marius was unable to answer; his teeth were gummed together.

As soon as the train pulled into the Imperial Railway Station, they jumped from the luggage wagon and ran along the concourse. Snow was falling as they crossed the Princess Euphenia Bridge, running back along the streets of the Old Town towards the hotel. They found the Band of Blood eating in the dining room.

'Yurgen?' said Gustavo, rising from the table, puzzled by the look of fear in the boy's eyes.

'Where's Merla?' demanded Yurgen.

'In her room,' said Cosmo. 'Where she always is. Why, what's wrong?'

Yurgen turned and ran from the room, racing up the staircase with Marius, Cosmo and Gustavo close behind.

Merla's door was locked shut.

'Merla,' shouted Yurgen, hammering against the door. 'Open up. We need to speak to you.' There was no answer. 'Merla?' He crouched down to look through the keyhole.

'What can you see?' asked Marius.

'Nothing,' replied Yurgen.

He fumbled for his skeleton key. Turning it in the lock, he opened the door. The room was empty. Merla had gone.

'Where is she?' shouted Yurgen. 'What's happened to her?'

'Nothing's happened to her,' said Gustavo, and an anxious laugh spluttered from him.

'Where is she then?' shouted Yurgen. 'Show me!' He seized Gustavo by the collar of his shirt and shook him roughly. 'Why weren't you looking after her?'

'Let me go, Yurgen,' gasped Gustavo. 'Please, Yurgen!'

Yurgen released the boy.

'What's happened, Marius?' demanded Cosmo. 'What did you find out?'

Marius related the tale of the journey to Offelmarkstein.

'It was a wax figure of Merla,' interrupted Yurgen, as Marius's story reached the china pumpkin patch. 'There was a label around its neck with her name written on it.'

Cosmo stared at the boys as if they had lost their senses.

'It's true,' said Marius. 'There were china pumpkins with wax figures inside. And Bollo from the Reformatory came in a motor van to take the pumpkins away.'

'Then Merla really is in danger,' said Cosmo.

'That's what I keep trying to get through your thick skulls,' growled Yurgen.

'All right, all right,' said Cosmo. 'But you're chasing ghosts if you think you saw Dolf.'

'I know what I saw,' replied Yurgen fiercely. 'And anybody who wants to call me a liar can say it to my face.'

'He wasn't saying that,' murmured Gustavo, eager to calm his friend.

'This isn't the time to fight,' said Marius. 'If Merla isn't here we have to find out where she's gone.'

'I know where she went,' said Heinrich, appearing from his room. 'She went to the cemetery. I watched her from my window.'

⋅—◆—⋅

Though the snow was now falling heavily, Marius, Yurgen and Cosmo could still make out Merla's footprints leading from the hotel, through the iron bars on Bone Orchard Street and winding across the cemetery to the grave of Count Von Hasselbach.

But there was no sign of Merla.

'Something heavy was placed on the tomb,' said Marius, running his hand around a circular impression in the snow.

'There's something else,' said Cosmo, pointing to a piece of cellophane that fluttered between Count Von Hasselbach's marble fingers.

'It's a wrapper,' said Marius, climbing up onto the tomb. 'There's blue ribbon attached.' He sniffed at the cellophane. 'It smells of chloroform. Like the bottle in Falkenrath's shop.' He jumped down and held out the wrapper for Yurgen to examine. 'Do you think it was the mad woman from the Festival of the Unfortunate Dead who took her? She thought Merla was her daughter.'

'I don't think so,' said Cosmo. 'There are more footprints here. Two people came. And look...these deep grooves...'

'It means she was kidnapped, doesn't it?' said Yurgen, pacing frantically and kicking at the snow. 'She must have been chloroformed and dragged away. But where's she been taken?'

'I don't know,' said Marius. He attempted to follow the footprints from the tomb, but the snow was falling so thickly that the tracks were soon hidden from sight.

'We'll never find her now,' said Yurgen, dropping to his knees and desperately trying to sweep away the fresh snow. 'It's hopeless.'

'No,' said Marius. 'It's not hopeless. At least we have clues now.'

'Clues?' said Yurgen. 'What clues have we got?'

'We know Merla was taken by two people, not one,' said Cosmo.

'And we know that Bollo's involved,' added Marius. 'But we don't know who he's working for. It's important that we try to think like Inspector Durnstein at all times.'

'We should tell Constable Sternberg what we've found out,' said Cosmo.

'Maybe we shouldn't trust anybody,' said Marius quickly.

'You're getting too suspicious,' said Yurgen. 'Sternberg brings us food. He protects us.'

'But that hasn't stopped members of the Band of Blood from disappearing, has it?' said Marius. 'And he knows our movements better than anybody.'

'You're mad,' laughed Cosmo. 'You've gone cuckoo. Didn't he take care of Heinrich when he was sick?'

'I know that,' said Marius. 'But—'

'He's one of us,' said Yurgen firmly. 'And if he's one of us, he can't be one of them. Can he?'

———◆———

When Merla woke the next day, she was entirely on her own, sitting on a chair in a small, bare room with boarded windows. Her head pounded from the chloroform. She climbed shakily to her feet, holding out her hands to steady herself as her eyes slowly grew accustomed to the gloom.

'Don't be afraid,' said a man's voice.

Though she strained her eyes, Merla could not make out the face of the man. 'Father?' she whispered.

The man laughed as he reached out to offer the girl a tray of chocolates. 'No, I'm not your father.'

'I'm not supposed to take chocolates from strangers,' said Merla.

'But I'm not a stranger,' said the man with a smile, pushing the girl gently back into the chair. 'I'm the one who abducted you.' He picked up a chocolate with a pair of silver tongs and wafted it under Merla's nose. 'A cloudberry crème. You like chocolates, don't you? Nice chocolates for good children—'

'And if I'm bad?' Merla interrupted.

There was a flash of silver as the man sliced into a second chocolate. Inside was the crunchy shell of a cockroach, its legs tangled in a thick web of fondant cream. 'Cloudberry crèmes for good girls and chocolate roaches for bad girls. Now, it's time to shave your hair.'

'My hair?' gasped Merla.

'And then we will give you a nice wig to wear on that pretty head of yours,' said the man, holding up a mop of plaited blonde hair.

'But I don't want to wear a wig,' protested Merla and kicked out wildly.

'But it's pretty,' said the man, his voice dropping to a menacing rumble as he advanced on Merla. 'You like pretty things.'

CHAPTER TWENTY-ONE

ARIUS AND Heinrich ambled slowly through the Old Town together. Yurgen was so worried by the prospect of another abduction that he would not allow any member of the Band of Blood to wander the streets alone.

'It's bad, isn't it?' said Heinrich, lifting the strap of his accordion over his shoulder. 'I think Yurgen's given up hope of finding Luca and Ava now.'

'I don't understand it,' said Marius. 'Who is Bollo working for?'

Heinrich took his usual place on the corner of the street outside Mr Kobec's shop. Leaning back against a lamppost, he began to play his accordion.

Marius entered the shop and selected tins of food from the shelves to take back with him to the hotel. There was a sudden yell from outside and Marius ran out in time to see Bollo's pumpkin motor van pulling away from the side of the street. Marius watched in horror as Heinrich's face appeared at the rear window. The boy hammered desperately at the glass, but as he did so a hand reached round and held a pad against his nose and mouth – and on the little finger of the hand was a golden signet ring. Heinrich's eyes closed, his head went limp and he disappeared from view.

Marius sprinted to follow the motor van down the street, but he could not keep up. He stopped suddenly. On the ground lay a chocolate, wrapped in cellophane, tied with ribbon from Hoffgartner and Akerhus's shop. He unwrapped the chocolate and sniffed hard.

'Chloroform,' he whispered. In desperation he turned and headed for the hotel.

Bag-of-Bones was prowling around the lobby, but the Band of Blood were out at work and the hotel seemed deserted.

'Help!' shouted Marius. 'Is anyone here?'

'Did you get the food?' asked Gustavo, entering from the kitchen.

'No,' panted Marius. 'It's Heinrich.'

Cosmo came running down the staircase. 'What's happened?' he asked. 'Is Heinrich sick again?'

'He's been taken,' said Marius. 'It's Constable Sternberg. I recognised his signet ring. And I think Akerhus and

Hoffgartner are involved. I found a chocolate that smelled of chloroform. Where's Yurgen?'

'He's at Oskar Sallowman's shop,' said Gustavo. 'It's only me and Cosmo here.'

'We have to get out,' said Marius. 'We're not safe.'

There was a scrabbling at the alleyway entrance and Marius swung round in time to see Sternberg emerging behind him.

'I knew you'd be trouble,' said the Constable, springing across the floor and grabbing Marius by the shoulders. 'Well, now you'll find out what happens to troublemakers.'

Gustavo leapt forward and tried to push Sternberg away, but the Constable only tightened his grip.

'Help me, Cosmo!' cried Marius.

Together the boys attempted to wrestle Marius free, but Sternberg only laughed. He jerked his arms viciously, shaking the boys away. Stepping backwards, he tripped against Bag-of-Bones and fell hard against the floor, taking Marius with him.

Marius blinked and sat up. Sternberg lay sprawled out beside him on the floor, lying motionless with his head back and his eyes closed.

'Are you all right?' whispered Cosmo.

'I think I hit my head,' said Marius, rubbing his temple with his fingertips.

There was a long silence.

'Is he dead?' asked Marius at last.

'He looks dead,' said Gustavo, pushing the man gently with the toe of his boot. 'But there's no blood. No blood came out.'

'There isn't always blood,' said Cosmo. 'We don't know what's gone on inside him.' He reached into his pocket and pulled out a shard of mirror glass, holding it beneath Sternberg's nostrils. 'There, you see?' he said, holding up the mirror. 'He fogged the glass. He's still got breath in him, which means we haven't killed him.'

Suddenly the man sat up and seized Cosmo by the wrist.

'I'm very much alive,' he grinned. 'You won't get rid of me that easily.'

Cosmo cried out and shook his arm so hard he was able to free himself.

Sternberg staggered to his feet, and Cosmo backed away in horror, turning and running towards the staircase, with Marius and Gustavo close at his heels. The ancient carpet rippled beneath their feet as they scrambled up the stairs, trying to outrun their pursuer. Gustavo tripped and fell heavily; hearing Sternberg close behind him he grasped hold of the banisters, hauled himself to his feet and carried on up the staircase.

Cosmo and Marius reached the landing first.

'Here! The old service shaft,' shouted Cosmo, climbing into the rickety laundry basket with Marius. 'They used it to take clean linen up to the hotel bedrooms. It still works.'

'I call it the express elevator!' said Gustavo, jumping in and slamming the hatch shut behind him. He hauled hard on the rope. 'Going up!'

The basket rattled slowly up the elevator shaft to the upper floors of the deserted hotel. Travelling as far as the laundry elevator would allow, they tumbled out of the basket, running desperately along the corridor, searching for a safe place to hide.

'Where do we go now?' wheezed Cosmo. 'It's a dead end.'

A window looked out over the Schwartzgarten Municipal Cemetery.

Marius reached out to lift the window but the wooden

frame was swollen from the damp and years of neglect and would not move.

'I want to look down to the street,' said Marius. 'We need to see if Sternberg's come alone. If we pull together we might be able to lift it.'

It took the combined strength of the three boys to shift the window and even then they could only open it a little way. Marius leant out and glanced down to the street below.

'Can you see anything?' asked Gustavo.

'Nothing,' said Marius, pulling his head back inside. 'The street's deserted. There's nobody out there.'

'So he was working against us all along,' said Gustavo angrily. 'And we trusted him.'

'Yes,' said Marius, fighting the urge to add, 'I told you so.'

'What are we going to do?' said Cosmo, pacing up and down. 'What are we going to do?'

'Calm down, Cosmo,' said Gustavo.

Cosmo turned on the boy. 'Calm down? How do you suggest I should calm down when there's a murderous maniac on the loose?'

'I suppose he's a kidnapper really,' said Marius. 'We

don't know that he's murdered anybody.'

'I stand corrected,' said Cosmo stiffly. 'We're being followed by a kidnapping maniac.'

Marius tried the doors of the rooms nearest the window but they were both locked.

'If only Yurgen was here,' said Cosmo. 'His skeleton key would open the doors with no trouble.'

'But he's not here, is he?' groaned Gustavo.

'It's going to have to be the window,' said Marius.

'What do you mean, "It's going to have to be the window"?' asked Cosmo.

Marius squeezed under the open window again and peered down over the stone ledge.

'What are you looking for?' asked Gustavo. 'You're not going to jump, are you?'

'I'd be smashed to pieces if I did,' said Marius. 'And there's too long a drop to the ledge below. We'd never make it.'

'So what do you suggest we do?' asked Cosmo.

'If we can't go down,' said Marius, 'then we'll have to go up.'

'Up?' said Cosmo, his eyes staring wildly. 'Can't we just

hide in one of the unlocked rooms? There are cupboards and...and fireplaces. There must be hundreds of places we could go without him finding us.'

Marius shook his head. 'He won't give up,' he said. 'We know too much for him to let us go. We've got no choice, Cosmo. We'll have to climb.'

'I'm going to die,' groaned Cosmo.

Marius wriggled out onto the broad stone window ledge and slowly climbed to his feet. A bitter wind whipped around the hotel and snow stung his eyes. He felt around with his fingertips and found a carved stone that protruded from the wall above him. 'I think we'll have to climb to the roof. He won't find us there. I'm going up.' Gripping the stone tightly he moved his foot to a narrow ledge at the side of the window and pulled himself across.

'But I'm no good at climbing,' said Cosmo, grasping Gustavo by the arm to hold him back.

'It's easy,' said Gustavo, gently shaking himself free of Cosmo's grip. 'Just don't look down.'

'It might be easy for you,' said Cosmo. 'But I'm an historian, not a climber.'

'You won't be anything if Sternberg finds you,' said

Gustavo, squeezing out onto the window ledge after Marius.

'I'm coming for you!' echoed Sternberg's voice from deep inside the hotel. 'I don't care how long it takes, but I will find you!'

The sound of slamming doors was growing closer with each passing second. True to his word, Sternberg was trying every room in his hunt to find the boys.

With trembling legs, Cosmo crawled out onto the window ledge.

Marius whispered down from above. 'It's not a hard climb, Cosmo. I'm nearly at the roof already. Once we get up there we'll be safe.'

'For now,' said Cosmo.

The slamming of doors was getting ever nearer.

'Just climb!' said Gustavo urgently.

Cosmo took a deep breath, stepped from the window ledge and reached up to the protruding stone that Gustavo and Marius had used before him.

Marius glanced down over the green copper roof of the hotel. 'I've reached the top,' he said.

'That's good,' said Cosmo bitterly, as he felt round for

a hand hold. 'It'll be an excellent place to watch from as I plummet to my death.'

'Nobody's going to die,' said Marius, who had reached down to grip Gustavo's arm and was now heaving the boy up onto the roof beside him.

'Keep going,' said Gustavo encouragingly to Cosmo, once he was safely next to Marius.

'I'm not going to stop, am I?' said Cosmo.

'And don't look down,' said Marius.

'Why do people keep telling me not to look down,' said Cosmo. 'I've got no intention of looking down.'

'Good,' said Gustavo. 'Because we're a long way up. You'd be sick if you knew how high we are.'

Sternberg's voice was closer now. 'Where are you, little gutter rats?' he shouted.

'Move your foot up, Cosmo,' called Marius urgently. 'There's a stone jutting out. You can just reach it.'

Cosmo took a deep breath and climbed up onto the stone.

'Come on, Cosmo,' said Gustavo, stretching out his arm – but the boy was still agonisingly out of reach.

'I can't do it,' said Cosmo.

'Of course you can do it,' said Marius.

'He's coming,' gasped Cosmo, as loud footsteps could be heard through the open window. 'He's going to get me!'

'No he's not,' said Marius firmly, pointing to a stone just above Cosmo's right foot. 'Just one more step.'

Cosmo's heart was pounding violently in his chest; he was certain he would fall to his death – but with a supreme effort he felt around with his foot for the final step. He climbed across, breathing hard.

'That's it,' said Gustavo. 'You've done it!'

Marius and Gustavo reached down and dragged Cosmo up onto the roof beside them. No sooner had they done so than the Constable's head appeared at the window below.

'Get away from the edge,' whispered Gustavo, and the boys pulled their heads back.

'Where are you?' hissed the Constable.

Marius peered cautiously over the roof edge. Below, Sternberg was leaning out from the window, trying to work out if the boys had found a way of climbing down. Without even thinking to look up, he pulled his head back inside and disappeared.

'He's gone,' said Marius. 'But he'll be back.'

'I did it,' panted Cosmo in disbelief, his eyes closed, not daring to look out over the roof. 'I did it.'

'That was close,' said Gustavo.

For the first time Marius noticed the view around him. 'You can see the whole city from up here. As far as the Imperial Railway Station.'

'Your arm's bleeding, Cosmo,' said Gustavo.

'It's nothing,' said Cosmo. 'I must have scraped it on the window ledge. It's not deep.' He pressed his pocket handkerchief to the cut and turned awkwardly to face Marius. 'So Sternberg *was* a traitor,' he said, 'and I didn't believe you. If I had, then—'

'Watch out!' said Gustavo, as far below the Constable stepped out from the alleyway alongside the hotel.

The boys ducked from view and watched as the man walked quickly to the end of the street and vanished from sight.

'He doesn't look happy, does he?' said Marius.

The boys laughed and Gustavo suddenly cried out in pain.

'Are you hurt?' asked Marius.

'It's my leg,' said Gustavo. 'I fell on it but I think it got worse climbing up here.'

'What are we going to do now?' said Cosmo.

'We need to get to Edvardplatz,' said Marius. 'Great-great-uncle Kalvitas can help us.'

Chapter Twenty-Two

IT WAS nearly dark by the time the three boys reached Edvardplatz. Gustavo was limping badly from his fall on the stairs and it was only with the help of Cosmo and Marius that he could walk at all.

'Just a few steps more,' said Cosmo. 'We're almost there.'

The blinds of Kalvitas's shop were closed and Marius hammered against the window with his fist.

The door was wrenched open and Kalvitas's frowning face peered out. 'What are you doing?' he demanded angrily. 'Trying to break my door down, are you?' His eyes picked out Marius standing in the gloom and his face softened. 'Marius?' he said. 'Marius, my boy! I was worried you'd been lost to the bears. Who else is there with you?'

'Cosmo and Gustavo,' said Marius.

'Come in, come in,' said Kalvitas, and Marius and Cosmo helped Gustavo inside. 'There's food on the stove if you're hungry.'

'Gustavo's hurt,' said Marius. 'It's his leg. He fell and twisted it.'

'Come out to the kitchen,' said Kalvitas. 'Can you walk that far?'

'I think so,' said Gustavo. 'But I can't go too quickly.'

'Sit him down beside the stove,' said Kalvitas, as Marius and Cosmo half-carried Gustavo into the kitchen and lowered the boy slowly onto a chair.

'And your head, Marius!' said Kalvitas. 'There's a lump there as large as a chocolate truffle.'

'It doesn't hurt,' said Marius.

'You'll need butter for that,' said Kalvitas. 'It will keep the swelling down.'

'There isn't time,' said Marius. 'The Band of Blood are in danger.'

'The Band of Blood are always in danger,' said Kalvitas with a smile.

'This time it's different,' Cosmo interjected.

Kalvitas stared hard at the boy. 'Very well,' he said. 'You'd better tell me all that has happened.'

'We haven't got time to tell you everything,' began Cosmo. 'It's a very long story. But it was on a dark night that the Band of Blood first encountered—'

'You're not writing a story now,' said Gustavo,

wincing with pain. 'Tell him the facts.'

'The facts are this,' said Marius quickly, before Cosmo could open his mouth again. 'The Band of Blood are being kidnapped to sell to the people of Offelmarkstein.'

'Have you been drinking?' asked Kalvitas gently.

'No,' said Marius.

'Because if you've got hold of my bottle of beetroot schnapps—'

'It's true,' said Gustavo. 'It's the men from the chocolate shop. Akerhus and Hoffgartner.'

'Ah,' said Kalvitas, as if everything had suddenly fallen into place. 'I knew something wasn't quite right with them. Their chocolate was too sweet.'

'They've got Merla,' said Marius. 'And now Heinrich too.'

'Then we must call for the police,' said Kalvitas.

'It won't do us any good,' said Cosmo. 'The police are in on this too. Or at least Constable Sternberg is.'

'We trusted him,' said Gustavo. 'But all the time he's been helping the kidnappers.'

'They should rip out his gizzard for that,' said Kalvitas grimly.

'You can teach us how to fight,' said Marius eagerly. 'We won't know how to rip out a gizzard unless you show us.' He lowered his voice so the other boys could not hear. 'You remember the stories your father told you. Of the battles he fought with Good Prince Eugene. You said yourself; it was as if you were there with him.'

'I can show you how to make chocolates,' said Kalvitas, his head dropping forlornly. 'But I can't teach you to fight. I've never swung a sword in anger. I've never even seen a battle. Except in here,' he continued, tapping the side of his head with his forefinger. 'Up there, I've seen every battle my father ever fought.'

But Marius would not be dissuaded. 'This is your chance to be a hero like your father,' he said.

Kalvitas rubbed the lump on Marius's forehead with a block of butter from the ice box. 'I'm old now,' he said. 'Battle's for the young.'

'You're not old,' said Marius, flinching from the cold butter. 'Not as old as you said you were anyway.'

'Seventy is quite old enough,' whispered Kalvitas.

The blood had clotted on Cosmo's arm and he carefully peeled away the pocket handkerchief. 'I've read about battles in my books,' he said. 'Maybe I can help to lead us to victory?'

'You couldn't even climb up the wall of the hotel without us helping you,' said Gustavo gloomily. 'What good will you be?'

Marius put his hand gently on Kalvitas's arm. 'Please help us.'

'My bones feel heavy inside me today,' said Kalvitas, his voice no more than a hollow whisper. 'If I twist too hard with a sword my fingers could snap clean off at the knuckles.' He stood and walked to the window, peering through the frosted glass panes, out onto the deserted expanse of Edvardplatz. 'My days of danger are behind me...not that they were ever truly in front of me. I'm just trying to get safely through my old age. And it's cold outside.'

'You can put on an overcoat,' said Marius, standing beside his great-uncle. 'And a hat. We have to get to Akerhus and Hoffgartner's shop to search for clues. We need you.'

Kalvitas's forehead was deeply furrowed from thought. 'What if I die?' he whispered.

'Then you'll die a hero,' replied Marius.

'And you'll have to die one day,' said Gustavo

philosophically. 'It might as well be now as later.'

It was not an encouraging thought, but nevertheless Kalvitas pulled on his coat and hat. He walked through to the shop and lifted down his sword from its hook.

It was impossible for Gustavo to walk more than a few steps, so Cosmo wheeled him outside on a trolley that Marius had discovered hidden away in a storeroom of the shop.

Kalvitas held his sword as high as his shaking arms would allow and uttered a hoarse cry. 'Forward, into battle!'

'He'll be dead before daybreak,' whispered Gustavo.

'I'm old,' croaked Kalvitas, swiping at the boy's head with the flat of his hand. 'I'm not deaf.'

It was a strange procession through the streets of Schwartzgarten; Marius leading, with Cosmo following behind, wheeling Gustavo in the trolley. Kalvitas took up the rear, the tip of his sword showering the ground with sparks as it dragged along the cobbles.

Akerhus and Hoffgartner's shop was closed for the night and the lamps in the windows had been extinguished.

The mechanical figures above the shop were motionless, though their eyes glinted strangely in the moonlight.

'We need to get inside,' said Marius, rattling the door handle.

'Move aside,' said Kalvitas. 'I can make short work of the lock.' He slid the end of his sword between the door and the frame, and levered hard; with a crack of splintering wood the door swung open.

The shop lay silent and all seemed innocent enough. Behind the counter was a steep and narrow staircase.

'Gustavo, stay down here and rest your leg,' said Marius. 'We need to search upstairs. If you see anyone coming, give the warning.'

'What is the warning?' asked Gustavo.

'Why don't you just scream, "Help, they're coming!"' suggested Cosmo.

Gustavo nodded and helped himself to a bag of cloudberry crèmes.

'The Band of Blood don't steal,' said Cosmo. 'What would Yurgen say?'

Gustavo shrugged and bit into one of the chocolates. 'I don't think it matters if I steal from kidnappers.'

Marius cautiously climbed the staircase, with Cosmo and Kalvitas following behind. He took the flashlight from his pocket, but it seemed there was little to illuminate – just a small and empty storeroom. There were no clues to be seen.

As Cosmo and Kalvitas turned to leave, Marius noticed something odd.

'There's a door here,' he said. 'Behind this cupboard. Help me, Cosmo.'

Together, the two boys dragged the cupboard away from the wall. Slowly and warily, Marius opened the door to reveal a second room with bare floors and boarded windows.

Marius opened the drawers of a tall filing cabinet. He lifted out a handful of wax figures, each with a paper luggage label tied around its neck.

'Do you know these names?' asked Marius, holding out the figures to Cosmo.

Cosmo nodded. 'Most of them,' he said. 'There's Dorf...and Izak. Some of the names I don't know.'

Two chairs had been bolted to the floor, connected to the wall with copper wires. Cosmo frowned, attempting to make sense of the scene before him. Curiously, he reached inside the filing cabinet and his hand alighted on a large, black book, bound with tattered cloth.

'It seems it's not only the Band of Blood who keep a Ledger,' he observed, as he lifted out the book and carefully turned the pages.

Even in the cold glare of the flashlight, Marius could see the colour fade from Cosmo's face. 'What is it?' he whispered. 'What have you read?'

Mutely, Cosmo held out the book and pointed at an entry that had been written neatly in purple ink:

THE BOY DOLF

DAY ONE: *Two sharp shocks administered to cure him of his temper.*

DAY TWO: *Three longer shocks to prevent him pulling at his leather arm restraints.*

DAY THREE: *Hair shaved and wig fitted, as requested by Dr and Mrs Königer of Offelmarkstein.*

DAY FOUR: *Fifteen shocks administered to begin process of memory replacement.*

Then, at the very bottom of the page:

DAY TWENTY: *Treatment successfully completed. Boy shipped by train to Offelmarkstein.*

<u>ORDER FULFILLED</u>

'What have they been doing here?' said Kalvitas, grasping the copper wires.

'They've been using electric shocks to brainwash their victims,' said Cosmo. 'I'd let go of those wires, Mr Kalvitas, unless you want to be fried like a veal steak.' He bent down in a corner of the room and picked up a dirty pink ribbon that had been trampled into the dust. 'This is Merla's,' he said. 'Shine the light over here, Marius.'

Marius turned the beam of light and Cosmo gasped. He clutched at the floorboards and turned hopelessly, holding out a handful of black hair. 'This is Merla's too,' he whispered.

'What's your plan then?' asked Kalvitas. 'What are we going to do?'

'I don't have a plan,' said Marius. He shook the flashlight but the battery was fading fast.

'But you must have a plan,' said Cosmo, his voice suddenly thin and reedy. 'How can we defeat Akerhus and Hoffgartner if we don't have a plan? Inspector Durnstein always has a plan.'

'I'm not Inspector Durnstein,' said Marius, leading the way back downstairs. 'I want to save Heinrich and Merla as much as you. And all the others. But I don't have any more ideas. I'm just a boy.'

Downstairs, Gustavo was holding up a scrap of headed notepaper. 'Look at this,' he said. 'I think they might have gone to their new factory in the Industrial District. We should go there. And fast.'

'Yurgen should still be at Sallowman's,' said Marius, setting off along the pavement as quickly as he could run. Cosmo followed, pushing Gustavo in the trolley with Kalvitas, colder than before, struggling valiantly to keep up.

They found Yurgen walking from Oskar Sallowman's shop with Lil. Boris scampered along at their side, a chicken wing clamped between his teeth.

'Sternberg was like a brother to me,' said Yurgen, when Cosmo had described their escape from the Constable.

'We've been double-crossed,' said Lil. 'And nobody double-crosses the Band of Blood!'

CHAPTER TWENTY-THREE

THE CHOCOLATE factory of Akerhus and Hoffgartner had been built in the Industrial District of Schwartzgarten, where the air was rich with the aroma of coffee beans from a nearby roastery. The factory building was vast and gleamingly new; its enormous glass roof glittered with electric light, and a plume of black smoke rose from a towering brick chimney stack. On a lawn leading down to the entrance, an ornamental stream wound through a small copse of aspen trees, gushing over rocks before disappearing beneath the glass walls of the factory.

Outside, the gates were guarded by Vigils, dressed in long black overcoats with their beaked raven masks.

'Look!' said Marius, pointing as Bollo's pumpkin van pulled up outside the factory.

Two of the Vigils stepped forward as Bollo opened the doors of the van and pulled a boy from inside.

'It's Heinrich!' gasped Yurgen. 'We've got to do something.'

'Where are you going?' said Cosmo, clutching hold of Yurgen's arm and holding him back. 'There are too many of them. If they catch us as well, what use will we be to Heinrich?'

'We need a distraction,' said Yurgen. 'Something to lure Bollo away from the factory.'

'The mechanical horse!' said Cosmo suddenly. 'Look, the tracks run straight past the factory gates!'

'What use will that heap of rust be to us?' said Yurgen. 'You're mad.'

Marius smiled. 'An iron horse would certainly be a distraction, wouldn't it?'

'I told you we might have a use for it someday!' said Cosmo with a grin.

———◦—◦———

The rails on which the iron horse had once steamed into the goods shed were still thick with choking weeds and decades of dirt, so Lil used an old spanner to clear a path from the wheels of the horse to the doors of the shed.

Marius, Yurgen and Kalvitas hurried backwards and forwards with buckets of coal, which Cosmo shovelled into the gaping mouth of the iron beast.

Sparks flew and clouds of steam filled the shed. There was a roar from inside the horse's belly.

'I think that's enough coal,' said Cosmo, wiping the perspiration from his forehead. 'It's hard to say for certain though. If I could calculate—'

'This isn't the time for maths,' said Gustavo, limping badly as he piled old wooden crates beside the mechanical horse to use as steps.

Cosmo climbed up into the iron saddle and took hold of the levers. He held out his hand and helped Gustavo to clamber up behind him.

Marius and Lil pushed against the heavy wooden doors of the shed. 'We can't open them any further, Cosmo,' said Lil.

'Iron is stronger than wood,' said Kalvitas. 'If the doors won't open wider then you'll have to break them down. Shovel in more coal!'

Marius piled more fuel into the horse's mouth.

'That will do,' called Cosmo at last, struggling to be heard above the thundering noise of the boiler. 'If we feed it too much it might explode. Then we'll all be killed.'

Marius dropped the shovel and jumped back in alarm as Cosmo pushed the direction lever. The legs of the iron beast moved slowly at first and it crept forward through the shed. The movement was accompanied by the deafening caw of ravens, shaken from sleep in the rafters by the sound of grinding levers and squealing pistons.

The nose of the horse nudged against the doors but moved no further.

'It's no good,' said Cosmo. 'We need more of a run-up.'

He pulled back on the direction lever and the wheels reversed along the track. The coal was now burning furiously in the boiler, deep inside the belly of the iron horse and Cosmo pushed hard on the lever. Like a steam train leaving a station, the great iron hulk quickly built up speed. Shuddering as it moved, it burst through the doors, splintering the wood to matchsticks.

'Good luck!' called Yurgen, as the iron horse passed along the rails towards the Industrial District.

'Can it go any faster?' asked Gustavo.

'I don't know yet,' said Cosmo, leaning hard on a second lever so the mechanical horse slowly raised its iron head.

It was not long before the chocolate factory was in sight. The motor van still stood outside.

'I can't see Bollo,' shouted Gustavo. 'But the Vigils are still there. He must be inside.'

'I think this might get his attention,' said Cosmo, pulling on the third lever and covering his ears as a shrieking whistle sounded from inside the horse.

The factory doors opened and Bollo appeared from inside.

'We know your plan, Bollo!' shouted Gustavo, as the mechanical horse rattled past the factory gates, following a bend in the tracks that led them on towards the New Town. 'You won't get away with it!'

Bollo jumped into the motor van with three of the Vigils.

'It's working,' said Gustavo. 'He's following us!'

The track from the chocolate factory was steep and Cosmo was not certain that there was enough steam to prevent the horse from rolling backwards along the rails.

'Come on,' he urged, as though the iron horse had magically sprung to life and could hear his words of encouragement. 'Just a bit further.' He pushed the direction lever as far forward as it would go and with a hiss of steam the wheels gained traction. 'Don't worry, Gustavo,' he laughed. 'I know what I'm doing now!'

The mechanical horse rolled on towards the New Town, gathering speed with every revolution of the wheels.

The city was ablaze with light. Along the pavements, smart women with fur coats and men with felt hats and cigars stopped and stared in disbelief as the great iron horse clattered along between the tramlines. Steam was rising in clouds from the ears of the mechanical beast and Cosmo tugged hard at the steam pressure lever. There was a sudden burst of speed and used coals tumbled out from the rump of the horse.

'It's going too fast!' shouted Cosmo. 'I don't know what to do!'

Bollo's motor van was weaving through the traffic and quickly gaining on them.

'He's catching up with us, Cosmo!' shouted Gustavo.

Cosmo pulled back on the pressure lever and flames leapt from the horse's nostrils and belched from its iron jaws.

A tram was hurtling towards them along the tracks.

'Look where you're going!' screamed Gustavo. 'It's a Reaper! We're going to hit it!'

The tram conductor rang the bell violently, but nothing could be done to slow the mechanical horse; the driver's eyes were tight shut as he pulled a lever and the tram switched onto parallel tracks. The driver of a patisserie van was not so fortunate; swerving to avoid the tram he lost control of the vehicle. The van spun round on the ice and the doors swung open, spilling boxes of cakes and pastries which bounced from the bonnets of passing motor cars; it was a strange snowfall of cream pastries. A chocolate cream torte burst against the windscreen of the pumpkin van, and Bollo switched on the wipers, which only served to smear the cake thickly across the glass.

'You can't outrun me!' screamed Bollo as he leant from the window. 'I'll get you sooner or later!'

The coals glowed red through the seams in the iron hulk of the horse. There came a shrieking whistle from the rear, like a thousand kettles boiling on a stove.

'There's too much coal,' shouted Cosmo. 'I think it's going to explode!'

No sooner had Cosmo spoken than the metal hatch

in the horse's rump was blown from its hinges, clattering down onto the cobbles behind them.

An avalanche of burning coals spilled out and Bollo spun the steering wheel desperately; but he was too late. The tyres burst and he lost control of the motor van, which careered from the street and into a lamppost as the horse rattled on.

'That's one problem out of the way!' laughed Gustavo.

But Cosmo was too preoccupied to listen. 'The direction lever's locked,' he shouted. 'I can't move it.' He pushed again, harder than before, and the ebony knob of the lever came away in his hands.

Sparks flew from the wheels and Cosmo clung to the neck of the mechanical horse. There was a sudden, violent explosion and Gustavo gazed up as the iron head was blown from the neck of the horse. It shot through the air, still steaming from the ears and snout, trailing flame as it arced upwards into the night sky.

The tram driver and conductor fled as the huge head plummeted to earth, crashing down on the roof of the tram, which buckled like a crushed tin can.

At last, Cosmo was able to move the direction lever,

forcing it back with both hands. Slowly, with a creaking of iron, the headless mechanical beast started moving backwards, along the tram lines towards the Imperial Railway Station.

———✦———

As soon as Bollo's motor van had set off in pursuit of the mechanical horse, Marius, Kalvitas, Yurgen and Lil slipped in through the open gates and stealthily approached the chocolate factory, following the ornamental stream with the aspen trees for cover.

'The entrance is guarded,' whispered Marius, pointing towards two Vigils who stood watch outside the enormous glass doors of the factory.

Boris whined and Yurgen patted him gently on the head.

'Then how do we get in?' asked Lil.

'I don't know yet,' said Marius.

'Why don't we just climb down the chimney?' said Kalvitas with a mirthless chuckle.

Beyond the factory, railway lines snaked away towards the distant forest. Empty goods wagons, marked with the names of Akerhus and Hoffgartner, stood stationary on the tracks.

'If we follow the stream, it will lead us inside,' said Marius. 'It might be the only way in without being spotted.'

'What about Boris?' asked Yurgen.

'We can't take him,' said Marius. 'If he barks he'll give us away. We'll have to leave him here.'

There was a large vent beside the stream, filtering air from inside the factory.

'You'll be all right, boy,' said Yurgen as he tied Boris's leash to the metal grating.

They climbed down onto the rocks that bordered the stream and waded out into the icy water.

'There's a fast current,' gasped Marius.

'We'll be swept to our deaths probably,' said Kalvitas, still dragging his sword behind him.

The stream grew suddenly deeper, until they were up to their waists in the freezing water. The glass walls of the factory loomed high above them, and they were forced to lower their heads as they entered the tunnel that led beneath the building. But their way was barred by a large metal grille.

'I've got a hacksaw,' said Yurgen, reaching down below the surface of the water and unhooking the blade from his belt. 'If we can cut away two of the bars that should be enough for us to squeeze through.'

'It's a good thing Gustavo isn't with us,' said Kalvitas. 'Or you'd have to cut through three bars.'

'He's got heavy bones,' said Marius defensively.

Yurgen worked the blade backwards and forwards until his fingers were raw. He cut through the top of the first bar and with Marius's help bent it to one side. But the hacksaw was not designed for such heavy use, and he was not even halfway through the second bar before the blade snapped and dropped into the water where it was swept away by the fast-flowing stream.

'Here,' said Kalvitas. 'Take my sword.'

Yurgen hammered against the bar with the hilt of the sword and eventually the metal snapped.

One at a time they squeezed through the hole in the grille and continued on along the tunnel. The ceiling grew lower so they had to stoop as they walked, feeling their way forward in the darkness.

'I've got a crick in my neck,' muttered Kalvitas.

'Chopping off heads is one thing, but a cricked neck is another thing entirely.'

At last the ceiling grew higher and they were able to walk upright once more.

'There's light ahead,' said Lil suddenly, her teeth chattering from the cold.

'Be on the lookout,' said Yurgen. 'There will probably be Vigils everywhere.'

The stream led out into a wide pool in the middle of a large glass hothouse where tall cactus plants grew. They climbed out of the water and across a shoreline of rocks at the edge of the pool. The air was hot and humid and their clothes began to dry on them as soon as they reached land.

Small red insects scuttled across the cactus plants and Lil watched with fascination as one of the creatures scurried across the back of her hand.

'Cochineal beetles,' said Kalvitas as he wiped the blade of the sword on the sleeve of his coat. 'They use the colour in their strawberry fondants,' he explained, pointing to a crushing arm at the end of a long conveyor belt that was pounding the desperately scuttling creatures, grinding them into a thick, red paste.

'Which way do we go now?' whispered Lil.

Yurgen opened a door that led from the glasshouse and out onto the factory floor. Wheels turned and pistons roared as the chocolate machines pounded out their deafening rhythm. The factory floor shimmered under the heat of enormous electric lights, and the chromium metal of the machinery gleamed.

'There's another conveyor belt,' said Yurgen. 'If we make our way behind it we should have some cover. As long as we keep our heads down.'

Nuggets of cherry nougat tumbled along the conveyor, passing beneath the enrobing machine which covered the sweetmeats with a fondant-thick coating of milk chocolate.

But as they rounded a large crate of chocolate boxes they discovered that they were not alone. A thin woman stood before them, dressed in a coat with a fox fur collar.

It was the woman from the train. She grasped Marius by the shoulders and as the boy opened his mouth to cry out she held her finger to his lips. 'Shh,' she whispered. 'Don't be afraid.'

'What are you doing here?' asked Marius, when he had at last recovered his senses.

'Who is she?' hissed Yurgen. 'Is she one of them?

'She raises money to save orphans,' said Marius. 'I met her on the train to Schwartzgarten.'

'And I met her on the eve of the Festival of the Unfortunate Dead,' added Lil.

The woman nodded her head. 'Collecting curselings for the poor children with neither mother nor father to take care of them.' She held Marius tightly by the wrist and leant in close. 'But things are far worse than we feared for the orphans of Schwartzgarten. Terrible things are happening. Akerhus and Hoffgartner have been kidnapping orphans from across the city—'

'We know,' interrupted Marius. 'We've been to their chocolate shop in the New Town. We found a hidden room where the children were brainwashed.'

'Then you know as much as I do,' said the woman. 'The entire, unfortunate truth. I have sent word to the police.'

Yurgen pulled back. 'If the police find us here we'll be rounded up and sent to the Reformatory.'

'But what else can we do, Yurgen?' said Lil.

The woman nodded. 'We must put our faith in the law.'

'We're looking for our friends,' said Marius. 'A boy

with an accordion, and a girl with grey eyes. They've been taken recently.'

'I think I know where they're being held,' said the woman, beckoning for them to follow her. 'I have seen Akerhus just now with a boy. In the chocolate mixing room – that must be where your friends were taken.'

They followed the woman into the mixing room. Hiding behind one of the copper vats, they watched as two Vigils dragged Heinrich towards a metal chair, securing his arms and legs with leather straps.

'What are they doing to him?' asked Yurgen, as Heinrich squirmed, fighting to slip his arms from the leather restraints.

'Please don't struggle,' said Akerhus. 'There's no way you can possibly escape.'

'We have to do something!' whispered Lil.

'I have alerted Constable Sternberg from the Department of Police,' said the thin woman with a smile. 'Help will be here soon.'

'But Sternberg's one of them,' spluttered Marius. 'They're in this together.'

'Have I made a mistake?' said the thin woman. 'Have I

put you all in terrible danger?'

'I think that's exactly what you've done, Hoffgartner,' said a voice.

The children turned and there stood Constable Sternberg, his head bandaged.

The woman wiped away her make-up and pulled the wig from her head – revealing the grinning face of Hoffgartner beneath.

'I knew it!' said Marius, reeling back in horror. 'I knew there was something familiar about her!'

'Look, Akerhus,' shouted the man. 'It's Kalvitas, the Chocolate Maker. He's brought an army with him!'

Akerhus laughed. 'And with his sword as well!'

'You shouldn't have come here,' shouted Heinrich, twisting in his chair.

'They know our plan,' said Hoffgartner, removing the last of the make-up from his thin face. 'They know that we've been brainwashing the children.'

'And what can they do about it?' said Akerhus. 'They can hardly stop us now, can they?' He grinned at the children and held a copper wire to Heinrich's head. 'Perhaps you would like to see a demonstration? We have perfected our art. We can erase the boy's memories, but he will still be able to play music like a maestro.'

Heinrich kicked out violently. 'I don't want to be brainwashed!' he cried.

'You only make it more difficult for yourself,' said Akerhus. 'Why resist the inevitable? I will attach the electrode here—'

Heinrich jerked his head forward and bit the man's finger.

'I'm bleeding!' screamed Akerhus. 'The little gutter rat bit me!'

'It serves you right!' shouted Heinrich. 'You smashed my accordian!'

'Don't you see the good we're doing?' said Hoffgartner with a weary sigh. 'The people of Offelmarkstein are sick. The river Offel runs black and the choking fog from the factories fills their lungs. There are no children born there now. The people of the town wanted families and the orphans of Schwartzgarten needed parents.'

'They had the Band of Blood,' said Yurgen. 'They didn't need parents.'

'But they lead better lives now,' said Akerhus. 'Would

you deprive the childless couples of Offelmarkstein the chance of happiness? You think your friends wanted to live out their days in the Band of Blood?

'It wasn't up to you to decide for them!' shouted Marius. 'You're kidnappers!'

'We're *kind*nappers,' said Hoffgartner.

'I suppose it was you who killed the Chocolate Makers?' growled Kalvitas.

'It was necessary,' said Akerhus with a frown. 'If we can drive the Guild of Twelve from Schwartzgarten, just think how successful our factory will become. The more chocolate we sell, the larger our factory will grow and the more orphans we can mould. And Sternberg will make sure that no one asks too many awkward questions.'

'I should chop off your heads right now!' bellowed Kalvitas. He gripped the hilt of his sword with both hands, but his arms had grown weak and his hands trembled.

'I don't think we've got much to fear from the old man,' laughed Akerhus. 'He hasn't got enough strength even to lift his sword off the ground!'

There was a loud cackle of laughter from the Vigils.

'It's not just the orphans of Schwartzgarten that we

can help,' declared Hoffgartner. 'By harnessing the power from the chocolate machinery it is enough to brainwash the orphans of the entire Northern Region.'

'And perhaps you have seen our railway wagons outside,' said Akerhus. 'We can transport the orphans directly from the factory to their new families in Offelmarkstein and beyond. And with the chocolate machinery at work nobody outside can hear a single scream.'

'At capacity we can remould and sell a hundred orphans each and every month,' said Hoffgartner proudly.

'A hundred children?' gasped Marius.

Akerhus nodded. 'It is a beautiful plan, don't you see now? It will make us our fortune.'

With a loud scream, Merla stumbled into the room, her hair shaved from her head and her eyes staring wildly. She clutched two small children by the hands.

'It's Ava and Luca!' cried Marius.

'You were supposed to be looking after the girl,' snarled Akerhus as two Vigils entered, running to catch up with Merla.

'She's like a wild animal,' replied the first Vigil, rubbing his leg. 'She ought to be caged.'

'Merla, it's me,' said Yurgen. 'Don't you remember?'

But Merla shook her head and howled.

'There's no use for her, I fear,' said Akerhus. 'Her mind has gone too far to bring it back again. Her brain must have been troubled before we set to work. She was to have lived with Baroness Smelteva, who had requested a girl of noble birth. But that is out of the question now, of course.'

'I should cut out your black hearts!' shouted Great-uncle Kalvitas, holding his sword as high as his shaking arms could manage.

There came a loud scrabbling sound from above, echoing through an air vent high in the factory ceiling. With an ear-splitting volley of barks, the metal grate that covered the mouth of the vent crashed down to the ground, narrowly avoiding Akerhus. With a triumphant howl, Boris sprang from the open vent, still trailing his leash, which flapped behind him as if it had a life of its own.

Hoffgartner cried out as the dog landed heavily on his bald head. 'Catch that wretched mutt!' he screamed, as Boris leapt down and scampered across the floor.

'Nobody touches Boris!' shouted Yurgen, darting forward and snatching the dog up in both hands.

The Vigils were closing in and he backed away towards the wall.

'Give up, boy,' said Akerhus. 'There's nowhere left to run.'

'There's a ladder behind you, Yurgen!' shrieked Lil.

Yurgen turned.

'You'll have to climb!' shouted Marius.

With Boris clasped tightly under his arm, Yurgen clutched hold of the rungs and climbed the ladder.

'What are you waiting for, Sternberg?' shouted Akerhus. 'Follow him!'

The Constable ran across the floor and followed Yurgen up the ladder.

Yurgen stepped out onto a narrow metal walkway that crossed over one of the enormous copper vats, the metal beaters turning beneath him as they churned a batch of thick, milk chocolate.

'It's a dead end, Yurgen,' said Sternberg, reaching the top of the ladder and pursuing the boy onto the walkway. 'There are Vigils everywhere. You're trapped.'

'It was you that took the Ledger, wasn't it?' said Yurgen. 'That's how you knew where Heinrich would be working.'

'Of course I took it,' said Sternberg. 'The night Heinrich was sick, I wrote down what I needed to know. I even returned it for you at The Bureau of Forgotten Things.' He took another step forward.

'Stay back!' shouted Yurgen, swinging his grappling hook above his head. 'I'll knock your teeth out if you come any closer!'

'Poor Yurgen,' grinned Sternberg. 'What a tragic life you've led, and what a tragic end I've got in store for you,' he said, glancing down into the vat of chocolate. 'I knew you'd be trouble. No wonder your Best Beloved didn't want you.'

'They did want me!' shouted Yurgen, spinning the grappling hook faster and faster.

'Lies,' said Sternberg and took another step further. 'All lies. You're not an orphan, you're just unloved.'

'Shut up!' screamed Yurgen. Boris barked violently and jumped from beneath the boy's arm. Diving to catch the dog, Yurgen stumbled and slipped from the side of the walkway. 'Help me!' he gasped, clinging desperately to the rails, his legs dangling above the revolving chocolate beaters.

'Help you?' laughed Sternberg, approaching slowly. 'Now why would I do that?'

Marius could only look on in horror as Sternberg reached down to prise Yurgen's fingers from the rails.

———

Meanwhile, the mechanical horse was rattling along the tracks towards the Industrial District, picking up speed with every passing second.

'We've got to get off, Cosmo!' shouted Gustavo, as the wind whistled past their ears. 'If the horse topples over and we're still on it we'll be crushed to death.'

'It's a long way down!' yelled Cosmo. 'If we jump we'll break our necks. We're travelling too fast.'

Gustavo tightened his hold around Cosmo's waist. 'So we're dead if we stay on and we're dead if we leap off?'

With a terrible clanking and jolting, the horse jumped from the tracks. It burst through the iron gates of the factory, and bounced across the grass beside the ornamental stream.

Gustavo closed his eyes. 'We're going to crash into the building!'

'Keep your head down, Gustavo!' screamed Cosmo.

The wheels gouged deep tracks in the grass, but still the mechanical horse did not slow down.

'We're going to die!' yelled Gustavo, ducking his head as the iron rump of the horse smashed in through the glass wall of the factory.

Gustavo was thrown from the saddle, his fall broken by heaped sacks of cocoa beans. But Cosmo still had tight hold of the creature's iron neck.

The shower of shattering glass sent the Vigils fleeing for cover as the horse skidded across the polished floor, spilling red-hot coals. Cosmo pulled desperately at the ebony levers but there was nothing he could do to stop the horse. He slid from the saddle and tumbled down onto the floor.

Flames burned brightly through the gaping neck of the decapitated creature. With a terrifying shriek of steam, rivets burst from the iron belly, firing against the factory floor like bullets from a gun. The horse rolled on and struck the side of the copper chocolate vat with a dull metallic clang, as mournful as the chime of a cracked and ancient bell. The vat shuddered and the metal walkway trembled beneath Sternberg's feet. He struggled to keep his balance, but it was no good; he lost his footing and fell, plunging down into the bubbling chocolate.

The Constable reached out desperately, fighting for air, leaving long streaks of chocolate as his hands flailed wildly against the side of the copper vat. But the metal beaters churned and swirled the mixture, creating a tide that was impossible for the man to swim against. He gasped for breath and his mouth filled with the hot, sweet chocolate.

'Help me!' he spluttered.

'We've got to do something,' said Lil. 'We can't just leave him to drown!'

'He deserves everything he gets,' shouted Yurgen, swinging his legs up onto the walkway and pulling himself to safety. 'Death to the traitor!'

'Please, Marius!' cried Lil. 'It doesn't matter what he's done. If we don't do anything to help him then it makes us as bad as he is.'

Marius quickly climbed the ladder to the vat. 'I can't see him,' he said. 'He's gone.'

Suddenly the Constable's head breached the surface. Marius leant down from the walkway, reaching out his hand; but it was too late. With a sickening gurgle the Constable sank back and disappeared beneath the surface.

Sensing that the battle was lost, the Vigils were fleeing through the shattered hole in the glass wall.

'Come back, you fools!' shrieked Akerhus. 'Are you afraid of children and an old man? Get back here!'

'They know you're beaten,' shouted Marius. 'That's why they're running.'

Kalvitas whirled his sword gleefully as the sound of police bells could be heard from outside.

Akerhus and Hoffgartner had no choice but to flee as well, running from the police who were now pouring in through the hole in the wall.

'We can't let them get away!' shouted Yurgen.

Kalvitas looked round frantically, attempting to find some way to slow the murderous Chocolate Makers. He pulled at a red lever, and high above the chocolate vats a large copper bowl jerked forward. As if in slow motion, a scalding sea of molten caramel cascaded down onto the factory floor.

Akerhus was swept from his feet, choking and waving wildly as he drowned in the puddle of caramel.

But Hoffgartner remained upright. He ran on, his skin turning crimson beneath the sticky layer of boiling caramel as he blistered and burned. He made strange motions with his hands, as if he was trying to swim – though in fact he was fighting to claw his way out from the molten caramel shroud. A hand broke free, clutching desperately for help and caught against another lever on the wall. There was a snowfall of crystallised cloudberries, which scattered down upon him like edible confetti.

As Hoffgartner breathed his last breath, a bubble of caramel formed at his lips and set hard.

'Death by caramel,' murmured Gustavo. 'What a delicious way to die.'

Two police constables tugged at a long power cable and the chocolate machinery fell silent.

The Inspector of Police approached Hoffgartner slowly; the caramel was already hardening. 'He looks good enough to eat,' he said.

The pain of standing upright was too much for Gustavo and he sank down onto a stack of metal chocolate moulds. 'My leg's bad.'

'You'll live,' said Yurgen.

'Orphans, are you?' asked the Inspector..

'They are the Band of Blood!' shouted Kalvitas.

'Is that so?' replied the Inspector, and his mouth twitched into a smile. 'Easy now,' he said, as Merla uttered a terrible moan and staggered across the floor, her grip on Ava and Luca still strong. 'You come with us. We'll find you a safe bed in the Asylum.'

'No,' said Kalvitas, taking Merla by the hand and gently pulling her and the little ones towards him. 'She stays with Yurgen. The Band of Blood will look after them now.'

CHAPTER TWENTY-FOUR

EVERY DAY for the next two weeks, Marius crossed the great city to visit the Band of Blood, watching as Yurgen patiently nursed Merla with hot broth made of chicken bones from Sallowman's shop. The girl was happier and calmer now, with Bag-of-Bones as her constant companion. Luca and Ava also stayed by her side, not wanting to leave the girl who had saved them. Heinrich, mourning the loss of his accordion, had found a tin whistle, and was fast driving the Band of Blood from their senses, as he taught himself tunes from a book of Schwartzgarten folk ballads.

Though Kalvitas had not succeeded in chopping off a single head, he was still rewarded for his bravery with a gold medal presented by the surviving members of the Guild of Twelve. At night, Marius worked with his great-uncle in the chocolate kitchen, making Pfefferberg's marshmallows and diabolotines for the shop. Marius wrote to Mr Brunert, explaining in detail the peculiar events that had unfolded, but reassuring him that he was quite safe and studying his algebra and mathematics every evening. Mr Brunert replied by return of post with news of his own – he was to set up a school in Blatten, funded by Marius's great-great-great-aunt. She had finally succumbed to extreme old age, and Mr Brunert had been astonished to discover that the woman had made him a small bequest in her will, to make amends for the fact that Marius's parents had left the man with barely a curseling to his name.

At the end of the month, the caramel-coated corpses of Akerhus and Hoffgartner were placed on display in the Black Museum at the Department of Police, and Marius paid a visit with Cosmo, Gustavo and Great-uncle Kalvitas.

'It probably served them right to end up that way,' said Marius.

'It probably did,' concluded Kalvitas, snapping off a fragment of the caramel to keep as a memento of his adventures. 'Their chocolate was always too sweet.'

After a supper of caramel hot chocolate and sugar biscuits, Marius made his way slowly up to bed, feeding the budgerigar a piece of dried cuttlefish as he went.

Climbing into bed and lying back against the pillows, Marius turned to the final page of his guidebook.

Messrs Muller, Brun and Gellerhund hope you have enjoyed your stay in Schwartzgarten.

He took out his fountain pen and added three words:

Yes and no.

Closing the book, Marius blew out the candle and settled down to sleep.

THE END

EVER WATCHFUL

Check out more **GRUESOME**
goings-on in the city of
Schwartzgarten!

Turn the page for tonight's
late edition of

The Informant

The Informant

One Curseling   Late Night Edition

ANOTHER GRISLY DISCOVERY IN LÜCHMÜNSTER

Who are the Brothers Boffkin? This is the question on the lips of all law-abiding citizens of Lüchmünster tonight, following the discovery of the third corpse in as many days within the city walls. The latest victim, Chairman of the Northern Inspectorate of Schools, was poisoned in his apartment in the early hours of this morning. The words BROTHERS BOFFKIN, daubed in red paint above each of the three bodies, is the only evidence pointing to the identity of the killers. The police readily admit their bafflement in the face of these heinous crimes.

CARAMEL CORPSES ON DISPLAY

The Department of Police have announced that from tomorrow the caramel-entombed corpses of the chocolate makers Akerhus and Hoffgartner will be on general display in the Black Museum, along with other artefacts relating to their despicable crimes. The Governor of Schwartzgarten has let it be known that responsible parents should take their offspring to the museum as soon as is practical, in the hope that the exhibits will perfectly illustrate the inevitable outcome of a life of wickedness.

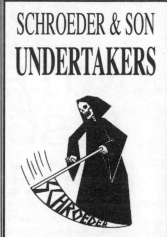

M. KALVITAS AND GREAT-GREAT-NEPHEW

M. Kalvitas of Edvardplatz, that celebrated conjuror of chocolate confections, has added a second name to his familiar shop sign - that of his great-great-nephew, Marius Myerdorf. The Myderforf boy, who hails from the mountain town of Blatten (noted for the manufacture of Brammerhaus tweed), has quickly established himself as the heir apparent to his aged uncle and has this week unveiled a new variety of the renowned Pfefferberg's Nougat Marshmallows, now with a filling of the creamiest caramel. It seems quite certain that this youngest member of the Guild of Twelve has many sweet surprises planned to tantalise the taste buds.

LUNATICS AT LARGE ONCE MORE?

It would seem that barely a week can pass without the discovery of another poisoned or mangled corpse somewhere in the Northern region. No sooner has one case closed than the next springs open. Now this murderous epidemic has spread to the university town of Lüchmünster, with three killings in one week perpetrated (or so it is said) by the mysterious Brothers Boffkin. It calls to mind the activities of the Schwartzgarten Slayer, the diminutive Osbert Brinkhoff, who has not been seen these past months since escaping from his cell. With the police scrabbling blindly for clues, we should not doubt that the Brothers Boffkin, whoever they may be, will very soon turn their attentions to the Great City of Schwartzgarten itself.

The Editor

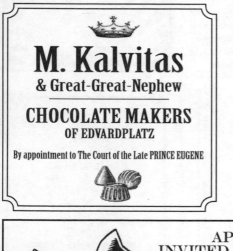

If you prefer **CLEAVERS** to kittens and **FIENDS**
to fairies...then you'll love the

GRUESOMELY FUNNY

TALES FROM SCHWARTZGARTEN

ISBN 978 1 40831 455 5 pbk
ISBN 978 1 40831 668 9 eBook

ISBN 978 1 40831 456 2 pbk
ISBN 9781 40831 671 9 eBook

ISBN 9781 40831 457 9 pbk
ISBN 9781 40831 672 6 eBook

ISBN 9781 40833 182 8 hbk
ISBN 9781 40831 673 3 eBook